Praise for the work of Annette Blair

NEVER BEEN WITCHED

"A superb tale . . . Whimsical but heart wrenching . . . Magician Annette Blair provides a terrific finish to an entertaining saga."
—*Alternative Worlds*

"The author combines magic and love in such a way that even a statue would find its heart moved . . . A perfect ending to a witchy trilogy. Annette Blair's writing is pure magic! Highly recommended!"
—*Darque Reviews*

"A wonderful tale of love, understanding, and forgiveness told with passion and humor. The reader will be captivated from the first page and will find it difficult to put this enchanting story down . . . [*Never Been Witched* includes] a good amount of hilarity and eroticism tossed in as only Ms. Blair can do."
—*Fresh Fiction*

"The last of Annette Blair's witch trilogy is definitely, in this reviewer's opinion, the greatest, and that is saying a lot as the two preceding tales are superb . . . There is mayhem and humor by the truckload in this very sexy and highly entertaining story. At the same time *Never Been Witched* is a tender love story of two extraordinary souls looking for the way to a happily ever after. Wow!"
—*Reader to Reader Reviews*

"A wonderful conclusion to a funny and enjoyable series."
—*Romance Junkies*

"I simply could not put this book down . . . The pacing of her books is absolutely perfect. They're fast, intense, and suck the reader in with a vengeance . . . The sweet paranormal touches, humorous language, and snappy dialogue are superb. Blair is setting a high bar for herself and future works, and I have no doubt she will rise to the challenge. This book rocked the house! Grade: A+"
—*Penelope's Romance Reviews*

"I highly recommend this series and especially this third book of the trilogy to anyone who loves magic, humor, and romance mixed together with delightful characters guaranteed to keep you entertained and charmed!"
—*Fallen Angel Reviews*

continued . . .

GONE WITH THE WITCH

"Yet another fun romp for Annette Blair!"
—*Fallen Angel Reviews*

"A spellbinding story that totally knocked my socks off!"
—*Huntress Reviews* (5 stars)

"Wonderful characters, a riveting story line, and a sensuous undercurrent are just a few of the things that made this such a phenomenal story." —*Romance Junkies*

"This story tugged at the heart . . . A definite addition to my keeper shelf." —*Fresh Fiction*

"I've read all of the 'witchy' tales from Ms. Blair, and found this to stand on its own, but [was] made even better [by] having known many of the characters previously. I would recommend them all for your reading pleasure." —*Romance Reviews Today*

"Annette Blair's second contribution to her triplet trilogy should come with oven mitts as it is hot, hot, hot . . . This is one road trip you do not want to miss!" —*Reader to Reader Reviews*

SEX AND THE PSYCHIC WITCH

"Sassy, sexy, and sizzling!" —*Reader to Reader Reviews*

"Ms. Blair's humor and wit is evident in many ways . . . A delight [that] will bring chuckles." —*Romance Reviews Today*

"A sexy, hilarious, romantic tale with fun characters, snappy writing, and some super-spooky moments. I've looked forward to this story since the introduction of the triplets in *The Scot, the Witch and the Wardrobe,* and it was well worth the wait!"
—*Fresh Fiction*

"More hot scenes . . . spine chills . . . outrageous stunts . . . A witchy climax that will warm your very soul. I can hardly wait until the next Cartwright triplet spins her spell. Out-Freaking-Standing!" —*Huntress Reviews*

THE SCOT, THE WITCH AND THE WARDROBE

"Sassy dialogue, rich sexual tension, and plenty of laughs make this an immensely satisfying return to Blair's world of witchcraft. Fans will welcome back familiar characters in supporting roles, but newcomers will take to it just as well." —*Publishers Weekly*

"Snappy dialogue can't disguise the characters' true insecurities, giving depth to Blair's otherwise breezy, lighthearted tale."
—*Booklist*

MY FAVORITE WITCH

"Sexy." —*Booklist*

"Annette Blair will make your blood sizzle with this magical tale . . . A terrific way to start the new year!"—*Huntress Reviews*

"This warmhearted story is a delight, filled with highly appealing characters sure to touch your heart. The magic in the air spotlights the humor that's intrinsic to the story. A definite charmer!"
—*Romantic Times*

THE KITCHEN WITCH

"A fun and sexy romp." —*Booklist*

"Magic. *The Kitchen Witch* sizzles. Ms. Blair's writing is as smooth as a fine Kentucky bourbon. Sexy, fun, top-notch entertainment." —*Romance Reader at Heart*

"Bewitching! Full of charm, humor, sensuality . . . An easy-reading, reader-pleasing story that makes you feel good all over."
—*Reader to Reader Reviews*

Naked
DRAGON

A Works Like Magick Novel

ANNETTE BLAIR

BERKLEY SENSATION, NEW YORK

THE BERKLEY PUBLISHING GROUP
Published by the Penguin Group
Penguin Group (USA) Inc.
375 Hudson Street, New York, New York 10014, USA
Penguin Group (Canada), 90 Eglinton Avenue East, Suite 700, Toronto, Ontario M4P 2Y3, Canada
(a division of Pearson Penguin Canada Inc.)
Penguin Books Ltd., 80 Strand, London WC2R 0RL, England
Penguin Group Ireland, 25 St. Stephen's Green, Dublin 2, Ireland (a division of Penguin Books Ltd.)
Penguin Group (Australia), 250 Camberwell Road, Camberwell, Victoria 3124, Australia
(a division of Pearson Australia Group Pty. Ltd.)
Penguin Books India Pvt. Ltd., 11 Community Centre, Panchsheel Park, New Delhi—110 017, India
Penguin Group (NZ), 67 Apollo Drive, Rosedale, North Shore 0632, New Zealand
(a division of Pearson New Zealand Ltd.)
Penguin Books (South Africa) (Pty.) Ltd., 24 Sturdee Avenue, Rosebank, Johannesburg 2196,
South Africa

Penguin Books Ltd., Registered Offices: 80 Strand, London WC2R 0RL, England

This is a work of fiction. Names, characters, places, and incidents either are the product of the author's
imagination or are used fictitiously, and any resemblance to actual persons, living or dead, business
establishments, events, or locales is entirely coincidental. The publisher does not have any control over
and does not assume any responsibility for author or third-party websites or their content.

NAKED DRAGON

A Berkley Sensation Book / published by arrangement with the author

PRINTING HISTORY
Berkley Sensation mass-market edition / January 2010

Copyright © 2010 by Annette Blair.
Excerpt from *Bedeviled Angel* by Annette Blair copyright © by Annette Blair.
Excerpt from *Blood Magic* by Eileen Wilks copyright © by Eileen Wilks.
Cover art by Arn0.
Cover design by Rita Frangie.
Interior text design by Laura K. Corless.

ISBN: 978-0-425-23200-2

BERKLEY® SENSATION
Berkley Sensation Books are published by The Berkley Publishing Group,
a division of Penguin Group (USA) Inc.,
375 Hudson Street, New York, New York 10014.
BERKLEY® SENSATION and the "B" design are trademarks of Penguin Group (USA) Inc.

PRINTED IN THE UNITED STATES OF AMERICA

10 9 8 7 6 5 4 3 2 1

AUTHOR'S NOTE

I took literary license with Salem, Massachusetts, in order to give my magickal supernatural ancients a place in the life of one of my favorite cities. Imagine that Collins Cove is barely cut into Salem, and that extra piece of land is a community known as Salem's End. McKenna's property is there, fronting the water. What's left of the cove is what I refer to as the old harbor. The caves where people hid during the Witch Trials, and survived, do exist, but they're in Framingham. I moved them to McKenna's land for the purposes of my story.

A SLIVER OF HOPE

*On the Island of Stars, on a plane beyond ours, a Roman legion
  exists.*
Cursed for performing their duty with spirit and might.
*Banished and exiled by Killian, Crone of Chaos and black-
  magick blight.*
Warriors still, breathing fire for sport
Casting shadows on the ground from the air, wings spread,
Bearing scales of gold, some silver, some red.
Dragons who hoped to be blessed with unlikely redress,
Humanity returned and put to the test.
*But trapped by an endless lava sea, this army of dragons seems
  doomed not to be.*
*One sliver of hope, a risk: bound moons shade white magick
  from black.*
*One dragon per phase **might** be turned and sent back,*
But who could be spared to make way for the rest? Who best?
The alpha, stepped up to save his clan.
Andra, Goddess of Hope, chanted her white-magick plan:
*"Shed horns, spines, claws, and webbed wings. Shrink scales,
  spade, and tail—"*
*Killian's counter spell struck like a fiery bolt. Bastian roared as
  he took the jolt.*
*But aborting now would mean certain death. No wasting time,
  not even a breath.*
*"Warrior to beast, now back again. Send this man to the plane
  he began."*
*Bastian roared as he twisted to shift from dragon to man in the
  steam from the rift,*
Blessed by Whyzind the elder with a dragon tear, a magick so rare,
Hope grew, despite the scent of death in the air.

ONE

❧

In a body that seemed too small to contain him, Bastian tumbled endlessly through bouts of darkness and spirals of light, hailstorms and lightning, surcease and fright.

She who cared for him and his brother dragons on the island appeared to him. "Killian failed to stop us with her counter spell," Andra said telepathically. "She will never forgive you for getting away, or me for casting the spell that released you. Be vigilant; her vengeance knows no bounds. She is an eternal, universal scourge on her enemies."

"Is there no hope for my brothers, then?"

"There is always hope. Never forget that. Every battle Killian loses, like this one, weakens her, as my losses weaken me. Every battle each of us wins strengthens us. But Killian toils for the dark and hopeless aspect of spirit, and I for the bright and hopeful. By virtue of your transformation, you are now one of my emissaries."

"And one of Killian's enemies. Where are you sending me? What do you ask of me?"

"You will understand in time." Andra vanished as Bastian's tumble through the ether continued.

Time passed. Gnashing teeth drowned sweet, soothing whispers.

Andra returned, her cloak of stars dimmer. "On earth, you will be both powerful and powerless. You will retain the gift of fire, but do not flaunt it."

Sleep came. Dreams: Bastian rode a swirl of stars, until lightning struck and his inner dragon rose up to rebel. He fought a darkness of spirit that angered him, and his dragon nearly rose up to take over his being.

The scent of rose poppies, Andra's scent, calmed him. "Fight your dragon's attempts to regain control," she whispered. "For Killian's counter spell may have altered your ability to shift back into a man, and that inability could destroy you and all you hold dear."

This time, Andra disappeared as fast as she'd arrived.

Toothy gargoyles took to nipping at his hind end while pixies screamed in his ears. He fought a horde of charging creatures. Flying ogres, smoke-winged and dark, licked his cheeks with slurp-slimy tongues. Goblins, with pointed ears, stink-burped in his face. After an eternity of torture, his transgressors were sucked into an icy darkness, leaving Bastian exhausted, his vigilance weak.

Andra returned, paler, smaller. "You are charged to find one particular earth woman, one whose hope you must strive to replenish. That is how we work, by spreading hope wherever we can, one creature at a time. That creature will in turn spread a contagious hope to the next. This woman you seek is your fate. Her heart is a mate to yours. She will be spirited and often alone. She may have rivers flowing from her eyes and seem shunned by men. She will not like who she is or how she looks. You can change that. But her heart will be pure and beautiful. Make her lifequest your own. She is the key to fulfilling your destiny and continuing my work."

"How will I know her?"

"Her heart will speak to yours, however much she fights you."

"She fights?" Anticipation rushed Bastian but he checked himself. "If I fail in this quest?"

"You will perish. As will your brother dragons. If you succeed, I will send them to you, one by one, each man-dragon with his own assignment."

Bastian hated to see Andra leave this time. She seemed to be fading away.

Alarm disturbed his dreams . . . or his reality. Color and light swirled to mighty winds that rippled his skin and shivered his teeth. He saw eyes and talons, sharp as double-edged swords. Night shifted to day and back again.

Andra's light grew dim, her scent, too, her hand against his brow a frail blessing. "I invested my magick in you," she whispered. "Succeed, and you return it thrice over. Fail and I will be too weak to save your brothers. Your destiny lies at the sign of the crowned dragon. Only your heart mate can lead you there. You will give her hope and she will give you life."

As her words faded, so did Andra, until she was nothing but a winged wisp; then she vanished.

When he woke, Bastian journeyed, still, toward a bright, distant light filled with rainbow wishes, vague dreams, and nightmare prospects.

As he spiraled toward an unknown destiny, he hoped the turbulence would not turn him inside out or jelly his brain before his arrival.

TWO

≈

He landed naked upon a sword bush in a circle of chanting women.

Bastian roared and shot to his feet. Dreadful notion on his part, because he had retained his dragon leap. After cracking his man skull and downing one poor tree, he ended flat on his back, bones rattling, the fading scream of circle-chanters floating back to him from a growing distance.

Pain teased his inner beast to the point that it tried to overtake him, a test of strength so powerful, shadow claws formed on his hands before Bastian stifled his inner rebellion and his claws receded.

After centuries of waiting, he'd nearly lost his humanity in less than a blink.

To keep Andra and his brother dragons safe, he *must* keep himself in check.

Bastian flexed his man hands as the scent of vegetation, of earth and its creatures—blessedly lacking the stench of lava smoke—filled his senses while awareness settled in. He had landed in an isolated spot, except for an amused banquet of birds on the limb above him, cawing and sprinkling him with *scorn*.

Small winged creatures had often blessed him thus. Made him feel a bit more comfortable in his surroundings and, well, *scorned* upon, but roasting and eating them did not seem prudent.

Bastian raised himself on his elbows and saw a group of human spirits watching him, their shadowy bodies fully formed as they stood by a cluster of caves and trees, pointing their shaking fingers his way.

The first humans he'd encountered in centuries offered no welcome, only warning. But why?

He should not be able to see them with either human or dragon eyes.

Had Andra's transformation spell given him this new ability? Or had the power come from Killian, who sent them to the island centuries before? *She* meant them harm. This he knew. So what had her counter spell wrought?

Nothing good, he feared. He did not expect to come out unscathed, not from an encounter with a sorceress as dreadfully strong as Killian.

He supposed he would know soon enough.

As Bastian tried to catch his breath, a tiny dragon slipped through the veil behind him, lively, blue, and barely bigger than his cupped hands. It seemed to air-hop rather than fly around him, sending out puffs of yellow smoke until the frolicker hovered above his head and looked into his eyes. "I am Jock," he said telepathically, "your guardian dragon. That was test smoke. The air here is safe for you to breathe."

Bastian would be dead if it were not, but no need to disappoint his eager, though seemingly useless, guardian.

Jock snuffled in a way that reminded Bastian of

Whyzind, his mentor, too old and sick to survive a transformation and journey through the planes. His blue guardian dragon's snuffle turned into a bout of laughter as Jock doubled over and pointed to the center of Bastian's man body.

Bastian raised his head, looked down at himself, and saw what *must* be the result of Killian's counter spell. He remembered enough about his human form to know that a man lance did not normally have such length, a flaw like movable scales beneath its skin, nor an arrowed tip like a dragon's tail.

Bastian lay back against his leafy, insect-ridden bed of dirt and dust. Was this his destiny, then? To arrive flawed and fighting the beast eager to reclaim him?

Killian had remained as shrewd as ever. His lance would never please an earth woman, though Andra had not mentioned his need for it, which did not stop him from anticipating its use, a hope he should probably relinquish.

Bastian sighed and remained on his back to regain his strength after so relentless and arduous a journey.

Several edible earth creatures approached. One, a delicious-looking morsel, whet his appetite as it climbed on his chest, regarded him with disdain, turned, and raised its striped tail.

"Wailing welks! The stench!" Bastian barely knocked a bird from the perch above him as he rose and shot a small streak of fire the striper's way.

Tail smoking, it scurried into a cave.

So this was rescue? Puncture wounds in his backside, reeking edibles, vengeful spirits, cold feet, and a flawed man spike?

Being human could not be worse. Bastian's head came up. Yes, yes it could. Killian could have taken his dragon magick.

To test one of his skills, Bastian placed the flat of a hand on each of his travel wounds, and within a human heart-beat, the bloody gashes became new marks on his scar-ridden hide.

"So far, Jock," he told his unexpected companion, "I have kept my leap, my fire, and my healing power, and I have *gained* the ability to see spirits."

Jock danced about his shoulder and snuffle-puffed a swirl of red smoke. "Red is for celebrating," his guardian said.

Standing among trees and smaller vegetation, Bastian did not know where to begin looking for his heart mate. He did not remember his life as a Roman warrior, but he expected more color than on the island, not less.

Except for a cozy cave or two, earth appeared to have little to offer. If this was indeed earth. It might not be.

As if to counter his frustration, a human approached, fragile of feature, hair and body cloaked, except for the sticks holding up the back of her feet. These creatures walked on their toes?

"My name is Vivica Quinlan," she said, telepathically, the softness of her voice giving away her gender. "You found a skunk."

"If it is known for its stench, then yes, I did."

Vivica's bright eyes danced as she handed him a cloak similar to hers, though his was as dark as a place without suns and as soft as a bustard's ear. Broad as his shoulders and tall to the ground, it covered him. He held it together up front to hide his flaw.

His greeter seemed unfazed by the air-snacks whirring about her head like a crown, making her look both regal and ridiculous. The hummers, red and green, looked no bigger than his thumb. The ugly black stick creatures with wide eyes, bony legs, and wings too big for their bodies emitted pings that bounced between one another and the objects around them.

He had also retained his keen dragon hearing.

Andra said he needed to find a crowned dragon. Instead a female crowned in winged snacks had found *him*.

What other eerie and unexpected surprises would this centuries-overdue journey bring?

THREE

Beside Vivica Quinlan stood a steadfast and regal creature with white fur and black spots, a whirring deep in its being. Loyal, judging by its stance, it stood as tall as its master's caressing hand.

No snack, this, but a prize. Whiskered and long-legged, it wore the same covering as Vivica.

"Your creature is unknown to me," Bastian said.

"She's a Savannah cat, a feline," she said, petting its head, cupping its twitching ears. "Isis is half wild, half domestic, and especially big for her kind. I'm honored to say that *she* chose me."

"But you wear the same fur as your feline."

"My cloak, you mean? Fake fur. I had it fashioned to look like Isis's coat. No animals were harmed in its making."

Bastian thought of his dragon brothers. "I should hope not."

"We're a pair, Isis and me, advertising my employment agency wherever we go."

"A pair," he said, reading her with another of the senses he happily retained: the ability to read others. "You are *not* my heart mate."

"I am not. I am here to welcome you."

"You speak and understand dragon?"

"Telepathy transcends languages, but to survive here, you will need to learn English. My employment agency, Works Like Magick, is a safe house where I will acclimate you to life on earth, and prepare you to take your place among us to earn your keep."

This female instinctively comprehended the import of his arrival. "Do you not fear me?"

"I am never fooled by outward appearances. I have the sight. You are bold of spirit, fiercely protective, and pure of heart. I expect your journey was a long one?"

"I traveled from the farthest life plane, before the nearest death plane." Or so Andra told them when they arrived on the island centuries before.

"I will need you to share your history with me during the days or weeks of your acclimation, so I may place you in a suitable work environment."

"That would seem prudent." Bastian towered over his greeter, yet his cloak fit his length, so she must have anticipated his arrival in some way. "You possess magick of your own, do you not?"

The tilt of her lips and the depth of her vision revealed wisdom and knowledge. "When the air shivers and the bats awake by day, they come for me with the hummingbirds, and I know the veil between the planes has been breached. Together, we greet the magickal, supernatural ancients, the chameleons of the universe, and we offer you our hospitality. You do realize that a small blue dragon and a teacup faery breached the veil with you?"

"A faery?"

"She hides behind you."

"That would account for the annoying wing whir in my ears." Bastian kept his roar to an annoyed growl as he turned to catch the sprite by her wings. Contrary to popular belief, faery wings did not break. Holding them was the only way to catch so lively a creature.

She struggled uselessly to free herself from his hold. "May you grow wooden limbs and attract woodpeckers," she cursed.

"Nice talk," Bastian said, while Vivica bit her lip to hide her amusement.

The tiny, annoying faery resembled a human female but with ear peaks, hair the color of silver stars, long, straight, and flying in the breeze, and wings bright and colorful as a flutterby. Feet bare, she wore a dress of sweet-scented flower petals, and a dewcup hat, stem up. Endearing in looks, perhaps, but completely lacking in manners. "How does one rid oneself of a flutterby faery with attitude?"

"I believe it's up to her. She might be with you to the end of your days."

Bastian groaned while the faery boxed his earlobe, her laughter mocking.

Vivica cleared her throat. "And I think you meant 'butterfly' faery."

"Did I? Our human words were lost or mangled over the centuries but we knew what we meant." Butterfly or flutterby, he thought, the tiny brat could be an enemy in disguise. In true form, she might be a roachwart with red swine bristles and a heaving stench.

The sprite could also be a beacon signaling his presence to good and evil alike. Killian's personal scout, perhaps. Bastian regarded his greeter—Vivica, she called herself—and supposed *he* should know where he landed before anyone else did, human or magickal. "Where exactly do I find myself?"

"Salem's End. Earthside Plane. Welcome."

FOUR

Holding his cloak together, Bastian bowed. "I accept your hospitality and your welcome as a gift."

"Some call it a curse. I am descended from Ciarra Mc-Kenna, a powerful witch who lived in one of these caves to escape the hanging times—the witch hysteria, which you'll learn about—though family legend says the caves were masked by a deep layer of thorny thickets and a spell or three. The land is now owned by one of Ciarra's non-magickal descendents, a distant cousin of mine. Since it is now considered hallowed ground, the owner allows Salem witches to gather here."

"Witches are befriended these days?"

"Yes, we are. Magick is not only tolerated but often desirable."

"I come from magick," he said.

His greeter nodded as if she knew. "We have that in common."

"I frightened a circle of women when I arrived."

"Witches, yes, I passed them on my way here. Most believe they went into a trance. Hopefully, none will guess that you are real."

Bastian followed his greeter from the grass and trees to a place with many paths. On them, trapped humans filled colorful noisemaking machines with stink powder coming out their hind ends. Vivica did not seem alarmed by the sight.

"This is Salem proper," she said. "Salem's End is on the outskirts of the city, the Witch City, some call it."

Walking beside Vivica, scents and sights warred for prominence. People, human and not, wore cloaks similar to his. On some, shadow remnants of claws, spikes, fangs, snake hair, and such remained. Those without cloaks dressed different from one another.

"Can they see the remnants of my past life?" Bastian asked. "Like my wings or horns?"

"I can," Vivica said, "but usually, neither humans nor supernaturals can see what is magickally hidden. Do you see the remnants of their past lives?"

"I do. Is that bad?"

"I'd say it's desirable."

"Some have black hearts," he noted.

"Never trust a black heart."

"This I know." He peeked at the trail of bony females behind them, many with legs exposed. They needed feeding and badly. "Vivica, why do females follow you?"

She shook her head. "They're following you, Bastian. You're a fine specimen of manhood."

He looked back, locked gazes with each, but found none with a heart that spoke to his. "Supernaturals with good hearts seem happy here."

"The chameleons of the universe adapt to the mainstream, though there are gathering places where they socialize with their own kind. Underground clubs and such."

"How do they crawl beneath the dirt?"

"You are a literal thinker, I see." Vivica tapped her lips with a finger. "For you, I will have to pull out all my magick and give you the super deluxe mainstreaming culture acclimation package—language, customs, technology, and so forth. Ciarra also acclimated the magickal supernatural ancients," Vivica said. "There were fewer of you back then, but these days, human magick has thinned the veil in Salem to a permeable mist."

FIVE

"It's raining men! Naked men to be precise. No, don't adjust your TV sets, ladies and gentlemen. You heard right, and you heard it here first."

McKenna Greylock stopped mixing spackle and turned to the small TV on her kitchen counter.

The sensationalist reporter flashed his best grin. "Several sources," he continued, "have reported sightings in the past week of magickal beings entering Salem . . . without a spaceship. A spokesperson from a local coven believes that paranormals from other planes could, indeed, breach the veil into our own and live among us. How well do *you* know your neighbors? In other news—"

McKenna turned off her TV. "I hate that reporter," she said. "Lizzie, did you hear?" she called. "More otherworldly pod people breaching the veil."

"I heard," Lizzie said, spackling one of the bedrooms. "Why don't they just call us Roswell and get it over with?"

"Tell me about it." McKenna turned to a knock at the kitchen door but wished she hadn't.

Beelzebub calling.

Face like an angel, a smile that could charm a rock, beneath which he lived. Blond. Blue eyes, empty, like his heart. Elliott Huntley, developer from hell.

"Good morning, McKenna. May I come in?"

She couldn't believe she went on two dates with this gotta-like-me reptile, until she realized he was attracted to her land, not her. Would she *never* learn?

She stepped out to her kitchen porch and closed the doors at her back. Otherwise, she'd have to fumigate. "You still can't have my land."

"As spunky as ever." He offered his hand, but she ignored it and walked to her porch rail at the side to look out over the old harbor in the distance. "Waterfront and water view," she said. "That's why you want it. I'll bet condos here would go for plenty."

He flashed her one of his all-American-boy smiles. "I'm here to brighten your day."

"Sure you are."

Huntley was the kind of guy you could imagine wearing Uncle Sam's top hat and kissing babies. "Hear me out, my friend," he said. "You might be surprised."

"We're not friends."

"Still, I'd hate for you to end up with nothing. I'd like to see you come out ahead for a change. How about I pay you a cool million, and you walk away from this property with your head high."

"If I walked, I'd be ashamed to raise my head."

"A million dollars, McKenna. It's nearly August. Your ninety days are ticking down to your inevitable foreclosure. After the bank takes the place, I buy it from them, not you." He ran his gaze over her porch. "A bed-and-breakfast, eh? It would take a lot of paying guests to keep you afloat, given your overdue mortgage and tax payments."

Which he should *not* know about.

"And before you open to guests, there's the little matter of getting the building inspector's approval. Nice guy, the inspector. Lousy poker player, though." Huntley compromised his perfect manicure by scratching a paint flake off her porch rail. "My condolences on the loss of your contractor, by the way. Bad luck, that."

She refused to satisfy the leech with a show of emotion. "Steve Framingham is still my contractor and he's recovering nicely, thank you. He'll be fit in plenty of time to get me up and running." She so wished that were true. "I won't sell, Huntley."

"I'm good at waiting. Haven't you heard?"

"Haven't you heard that money isn't everything? Or are you too far gone?"

With a smile, he tipped a hat as fake as his manners. "The offer's good for two weeks. Come August, I won't be as generous. You're losing money by the day."

You're losing your soul, she thought. He wouldn't know generous if it bit him in the balls. McKenna looked up and asked the universe to arrange that bite, please.

Huntley waved as he backed his sleek, silver Aston Martin down the drive.

She shivered. Seventy-five days left to turn this place into a bed-and-breakfast, and the only contractor she could afford was now confined to a wheelchair.

Her debt had come to light with her mother's death a couple of weeks ago, and she hadn't had time to grieve, because she had to save a centuries-old legacy steeped in history.

Yes, her heritage was up for grabs.

Panic caught her by the throat and stole her breath,

until she forced herself to calm and assess the situation rationally.

Huntley had done her a favor by showing up today. He'd not only given her a shock, he'd given her a lowball clue as to the monetary value of her property, her priceless heritage aside.

She understood, better than ever, that she couldn't wait for Steve to get better; neither could she stage a one-woman fight against a powerhouse development company.

Screw pride—she needed help.

She grabbed her truck keys. "Lizzie, I'm going to look into selling my produce, then I gotta see a witch about a handyman. I won't be gone long."

"I'll probably still be here spackling when you get back."

"Thanks, friend." Huntley, aka Dirtbag, had made one true statement. No time to waste. She needed a consistent influx of cash and she needed to hire someone Steve could direct from his wheelchair. Where better to find the perfect employee than at Works Like Magick?

After she talked to a local grocery store buyer, McKenna went to Vivica's employment agency. There, she passed lines of employers and employees waiting their turns and entered a door marked private. She cut through an open office with rows of desks surrounded by workers in open-ended cubicles.

In a high glass office overlooking the scene, Vivica rose from an executive chair behind her antique desk. "McKenna! It's been a while. I'm so happy you stopped by."

"Where else would I look for an employee? Works Like Magick provides the best. Everybody knows that." McKenna took the chair Vivica indicated. "Besides, we're related somewhere down the line, you and I."

Vivica had inherited the magick in the family, and she, McKenna, had not. *She* wouldn't know what to do with magick, if she had any. Fact is, she didn't know what Vivica did with hers, unless it accounted for the success of her famed employment agency.

Vivica's secretary brought chai tea for two.

"So, McKenna, have you turned your house into a bed-and-breakfast yet? I haven't seen any ads for it."

McKenna sighed. "Let's just say, at this point, I might well name it the Rotting Victorian, Mice Are Us, or Termites Inn."

Vivica raised a brow. "Catchy, literally. You'll have tourists fighting for . . . antibiotics and tetanus shots."

"Exactly. So what I'm looking for is a strong, honest, hardworking jack-of-all-trades who needs a place to live, three squares a day, poverty-level wages, and preferably isn't running from the law."

Vivica nearly choked on her tea. "You know," she said, setting down her mug. "Most job hunters expect good wages *and* benefits."

"Benefits." McKenna perked up. "I raise beef. I can serve steak every day. That's a perk."

"Literally, yes, but I meant—literally, hmm, who does that remind me of?"

McKenna sat forward. "You make great matches, so if you can ferret out the best employee for me, I'd be grateful."

Vivica raised a brow. "Beware my psychic abilities, because I do make the best matches, even when an employer, or employee, doesn't *know* what they need."

McKenna ignored the unease rippling through her. "So do you have some magick for a poor—and I mean that literally—cousin and potential bed-and-breakfast owner?"

"You're playing the cousin card? No fair. I'm a witch, not a miracle worker."

McKenna sipped her chai. "My mother's family, *our*

family, has owned that property for centuries. I can't lose it, Viv. Turning the place into a B and B was my grandmother's dream."

"*That's* why you got your degree in hotel/motel/innkeeping management."

"Yes, but I never thought I'd use it. I was so busy taking care of Gran, then Mom. Since Mom didn't live long enough to make the dream come true, I'm the last apple on the family tree, the McKenna branch. Bad enough I nearly gave the freaking tree dry rot by being born a girl. I can't let the thing topple, trunk, roots, and all."

"Weird how you're descended from Ciarra herself, while her brother is my ancestor, but my family inherited her magick."

"Don't feel bad. The universe made the right choice."

"Thanks. If it's any consolation, I envy you getting Ciarra's family name as your first name. Listen," Vivica added, setting down her cup. "I wanted to invest in your B and B, but when I thought seriously about it, my psychic instincts kicked in big-time, and I believe strongly that I would interfere with your destiny if I did. I'm sorry, McKenna, but it's against my deepest beliefs to screw with fate."

"We can't have that." Fate, schmate, damn it. McKenna sighed inwardly. At any rate, she didn't need Vivica's money. She needed a guardian flippin' angel.

"Kenna, I know you're the last of the line in a way, but I have something to tell you, and it's important."

"Shoot, I think."

"I sense that you have some connection or influence—more than a little—over the McKenna champion our ancestors have been waiting centuries for. Does that make any sense to you?"

"So not." McKenna sighed. "Pile on the pressure, why don't you?"

"Look, I'm going to find you the perfect worker. I promise. Because, girl, I don't envy you your enemies."

"You mean Dirtbag?"

Vivica covered her hand, the connection instilling courage. "Huntley is more ruthless than you think. He'll do anything to get his hands on your land. It's the best piece of real estate north of Boston. He's nervous. He knows a B and B will thrive there, and once you thrive, you'll never sell."

"The same way his condos would thrive. Vivica, I need paying guests. If I don't fix the house so it will pass the building inspection and pay the mortgage my mother took out to pay Gran's medical bills, Huntley will get my land for a song."

Vivica retrieved her hand and sat straighter. "You realize, don't you, that your mother never mentioned her illness to you or a doctor so she wouldn't leave you the kind of debt Gran left her?"

McKenna's throat closed. Their fingertips met for a second more.

Vivica's hand fell away as she straightened. "I'll do whatever I can to help, McKenna. I mean it. Call on me anytime. What's your time frame?"

"I'm guessing the foreclosure paperwork's done. I default at midnight on October twenty-fifth, grace period included. I'm betting Huntley will be ready to sign on the dotted line at twelve-oh-one a.m." McKenna sighed. "Any chance you can nose around to see if the building inspector's clean? Huntley plays poker with him."

Vivica made a note on her to-do list. "Elliott Huntley is out to claim Salem, acre by acre. Somebody's got to stop him. Too bad our clan treasure's a myth. I cut my teeth on the family legend."

"Me, too, but I gave up on fairy tales a long time ago.

I'm just grateful to have you on my side. All I need right now is hard work, elbow grease, and a Works Like Magick handyman, accent on the magick."

Vivica sighed. "When I heard you had Steve Framingham as your contractor, I thought, 'Take that, Huntley.'"

"I know, but Steve no sooner took out my permit than he fell off a roof."

Vivica sat straighter. "A bit fortunate for Huntley, wouldn't you say? Is Steve badly hurt?"

"Only time will tell. He hates the wheelchair, of course, and he often feels useless, but he'll stand by my building permit and oversee the job, if I can find a quick study with muscle."

Vivica balanced on the back legs of her chair and steepled her fingers. "A literal thinker," she said, "a quick study with muscle."

Her chair popped forward as she homed in on a hunky male office worker wearing headphones and looking their way from the far end of the room. Vivica narrowed her eyes and turned to her computer. "Let me see if the man I'm thinking about is still looking for work."

McKenna watched the eye-candy office worker, but when their gazes locked, she turned away. "Given the fact that my offer sucks," she said, "what's *wrong* with the guy you think might be interested?"

"Nothing. He's a quick study in some ways, honest and hardworking, fast, strong, but English isn't his first language, and he tends to be frustratingly literal. He hasn't been here for long, but his paperwork's in order."

McKenna's heart raced, probably without cause. "When can I interview him?"

"If he's interested, I'll send him out in the next few days. If not, I'll let you know. To your benefit, he's not from this . . . area, and his perception of money is skewed, so you might be able to pull it off."

Guilt reared its ugly head. "Don't you have a responsibility to tell him how little I can afford to pay?"

"Absolutely. I'll tell him it's not enough to pay for rent, food, or utilities, but you're providing those."

"I like the way you think."

Vivica walked her out. "I'm glad you're stubborn and determined, McKenna."

"Thanks."

As she drove home, McKenna found herself humming "New World in the Morning," one of her mother's old favorites.

Hope-filled or not, in her experience, one's "new world" rarely arrived in the way one expected.

•

SIX

A few days later, Lizzie stood waiting on McKenna's kitchen porch, spackle tool, once again, in hand. "I thought I heard your truck turning up the drive."

"Thanks for keeping up with the grunt work while I went paint shopping, though I thought you'd have gone home by now."

"I'm happy to help, and frankly, leaving Steve with his mother and the kids makes him feel useful. He thinks he's taking care of his mom, and Nana thinks she's taking care of him. Everybody's happy. We talked on the phone a couple of times. In that wheelchair, he feels the need to prove himself, even if it's only that he's a good son and father." Lizzie's eyes filled, but she blinked away her tears and cleared her throat with determination. "Before I forget, Vivica called. She has a handyman prospect for you. Bastian Dragonelli. He'll be here today or early tomorrow. She's sorry it took so long."

McKenna resisted the urge to hug her friend. Sympathy would only bring on the waterworks, Lizzie had warned. "Long is right. I'm at seventy days and counting."

"Stop thinking work and think 'man,'" Lizzie said. "I'm hoping this guy is, well, handy, cute, unmarried, and in the market for—"

"A sturdy farm girl? Do you never stop matchmaking? Lizzie, look at me. I threw my scale through a second-floor window right before I put on barn boots to kick the crap out of my full-length mirror."

Lizzie's eyes crinkled with her hidden smile. "Sounds like a cathartic experience."

McKenna posed, hands on hips. "What you see is what you get."

"I like what I see. You're a knockout in your mom's flowered old hippie dresses. Feminine and—"

"I'm not going for feminine. These dresses have tent appeal. They cover the flaws."

"*And* they make you feel closer to your mother."

"She accepted me the way I am. Men, not so much." McKenna offered Lizzie a Creamsicle and took one for herself.

"What am I going to do with you?" Lizzie chided her with the kind of look she often gave her children. "McKenna, you have an hourglass figure and lush, full breasts, the kind that millionaire plastic surgeons create."

McKenna put on her apron. "No matchmaking! I want a hardworking grunt who doesn't think with his zipper brain. Not that I'll tempt him to."

"I'd kill to have long, sexy, red hair falling in waves to my shoulders like yours."

"Yep, can't argue with perfection . . . above the neck."

Lizzie tilted her head and looked lower.

"Okay, above the breasts, then." McKenna checked her

cleavage. "The girls *are* pretty amazing, aren't they? As for my hair, I wear it in a ponytail, so what difference does length make?"

"In a man or a woman?" Lizzie asked. "Haven't you ever looked in a mirror? Men drool over curves like yours."

"Are you coming on to me? Because I'm not into—"

Lizzie threw the putty knife at her.

McKenna's palm got slimed, and her old daisy wallpaper got splattered. "Listen to me, my kind friend," she said, wiping her hand on a dish towel. "I'm a hermit with attitude. I eat whatever the hell I want, and I like it that way. I don't *need* anyone."

"You need me."

"Okay, but I don't need a man."

Lizzie touched her arm, so gentle, so caring, so . . . primed to interfere.

"Spit it out, Framingham."

"Honey, you put up walls. Not to keep others out, I know, but to see who cares enough to tear your walls down, no matter how hard you beat him off."

"Up yours, LizBeth."

"Low blow. I hate my real name."

"I know you do. With the same intensity that I *like* my walls. Stop psychoanalyzing me and let's spackle."

"I'm just saying—"

"Shut. Up!" McKenna turned and walked away.

Lizzie caught her arm. "Don't you think we should patch the roof before we spackle the walls?"

"Upstairs, in the land of drips and buckets, yes. Down here, no problem. In this house, we paint, spackle, and glaze whatever we can, so we don't have to pay someone else to do it."

"Just once in your life," Lizzie said, "I'd like to see you stop being practical, throw caution to the wind, and chase a rainbow."

"Fat chance." McKenna caught movement outside. "I wonder if Vivica sent *him*?"

"Who him?" Lizzie looked up from her work.

"He who wanders in dumb circles through my woods. He should get directions from the stick insects following him. God save me from the kind of man who attracts women like the Pied primping Piper." She hadn't *really* been attracted to the guy in Vivica's office, McKenna told herself. She'd been . . . curious.

This wood wanderer, and Vivica's hunky male office worker, could *not* be one and the same.

Lizzie came to stand beside her. "Is he coming here? Are you sure you can afford a handyman?"

McKenna shrugged. "Whoever Vivica sends will be strong and willing to work for room, board, and a hundred dollars a week."

Lizzie's eyes widened. "McKenna, did you say you're going to let him live here? With you? You, who trusts no one? Especially not hunks of the male persuasion."

"Desperate times and all that, but he'll get the basement bedroom."

"Putting distance between you, hey? Like a floor and a wall? But enough about your cowardice. I thought *you* were planning to sleep in the basement?"

"I'll move down there when I open the B and B to keep the maximum number of good bedrooms available to paying guests."

"So, after you open, you're thinking of fraternizing with your handyman in a very *big* way? Say yes."

"Cold day in August. After the place is finished, I won't need a handyman."

"I beg to differ, but I'll save that argument. At least the basement ceiling doesn't leak."

"Nor does it have cracked windows."

"Or any windows. Anybody who takes you up on your job offer, I hate to point out, can't be too smart."

"I want a hard worker in whom brawn will beat brains."

"You forgot staying power."

"Lizzie, you're about to pop babies numbers three and four, and you've only been married five years. I thought you wanted to put a cork in staying power."

Lizzie's gleam disappeared. "That was before Steve got hurt." She rubbed her burgeoning belly. "These could be my last." Her tears spilled over before she could stop them this time.

McKenna gave in and hugged her. "Steve's recovering, isn't he?"

"He won't let me go to the doctor's with him. And the insurance company is investigating as if he jumped off that damned roof for the fun of it. Unless they release his benefits, we're gonna lose our house. Sound familiar?"

"Oh, sweetie. I empathize. You know I do. If you weren't preggers, I'd suggest we crack open a bottle of Mom's preferred stock Cherry Manischewitz. Are you up to taking out your frustration on a wall?"

"You'd let me do that?"

"Well, I need to enlarge the kitchen."

"Which accounts for the sledgehammer by the door." Lizzie's watch alarm rang. "Oh, I gotta go. Steve's mom has probably had enough of him and the kids all day. I should bring her the wine."

"Whitney and Wyatt do tend to tire their playmates."

Lizzie rolled her eyes. "Nana doesn't seem to mind. For an arthritic seventy-year-old, the frisky girl keeps up."

Lizzie backed down the drive before McKenna spotted the blue plastic bat near the door. "Lizzie!" she called, running outside and raising it in the air. "You forgot Wyatt's bat!"

But her friend's old VW bus disappeared down the street.

McKenna went inside and stood it beside the sledgehammer. As she did, the floor shook beneath her feet, the echo of her crashing world reverberating around her.

She grabbed the sledgehammer and bat, and ran.

Either the place was falling down around her, foundation first, or Godzilla had just broken into her basement.

SEVEN

McKenna threw open the basement door and accidentally kicked a stair basket of laundry off the top step, too concerned about the disaster sending smoke and soot up the stairs to care about her underwear floating down ahead of her.

Halfway to the bottom, she stopped, stunned, and the sledgehammer slipped from her grasp to thunder and dent its way to the bottom, just missing her pained intruder's head on its final bounce.

In the middle of her basement sat the hunk from Vivica's office, the Pied primping Piper himself. Except Bastian Dragonelli looked more like a leathery tan pirate than a handyman—no primping involved—even with his butt stuck in her coal chute.

Shoulders thrown back, teeth bared, he stared at his raised hands as if they were on fire. Speaking of which, the bottom of her wooden stairs had been singed black, with no fire in sight, though the scent of smoke lingered in the coal-dusty air.

Vivica wouldn't send a lunatic handyman for her to interview, despite the evidence to the contrary.

Her archaic coal chute, now detached from her foundation, remained connected to the bricks the chute took with it during Mr. Handyman's Wild Ride. Also attached: an important section of drywall, the lack of which gave her basement bedroom an open-air view.

As intense as the man's inner struggle seemed at first, his hands and shoulders relaxed, as did every delineated muscle. A guileless half smile grew on his sculpted lips.

Difficult to contemplate killing an Italian Stallion, or so he appeared—except for his eyes, as violet as a summer sunset—especially when he seared her with his gaze to the point that she expected smoke to rise from her pores.

Despite the assortment of intimate apparel scattered about him, his gaze touched her in a place so deep, she hadn't known it still existed, and she hated like hell that it did.

The longer the eccentric stranger stared, the harder his stone-carved features became, until they sharpened to severe angles.

Never mind the sledgehammer breaking *him*, he could break the hammer with that look.

She, however, refused to surrender beneath the power of his gaze, though dashing up the stairs, locking the door, and nailing it shut sounded good, if only to annihilate the physical response scorching her. She pried her gaze from Weirdzilla's and raised her chin. "Take my bra off your head. You look like a perv."

He seemed surprised to discover her beguiling bargain up there, but after he removed it, he examined every red lace flower and finger-traced its shape, as if he'd never seen one before. With a fist in one of the cups, he frowned as if doing a math equation. Then he raised the bra by its straps, the points of the cups facing him, looked at her with a question in his eyes, then gave her a double take—her breasts, the bra, her breasts. That final look came with a lingering perusal and a stroking nod of approval, both of which made her nipples rise like cheerleaders at halftime, drat the girly traitors.

McKenna's heart raced. Her hands began to sweat.

Mr. Tall, Dark, and "Do Me" raised her bra as if to fit it to her contours. And, click, she saw comprehension dawn. He grinned.

She lost her knees and grabbed the stair rail. "What, assclown? You couldn't find the door, so you made a new one?"

He sobered. "Define assclown."

McKenna sighed. "I apologize. I'm being rude. You broke my wall"—*and penetrated my defenses*—"so I acted out."

"Out of where?"

"Out of pissed off, damn it. Your invasion is going to cost me."

"I don't know my own strength sometimes."

"I'd call that an understatement. Take a running leap, did you?"

"More like a thoughtless step."

"I beg your pardon?"

"Vivica sent me. I'm here for the interview."

"You're *not* hired!"

EIGHT

"Good," her intruder said, assessing his situation. "This place is dangerous."

McKenna tried not to let her jaw drop when Bastian Dragonelli, cold-day-in-hell employee and major studster, exercised the muscles in his quarterback shoulders to push against the coal chute and pull his tight, linebacker butt free. Then he rose like a warrior in a cloud of ancient coal dust.

Stretching to his full staggering height, he held her with his gaze as he squared his shoulders to a breathtaking span—like Lucifer, sighting prey and spreading his charred wings.

Dark. Disreputable. Depp without his pirate ship, but taller, broader. More dangerous.

Delicious.

The silent hunk lowered his chin to keep his head from an intimate encounter with a raw oak ceiling beam and stepped her way. "Vivica said you would interview me. She said I work cheap. You need cheap. I am also strong."

McKenna glanced at the hole in her house. "I can see that."

"So hire me."

"You just gave me the impression you didn't want the job."

He raised his chin—and swallowed his pride, she thought. "I need it."

Glued to the spot, three stairs from the bottom, she found herself standing nose to nose with the sex dream and tried not to fold under his hypnotic gaze. Good thing panic called for self-preservation. "I don't know you. You broke into my house. No, you *broke* my house!"

His physical strength, and the smile in his eyes, if not on his face, brought her to her senses. She took a minute to observe the paradox, giving him as bold and greedy a scrutiny as he gave her. Forbidding as he appeared dressed all in black, his leonine mane, an overlong tumble of sooty waves, humanized him.

"Did you use an eggbeater on your hair this morning?" she snapped, annoyed with herself for her speeding heart.

"On my way here, it started raining," he said, his voice low, gravel-rough, and as physically stroking as his gaze.

She wondered how it would sound as a whisper in her ear.

Mercy, McKenna, get a grip. "Don't touch the electrical wire in front of you, then, or you're a goner, wet or dry."

In the way every stubborn male listens to a smart female, the studster wrapped a hand around the end of the live wire and took the zap. But with some kind of bizarre inner force, he stood up to it.

The wire pulled from his hand, stood in the air, and burned itself up like a stream of gunpowder, electricity zooming back the way it came. When the wire vanished at the breaker panel—Zap! A crash and flash, and the lights went out.

"Good thing it's still daylight," he said.

"Do you *know* how much an electrician costs?" But with his smile, attraction zapped *her* like the electricity through that damned wire, which pissed her royally. "Unless you're the jolly dumb giant, or you were shot from a cannon at gunpoint, I'm gonna sue your sorry ass, mister!"

The idiot's eyes widened. "You *do* fight."

"You find me amusing?"

"I find you breathtaking."

"Blind and dumb."

"What is dumb?"

"You are, buddy, for coming on to me after adding to the cost of my renovations. I don't buy flattery. I'm no frail female, and I *do* own mirrors." A small one. To pluck her brows.

"I like fight in a woman."

McKenna stepped back, resenting her traitorous body and the warm tingles headed to all the wrong places. "Holy smackeroonie," she said. "You can probably *walk* through the kitchen wall, no sledgehammer needed. Or you can look at the wall, hard, and it'll fall at your feet."

Hell, he could walk through *her*, topple years' worth of walls, and leave her in a crumbling mess.

Don't let him stay, her sane self warned. This man is his own ammunition. "You can't—"

"I'm sorry about your wall," he said in all sincerity. "But I can fix it."

McKenna saw now what she'd missed when she lost her bones. Dimples. Oy vey Maria. "Walls, plural," she snapped. "Foundation wall, there." She pointed behind him. "Bedroom wall, that way." She thumbed his gaze toward the right.

Emotional walls. In here. No mention necessary.

But if he could do the job she needed him to, at the price she offered, she might be able to ignore his studlyness, if it weren't for the scars that added *beast* to his mirage of male perfection.

Must be a mirage. After all: he is man, hear him run.

He bowed. "Bastian Dragonelli at your service."

"McKenna Greylock," she said, her hand disappearing in his firm, secure one, while an unwanted sense of peace filled her.

Time stopped . . . for an infatuation hallucination.

NINE

～⟍～

Despite her warring emotions and spinning head, Bastian Dragonelli's knowing smile nearly knocked her on her ass the way that live wire should have knocked him on his.

Did he sense her haywire reaction?

What reaction? She never fell for a handsome face, remarkable or not.

Okay, so rejection had done a number on her. Her deadbeat grandfather had flown the coop. Her dad died young. Not his fault, precisely. And the few guys she'd liked, well, they wanted skinny. Then she let down her guard for an honest, "baseball and apple pie" face—Huntley—and all he wanted was her land.

No, she wasn't a woman who played "the game." Not anymore. Giving up her invulnerability and showing emotion would be like grabbing the hot end of that wire.

The squeals and snorts of piglets near the hole in her

foundation injected a shot of reality into a bizarre unreality, which allowed her to relax and breathe again.

"Hey," Dragonelli said, turning to the piglets. "Snacks! I'm hungry."

Before she could tell him he didn't have a right to be hungry in her house, unless she hired him—if she hired him—an owl flew in through the gaping hole and landed on the house wrecker's shoulder.

"Is that yours?" she asked.

Dragonelli eyed the small, bold, brown-and-white owl. "No. Is it not yours?"

McKenna shook her head. She may not have inherited the family's magick, but she had a healthy respect for animal totems. Owls were tied to wisdom. So if the little guy chose Dragonelli, did that mean *she* should? Of course, owls were also tied to seduction and fertility, not at issue here.

"I don't know what to say. They don't normally go near people."

"I'm not . . . people," her intruder said, stroking the owl, which emitted a *hoop, hoop, hoop* sound. "Winged creatures," he said, "they like me, whether mocking or blessing me. In ancient Rome, it is thought that to place an owl feather on a sleeping person is to learn their secrets. As a night bird, the owl symbolizes the darkness within us, the place where we hide our secrets."

"Have you been talking to Lizzie?"

"Vivica. I have been talking to Vivica. So do I get the job as your handyman?"

Loaded question. McKenna envied the owl stroked by that hand. Look at her, drooling over a man who just cost her a fortune. "I already said you're not hired."

"You don't know what I can do."

She swiped coal dust from her clothes. "I think you're a bit too clumsy to be working with tools."

"Like the one you threw at me?"

"I didn't throw it. I dropped it."

"Define clumsy."

Smart-ass. "You broke my foundation!"

"You nearly broke my head."

"I could sue," she snapped.

Bastian's shrug ruffled the owl's feathers. "What do you do here?" he asked, "that you need a handyman?"

"I'm turning the house into a B and B. You know, a bed-and-breakfast?"

"Breakfast is a meal," Dumb as a Stump said, doing an equation as difficult as bra identity. "And a bee is an insect." His damned violet eyes widened. "So you eat bees, here? In bed?"

English, *not* his first language. Takes things literally. "Tell me why I should hire a man who put a gaping hole in my house."

"I have read two books about shingling a roof."

"Except, you couldn't find a roof or a front door, if your life depended on it. Weren't you lost in my woods for half an hour?"

"I admit it, I am directionally challenged. Vivica says I understand direction better as the crow flies. My feet, they get lost on roads that go sideways when I need to go straight."

"Why didn't you ask one of your groupies how to get here?"

"Groupie?"

"The women following you."

"Those chirpy things? Annoying, hungry creatures. I shooed them away. Hire me and save me from them."

"Charm will get you tossed out on your ass."

"Define charm."

TEN

Bastian followed McKenna Greylock up her stairs, watching the sway of her hips while trying to keep his eager hands from cupping her fine bottom. Being near her, inhaling her woman's scent, he remembered something he had forgotten as a dragon, a truth that came rushing back to him for the first time since breaching the veil. As a man, he had *loved* women. The shape of them, their tastes and scents, the way they felt beneath him, above him, gloving him.

No woman, since his arrival earthside, had stirred either that buried knowledge or this strong physical response in him.

He had loved women centuries before. He loved them still.

McKenna Greylock made him remember bits of his life as a man. She made him want.

She made him want *her.*

He ached to press his face to her hair, feel its texture beneath his hands. Like so many other parts of her, he wanted to touch.

Halfway up the stairs, the owl flapped, dropped a feather, and flew out the way it had come, *hoop-hoop-hooping* all the way. Bastian pocketed the feather and returned his attention to McKenna. She smelled of joy flowers and dough-nut crumblies. One, a happy smell from his island home, and the other, a new sweet scent he had come to appreciate here.

While he took in every curve of her extraordinary body, the shape of her made him want to taste. At a nod from him, Jock air-tested her with yellow smoke.

She passed, praise be, so his guardian dragon snuffle-puffed a cloud of red celebratory smoke. A whoop of joy filled Bastian's lungs, but he refused to release it. He saw McKenna as a fortress he must breach, which he should keep to himself. But breach her he would, and make her glad he did.

A pleasant development, this need to breach, however embarrassing.

Killian had definitely failed to dethrone him. She may have altered him, but she had not broken the stiff object attempting to point McKenna's way beneath its firm denim confinement.

Dewcup, the faery pain in his unscaled rump, distracted him—which might be good, given the embarrassing size of his man lance.

The faery sniffed and nosed her way into every small thing in McKenna's house. Good thing his employer could not see the impolite pixie getting stuck nose-down in a drinking glass, after slurping the dregs from the bottom.

Bastian picked up the glass, held it behind him, turned it upside down, and shook it to release the imp while he pretended to admire the cooking room. No, the kitchen. McKenna spoke to someone on something like a phone, though her big speaking piece hung on a wall, rather than being kept in her pocket or in her ear like a bug.

Bastian admired her every move. She had hair the color of the red fire moon and a body with a shape that called to his lips and fingertips, both tingling with a necessity to touch. Following behind her made him quiver with all kinds of desires.

Around her, his broken man lance functioned remarkably well. Uh, perhaps too well. He held the glass in front of him. Empty.

He turned, whisked the dizzy faery off the floor, and pushed her into a tight-necked glass jug. Escaping would keep her busy and out of his hair for a while. She said hair made the softest beds.

He hated that most about Dewcup, getting her out of his hair.

Dewcup screeched for being stuck. "May your lance grow so long that you trip on it and break your ear wings!"

The faery, he could ignore. McKenna Greylock, he could not take his gaze from. Her defensive demeanor worried him a bit, as if she were an army of one who refused defeat. Which must have to do with her quest that he would make his own . . . in the event he had found his heart mate, which he believed he had, though he saw no sign of a crowned dragon.

McKenna hung her speaking piece on its perch and turned to him. "Okay, Steve is willing to teach you how to fix the foundation, which means that I get to remove the coal chute from my to-do list. He'll also tell you how to repair the wiring, fix the plumbing, replace the roof, and so forth. If I hire you, you'll have to sleep up here for a while, because the downstairs bedroom was supposed to belong to the help.

"Always, and I mean *always*, remember this: I give the

orders and, evidently, I do the errands, or lose you to the wilds of Salem."

She boldly pushed a finger against his chest, and Bastian remembered a day as a dragon when he would have taken a bite out of an aggressor for such disrespect.

"You," she said, poking him as she spoke the word. "You are the grunt. Nothing more. No opinions. No taking the lead. Jack-of-all-trades, master of nothing and no one, especially not me. Got it, Buster?"

"Bastian," he said. "My name is Bastian." She *must* be his heart mate. Her spirit and fight called to him as strongly as her heart. As strongly as her body, though he did not yet know her quest.

She looked at him with her winged brows raised, and he found himself moved again by her beauty.

"Your eyes are violet," she said.

"They're dragon-elli eyes. Dragonelli. All my brothers have eyes this color."

"It's in the genes, then?"

"No, that is my man lance in my jeans. I am sorry if it distracts you. It is a bit out of control today."

ELEVEN

Unfortunately, McKenna stared at that spot on his jeans, beneath which his lance danced, the more ardently given her admiration.

When her head came up, her cheeks were stained island-sky pink. "Not jeans," she said. "Genes." She spelled the word, placed a hand on her hip, and raised her chin, as if to keep from yielding to her curiosity and taking another look. "It's that literal thing, again, isn't it?" she asked. "Congratulations on the big bazooka, by the way. I take it you live large?"

"Bazooka?"

She cleared her throat. "Stop distracting me. Go back to the basement and wait while I get a tarp. We need to cover the hole in the foundation."

Bastian tried to define tarp as he went back downstairs. He hoped McKenna had a computer so he could look things up as needed. After seeing her at Works Like Magick, he had taken as many lessons as he could stand until he abandoned Vivica's mainstreaming learning series to take this job. Vivica called the series her "canned lessons" because she had designed them herself, utilizing all forms of technology. They were brilliant, he was sure, but McKenna, she was . . . magick.

While he waited for her to bring the tarp, he figured out the puzzle of the wall and began to replace each hard red block, and each clunky chunk that fit between, to close the hole he made when he overleapt his mark.

He fit the pieces together as well as he could, including the attached trough, which he would think might be for horses to drink, if it were not inside the house.

He shrugged when he finished. True, the wall could not stand a tumble through the veil, but it would keep animal snacks out.

When McKenna joined him, she carried something flat and blue under her arm and two small foreign objects in her hand. "Here," she said. "You said you were hungry. Have a Creamsicle before we start. Oh, you already started. Great. A little mortar and we've got a temporary fix. I guess you're hired. No, wait. You're hired on a trial basis. Two weeks. If I like what you do, we'll make it permanent."

"Okay," he said, as Vivica instructed him to say when, as Vivica put it, he had no clue. He accepted his Creamsicle and took a bite. It burst cold in his mouth with a flavor reminiscent of ory flowers. The long, thin center, also flavorful, reminded him of his days of foraging on the island when meat was in short supply.

"Uh, you ate the stick," McKenna said.

"Okay."

She gave him a sidelong glance and offered him her own long, chewy center.

"You do not want it?" he asked.

"No. Go ahead."

He accepted it, enjoyed its special flavor, and licked his lips. "I like this part best."

"What planet are you from?"

"Ah, planets and solar systems. I studied them."

"As did we all. You really take the fiber thing seriously, don't you?"

"Okay." He admired the sparkle in her eyes.

During his acclimation at Works Like Magick, he had looked for the heart mate Andra meant for him. He looked in the women who buffed his nails and tried to groom his hair—though he would not let them slice it with those double-edged swords. When he and Vivica walked to restaurants for eating lessons—not his favorite sport, juggling knives and other pronged weapons not fit to slay pixies— he looked for his heart mate in the women on the streets and in restaurants, as well.

On their way to Boston, in a tube car in a long underground cave Vivica called the T, a fast-moving place with body odor and cranky humans, he made the mistake of asking one woman if she had a heart. His face still stung remembering her slap.

While being acclimated into the mainstream at Works Like Magick, he had examined every woman who came looking for a job or for an employee. But they all seemed ordinary and of little interest . . . until the day McKenna visited.

Vivica had popped him a computer note on top of his lesson. "I see you watching. Can you work for this woman?"

He had replied: "I can do anything for the right woman, and the one talking to you is the first who sparks me." He wanted to come right away but took several more days of lessons, at Vivica's urging, before he set out to find McKenna, Jock cavorting about his head and Dewcup, the unwanted, cursing him all the way. If Dewcup's curses came true, he should have three man lances by now.

As he had neared McKenna's house, the spirits who witnessed his arrival, and more, showed themselves, some more stern in their warnings while others slapped their hands together or cheered.

He did not understand any of it.

Warnings aside, given McKenna's pure and beautiful heart, he would be as careful with her as the spirits protecting her were.

From McKenna Greylock herself, she who he did not yet know, what he wanted he could not yet name. Something larger and wider than his dragon being—which had been enormous—an undefined connection as remarkable as his tumble through the planes, but greater, deeper, and connected to the region of his chest.

Bastian feared this want with a different kind of dread than of failing Andra and his brothers.

In meeting McKenna, he feared that he had found another he dared not fail. Failing her implied a consequence worse than death.

TWELVE

Bastian studied McKenna's actions as she fastened the hard blue blanket she called a tarp over their foundation puzzle repair using objects she called a hammer, nails, duck tape, and two-by-fours. When her actions made sense, he worked with her.

When they did not, he stood back, watched, and learned. "How do ducks make this tape?" he asked, pulling some off the roll. "Or is it made for their use? Ducks are yellow and quack, are they not?"

"Literal," she said with a sigh. "Ask me when I don't want to crown you."

"I have already been crowned, thank you." With three horns.

She raised both brows. "Sure you have."

He did not appreciate her tone.

After they finished, he admired their tarp wall. "Should we not fasten another on the opposite side, outdoors, to keep the blocks in place? The wind, it frolics today."

"It *frolics*?"

The sound of McKenna's lilting mockery astounded him. He should be outraged, an alpha warrior mocked by a female with fiery hair and flowers on her gown. "What do you call what you are wearing?" he asked. He had not stayed at Works Like Magick long enough to study women's clothing, not that he cared to learn, except perhaps about the clothes McKenna took off.

She looked down at herself. "It's a flower-child dress, high waist and hem to the ground. It was my mother's. Why?"

"You look good."

She made a noise like a swooping bustard and shook her head as she went upstairs, and he followed. "Be honest," she said. "You've been in prison, haven't you, for, like, skady-eight years? You were the fall guy. Not guilty, but you took the heat, because you have a big heart."

Big and getting bigger. And not only his heart. "Okay."

"When you say okay, I feel as if you're patronizing me, like you're smarter than you let on."

"Define patronizing."

"All right, so you're a mystery man, an enigma, and you like it that way."

"Define enigma."

Near the top of the stairs, she turned back to him. "You're a pain."

"Pain, I understand. I apologize."

She waved off his apology. "On the way outside, I'll give you an abbreviated house tour, and after we secure the foundation, I'll show you the property. I intended the bed downstairs, covered in drywall and dust, for my handyman, but until we can fix that mess, I'll find you a bedroom upstairs."

When they got to the top, she bit her lip, and Bastian could swear that he felt how hard she did, because his bottom lip hurt in the same place. Unusual, that. He coaxed her bottom lip from between her teeth, and looking wide-eyed and surprised, she let him. *His* lip stopped hurting. "I hate to see you hurt yourself," he said, puzzled. "I thought you would draw blood."

She backed into the edge of the open doorway leading to the basement and he caught her by the shoulders so she would not fall. They stood fast heartbeat to happy man lance for a minute before she pulled to the side and smoothed her dress. "Thank you."

"You're welcome."

As they turned into a hall, a meowing snack jumped out at them, a swirled one, almost as ruddy as his scales had been, Dewcup riding it, though Bastian did not think this snack was meant to be ridden. It reminded him of a smaller and rounder version of Vivica's Isis, with swirls in its fur, instead of spots.

McKenna caught the silly snack to her heart. "No matter how many times she attacks like that, she still makes me laugh."

Good thing McKenna could not see the faery on her snack's back. "I like her color," he said, never having seen anything quite like it.

"She's a red mackerel tabby. I tried to name her after some shade of red, but she's more of a dark terra cotta. Then when she tilted her head and looked at me, I named her." She held the snack up and looked it in the eye. "The name Jaunty popped into my head, and it fit, didn't it, sweetie?"

The ruddy-colored snack crawled into his arms, so he held on while McKenna petted the striking, whisker-faced beastie, accidentally swiping Dewcup off its back. Bastian could no longer see the faery, but he could hear her insults from across the room. Meanwhile, he enjoyed having McKenna so close that her arm stroked his chest as she scratched her pet behind an ear.

"Why does your snack wear a hat? Vivica's does not."

"This is a cat, not a snack," McKenna said. "She's been playing guerilla warfare for days. I think her tissue-box helmet is a hoot."

"A helmet? She is crazy, your snack—cat?"

"You can't blame a kitten for bonding with her bed," McKenna said, "after she's left on your doorstep in a tissue box at the ripe old age of newborn runt."

McKenna looked up at him, expecting his understanding, so he nodded, thinking he could get lost in the green of her eyes as deep as the sea.

"I guess I made her tissue-box-dependent by continuing to give her fresh boxes and tissue mattresses."

"I do not understand," Bastian said. "Why did she stop using them as beds and start wearing them as hats?"

"She got too big, split every box she tried to climb into, but kept trying to nudge new boxes into compliance. One day, she accidentally got her head stuck in one. When that happened, she stopped crying, and walked away happy. Now she's a pouncing, head-butting kitty warrior that sneaks up on me at every turn." McKenna petted her Jaunty. "She loves the half-full boxes best—the kind she grew up in. She thinks Mommy's in the tissues."

Bastian nodded. "A mother figure." Mothers. He had learned about those in his lessons. "I must have had a mother at some point."

McKenna paled. "I lost mine a few weeks ago."

"Then we should find her."

THIRTEEN

"You do take things literally," McKenna said, her eyes bright.

Unable to think beyond wanting to make McKenna smile again, Bastian was almost relieved when Dewcup remounted Jaunty, and McKenna's hat-wearing cat pounced from his arms, hit the floor, and ran up a wide set of stairs yowling, Dewcup screaming in delight.

"This way to your bedroom," McKenna said. "Don't expect much. This is an ancient old Victorian. My mother called it the house that Jack built, though Angus was the ancestor who built it a couple hundred years ago. My great-grandparents, on my mother's side, the McKenna side, did a big remodel in their day, and turned it into a primo Victorian, which will look cozy and inviting on my website brochure if I ever get the house painted. There's practically a porch off every room, which is perfect for a B and B."

"I like your house. It is a beautiful and wondrous home like I have only ever seen on Vivica's computer."

"A home, yes," McKenna said, "but wondrous? I think not. For one thing, I barely have time to clean. For another, I'm making a terrible mess trying to fix it, and while I try, it's falling down around me, which is where you come in. You're going to help me turn it into a bed-and-breakfast. This is one of my favorite rooms," she said, stopping. "The library."

"A grand room." Bastian went to the bookshelves lining the walls, loving their scents and textures. He anticipated learning from them, books being his favorite earth gift, so far, and reading, his best new skill. He chose a book. *"A Girl's Guide to Plumbing,"* he read, and looked at McKenna for an explanation.

"Those are my how-to books on home repair." She shrugged. "While I normally shun reading material that assumes a female's lack of knowledge, I detest admitting that I don't understand construction jargon, so the Girl Guides to everything in home repair work for me. Never tell Steve."

"The man who will help me learn? I will not tell. This plumbing is something I should know, then?"

"Absolutely."

Bastian flipped slowly through the book, wholly absorbing its knowledge at dragon warp speed. "Imagine that I know nothing about fixing a house," he said, "and pick out all the books you think I should read, please. Stack them here by the chair for later."

"First, I give the orders. Second, you do know how much, or how little, I'm paying you, right?"

"Yes, but you forgot to ask if I know anything about what you hired me to do."

"Oh."

He sensed her disappointment. "I will do the job. I learn fast. Vivica says I am a quick study. And I take my responsibilities seriously. I will know what to do when it is time. Show me the rest of your home."

"Again, I give the orders, though I do like the way you say home. You make me feel good about the place, as if I can do this. I haven't been proud of it in ages. You're right, though—it's more than an impossible project; it's a home. My home. My family's home. I nearly forgot."

Bastian followed her into a room where the spirits of two females stood beside a bed. Both wore dresses similar to McKenna's, the eldest woman's darker with long sleeves and a high neck, in contrast to the younger woman's bright short-sleeved dress. He recognized the spirits from among the deceased men and women who had acknowledged his arrival on earth and again today. "This room has a sense of love that lingers," he said with a nod to acknowledge their presence.

They thanked him telepathically and introduced themselves as McKenna's mother and grandmother.

Bastian realized then that McKenna *lost* her mother to death, and he felt bad for not understanding. He wished he could communicate in English as well as he could think in dragon or communicate telepathically.

He asked them to help him get to know McKenna better.

"This was my grandmother's room, then my mother's," McKenna said, unaware of her ancestors' presence as she touched random items with reverence. "This picture is Gran, and this is my mom."

The spirits radiated as much love for McKenna as she did for them.

Bastian looked closely at a set of tiny statues lined on a shelf. "Dragons?"

"The McKenna women have been collecting them for years. Some are as old as the family line. I believe that Ciarra carved that one herself."

"Ciarra had the Sight," the older of the two spirits told him without McKenna's knowledge. "Ciarra knew you would come."

Bastian's heart quickened. "Then I *do* belong to McKenna? Or, she to me?"

"I said we knew you would come. We canna' promise that she will keep you." The elder spirit winked. "She's stubborn strong, is our McKenna."

FOURTEEN

"What do you think of dragons, Miss McKenna?"

"I'm either Miss Greylock or McKenna. You can call me McKenna, as long as you remember which of us is boss."

"You are the boss. You give the orders. I am the grunt. I remember." Though he was the alpha meant to tame her. "So what *do* you think of dragons?"

"I find them fascinating. I always have. They're a creature you wish existed. They're . . . I don't know . . . magical. I grew up loving them. Do you know how to make a dragon stew?"

"What!"

"Keep him waiting! Hah! Sorry, I don't know why that came to me," she said. "It's a joke. My friend's son told it the other day. His name is Wyatt. He's five."

Bastian thought he should probably smile, and he tried, until McKenna turned back to the collection. "This dark red dragon is another Ciarra carved. It's the oldest. Gran rubbed its belly every night for luck. And I have to be honest, with time running out on getting my bed-and-breakfast up and going, I've taken to coming in here every night to rub his belly myself."

Bastian's man lance thickened. The lucky wooden figure could be a carving of himself as a dragon, though something had broken off the top. He only wished McKenna would take to rubbing his belly, instead.

McKenna's mother and grandmother chided him for the thought.

"Take your time with her," McKenna's gran said.

"Yes, be gentle," her mother added. "McKenna has been hurt by men and she's skittish. She needs to be accepted as she is, flaws and all."

"Well, who would not," he told them. "I, too, need to be accepted in that way."

The elder nodded. "She needs you to be her friend first."

"As my daughter's employee, becoming her friend will be difficult. Try to get her to relax once in a while."

"But don't try too hard. My granddaughter will dig in her heels and work that much harder if you try to steer her from her course. Take her on a picnic."

"But make her think it's her idea. She melts at a kind word, but she can smell a false compliment from across the valley. My daughter is no fool."

Gran sighed. "And she likes to laugh. Make McKenna laugh, and often. It's a beautiful sound."

Bastian shoved his hands in his pockets and pretended to be looking over the dragon collection. "Assuming I stay longer than two weeks," he told the women, "I will try to make her laugh."

McKenna's mother shook her head. "Don't be silly about it. Kenna can't abide foolishness. Laugh *with* her."

"Not *at* her." Gran shook a finger his way. "She's sensitive about her size."

"So am I. I feel like a clumsy ox, especially beside McKenna. I started as a small Roman, I became a huge dragon, and now I am a big man. Frankly, none of my skins fit right. I have been uncomfortable in all of them."

Her mother smiled. "McKenna needs a man willing to help shoulder her burdens, someone as tenacious as her and strong enough to breach the barrier around her heart."

"Bastian," McKenna said. "Are you listening to me?"

"Of course." He gave McKenna his attention while continuing to speak telepathically with her female ancestors. "As you see, I have already met *the barrier*. She can be stubborn *and* bossy."

McKenna's mother crossed her arms. "I hope you know how to back down from a disagreement, because McKenna won't."

"Don't misjudge her as weak," McKenna's grandmother countered. "She's prepared to meet her most dangerous enemy alone. Don't let her. She needs you."

"But she will never admit it, will she?"

The spirits smiled with approval.

Wonderful. McKenna, who did not know what she wanted, came with ancestors who read his deepest yearnings and disagreed with each other about how he should treat their descendent.

He did not stand a chance.

"Oh, but you have every chance. My daughter doesn't know yet, but I believe she's meant for you. Tell her as much and you'll *never* win her."

"We're leaving," Gran said. "You'll need to be strong; she's hard on men. Brutal. And if she doesn't kill you before you catch her interest, you'll need your privacy."

McKenna's mother cleared her throat. "Make no mistake. We're not really leaving until the time for privacy is at hand. If you find our advice confusing, treat McKenna like you would a wounded dragon with no reason to trust."

"*That*, I can do."

"We'll be watching," Gran warned.

"Until we trust you with our girl's emotions," her mother added. "Shout, if you need us."

Bastian shook his head as the spirits disappeared and he followed McKenna into a bathroom off the bedroom.

"Okay," she said, "let's get one thing straight. I'm not in the market for a man. I need a hardworking employee. That's it. 'Nuff said. On the other side of this bathroom is my current bedroom, soon to be yours. I'll move to Mom and Gran's room, here, but I'm locking the door between your bedroom and this bathroom. Your bedroom and bathroom are off the hall. This bathroom is mine and mine alone. Got that?"

Bastian saluted, his head still spinning from that overdose of opposing wisdom.

"I'll move to my new bedroom later tonight," McKenna said. "You get a room adjoining my bathroom because ours are the only two rooms with beds, except for the bedroom in the basement, which you destroyed."

"By accident."

"Weird accident, if you ask me."

He didn't say a thing. Not even an "okay" seemed to fit.

"Want to see the rest of the house now or after you see the property?"

"The wind seems to be picking up outside," he said. "Should we not seal the foundation?"

"Right. We'd better put that tarp over your clumsy mistake. Foundation first, then." Definitely mocking him. "Did you have lunch?" she asked.

"I ate a Creamsicle and a half."

"Sure you did. Listen, I don't want to take time to cook now, but I can zap you a couple of corn dogs."

"I did not think that people ate dogs."

"*Not* funny," she snapped, taking a package from the freezer.

Dogs, not funny, he noted.

Whatever he ate, he liked, hard centers and all. After he finished, they covered the foundation with a second tarp. Crossing her yard, he found patches of lemongrass, pulled some, and ate it for dessert.

"What are you doing?"

"Having a bit of lemongrass. Have you never tasted it?"

"No."

"Would you like some?"

"Uh, no, thanks. Ranks right up there with chewy Creamsicle centers for me."

On the way to her barn, a wild animal charged her, and Bastian snapped off a tree branch, got between them, and wielded the branch like a sword.

"Wait!" McKenna shouted. "You'd fight an unarmed pig?"

"That's a swine?" He lowered the branch. "It can't be. It's as big as a horse."

"Not quite. Want to compare? Come inside and meet my horse."

"A horse! Can I ride? It's been centuries."

FIFTEEN

❧

"Centuries, huh?" McKenna smiled inwardly, but when her hunky, weird employee started sweet-talking her mighty Belgian, her laughter stopped, and well, she wished he'd sweet-talk her. Okay, so she'd flatten him if he tried, but knowing it didn't lessen the band around her chest. A need she hadn't thought existed until "zap me and take me" rattled her foundation.

Get a grip, she told herself. "She's more than nineteen hands high."

"Horses are bigger than I remember and so much more beautiful."

Her horse fell under Bastian's spell, nuzzling him and listening intently to every whispered word.

Bastian boldly charmed Toffee while her stunning beast—well, both stunning beasts—wallowed in a show of mutual affection, and McKenna refused to look envy in the eye.

She loved that horse. Less a farm horse than a pet, Toffee was the only extravagance McKenna allowed herself.

Listening despite herself, McKenna felt the empathetic shiver of Bastian's whispers along each of her nerve endings, and the touch of his breath, almost caressing her from her dry lips to—

Shocked at her reaction, McKenna stepped away and hit the stall door at her back. Beguiled by a man, a horse whisperer who could break through a brick wall without a scrape, a scarred he-man who liked the taste of Popsicle sticks. One with a half grasp on the English language, and no filtering system for his thoughts.

That's my man lance in my jeans?

I'll take one to go, please. And will the traitorous girly girl taking over my libido please depart and leave my sanity behind.

Frankly, she should have tossed the house breaker out on his fine butt over the man lance comment, though it had sounded wholly innocent.

Did innocent men still exist?

Before Bastian Dragonelli, she would have said no. Still, the jury was out on that.

McKenna stepped aside, relieved to stop arguing with herself, so as to fall into step beside Bastian and walk Toffee from her stall.

"What's her name?" he asked.

"Toffee, for her color."

He stroked the horse's neck. "Perfect name. We'll only go for a short run, okay?"

"Bareback?"

"I won't hurt her. She's big and strong, is our pretty girl."

Our?

He walked the Belgian out into the sunshine, hopped on with an easy grace and familiarity, and they were off.

Bastian shouted as they raced away, not so much a whoop as a bloodcurdling war cry. Earthy, like a warrior, or a beast who'd ensnared its prey.

With uncontained energy, Bastian and Toffee practically flew across the valley, so in sync they made her think of a ballet, big and bold, the two becoming one.

The embodiment of primordial magnificence.

Intimacy. Raw and unrestrained.

McKenna unbuttoned a couple of buttons in the heat.

The tiny owl that perched on Bastian's shoulder in the basement, or its identical twin, flew over to perch on a fence rail beside her, a magickal creature tilting its head. *Hoop, hoop, hoop?*

"Okay," she said. "I get it. I'll keep him—I mean, I'll *hire* him!"

It gave a half nod, *hoop*ed, and flew away.

The heavens darkened, the temperature dropped, and lightning struck. One minute sun, the next a downpour so fierce, the raindrops felt like needles pricking her skin. McKenna moved to wait inside the barn door while she watched the wind lash a cluster of ornamental grasses. Purple Mexican bush sage whipped against feather reed, little bunny, and cherry pink silver grass. They bent, but they did not break. The sturdiest of her ancient trees, however, bowed to the storm's power.

That tarp would never hold.

Bastian whooped as he got close, and when he stopped, so did her heart, because he gave her a smile that about cut her off at the knees. It split his face and softened his harsh features. Made his scars appear natural.

Whoever he was—whatever his background, certainly more than a handyman—he played with a fervor she hoped he gave to his work. If he did, she had half a shot in hell at getting her bed-and-breakfast up and running.

Did he make love with the same rousing exuberance?

Yes, she had lost her mind, or Bastian Dragonelli had taken it from her with some type of primitive grasp. If her atypical reaction to him didn't exhilarate her so much, she'd be pissed as hell.

Surprising her, and adding to her elation, Bastian lifted her off the ground with an arm at her waist, gave another war cry, and with her in front of him, they took another lap around the valley, wind and rain lashing them, Bastian's hand steadying her, huge and strong.

Man and beast rode as one. Striking. Sturdy. In control.

For the first time in her life, McKenna felt small. Protected. Safe.

"Are you all right?" Bastian's long hair whipped against her face when he leaned in. "Do you want to go back?"

His rough-stroking voice electrified her. "No!" she shouted. "Never!"

He urged Toffee to fly, and they did, all three, and McKenna nearly lost her heart, in more ways than one. Nevertheless, peace raced beside them.

It went too fast, that ride, and she did not want Bastian to let go. She liked his arms around her, his hands splayed bold beneath her breast, but all good things must end.

No one knew that better than her.

At the barn, he lowered her to the wet ground like a porcelain figurine in silk slippers.

His skilled dismount, tempered by the worsening weather, brought her to her senses with a jolt.

He walked Toffee past her into the barn, found a blanket, dried the Belgian, and brushed her down with gentle hands and tender words; then he added molasses to her feed and gave her a well-earned midday snack.

Man and beast acted cocky and pleased with their bonding ritual.

McKenna felt left out. She could join them, but since she wanted back in Bastian's arms, she stayed away.

She'd known him for half a day. Less. Was she hard up or what?

No, was *he* hard, or what? Hung like a bull. Be still her racing heart. She'd felt his prodding assets behind her.

He whispered a last few compliments into Toffee's ear and the Belgian's head came up with a whinny. She nuzzled him, as if they were lovers. No other way to describe it. Toffee was besotted, and Bastian returned the sentiment.

Lucky damned horse.

Inside and out, thunder seemed to follow him as he crossed the barn and approached her. She'd liked their ride, her back against his front, with that "man lance" in his jeans prodding her with interest, as if she were worthy of attention.

Sexy? Her? Hardly.

She would not compare this sophomoric reaction of hers to the storm. She was no cliché. Nor would she be seduced by the foolish fantasy of a scarred warrior.

A scarred *stranger*.

SIXTEEN

Bastian shut the barn doors before McKenna could gather her wits, his hand swallowing hers once more, and together they ran toward the apple orchard.

"Why didn't we stay in the barn?" she asked, shivering, wondering if her apples would be damaged by the storm.

"To protect the livestock," Bastian shouted above nature's fury.

"Do they need protecting?"

Lightning struck the tree beneath which they stood, sending a falling branch like a spear into Bastian's shoulder. The weather seemed personal, each clap of thunder a warning, each bright bolt a threat, and Bastian did *not* seem the least surprised. Protecting the livestock? What was she, chopped liver? "Don't I need protecting?"

He put an arm around her shoulders and squeezed. "You've got me."

She should be so lucky.

The storm raged, an icy ring of hailstones forming

around the perimeter of the tree beneath which they stood, stones as big as her apples. Yet the ground around the rest of the orchard remained green and untouched. Barely wet. "This storm's directly above us," she said. "As if it's *aiming* at us."

"Do not doubt that it is."

His words sent shivers through her, and when the sky caught fire, she screamed.

She never screamed.

He pulled her full against him, her face against his chest. After a minute, she looked up at him. "Did you see that? It looked like five lightning bolts started down here and worked their way to the sky, instead of the other way around."

Bastian placed his chin on her head and she felt his nod. "As if each strike started at someone's fingertips and rose upward," he said. "Yes, I am afraid that I did see." He held her tighter.

"My apples will be ruined. On this tree, at least," she said, trying to gauge his mood.

"How could they be ruined?"

"They could freeze, and I can't spare them. I need the whole harvest this year for my B and B guests. I'll have to get my fire drums to warm the air around this tree and melt the ice forming on its branches."

Before she got to the barn, another overbold lightning flash warmed her back. She whipped around, surprised to see that the hail around the tree had disappeared. "Bastian, what happened?"

"It warmed up."

"That's impossible. Do you smell baked apples?"

"Uh, no." He looked odd then as he caught a falling apple and whisked his hand from beneath it. "Hot!"

Said apple hit the ground and split, its peel practically falling away.

"It's cooked! My apples got cooked on the tree? What the hell kind of storm is this? Could that cluster of lightning flashes have cooked them?"

"Saw that, did you?"

"Not really, but the world went bright at my back."

"Lightning. Right. Okay."

She gave him a double take. "Okay," McKenna said. "We're picking hot apples right now, you and me, and then you're getting a lesson on how to add the spices to turn them into applesauce. Jars and jars of applesauce."

"It's the least I can do."

"Why?"

"I mean . . . you are the boss. I am the grunt."

She eyed him skeptically, because he looked like . . . a kid hiding a pet snake. "We'll have to harvest the other apples, soon, before another freak storm hits. Are hail and lightning normally part of the same storm?"

They got right down to apple picking in the rain, but the sun came out as they finished. Bastian worked fast. Afterward, he carried several full baskets, one atop another, toward the house.

On the porch, McKenna looked at her home through Bastian's eyes and realized how badly it needed painting. She nearly apologized for the peeling paint, until she realized that the condition of her home accounted for this man's presence. Not a warrior, nor a god, no matter how many baskets he could carry, or how primitive and magickal he felt on a horse behind her, but a handyman, human, flawed, and in her employ.

She had nothing to apologize for.

She shivered, and not from being cold and wet, or even from getting her apples flash-baked. *Get a crush on the help, why don't you? First damned day.*

She should get that vibrator Lizzie jokingly suggested. When McKenna flipped the kitchen light switch, nothing happened. "I forgot, the electricity is out—your fault—but you can still shower to warm up. There should be plenty of hot water left for both of us."

"Both of us?"

"Yeah. You, in your shower. Me, in mine."

"Oh, sure."

She led him to his bathroom and gave him fresh towels. "You'll have to feel your way around."

"May I?"

She didn't need light to hear the suggestion in his voice. "Of course not!" But his interest sure did boost her ego, especially during their wild ride.

"Can you start the shower for me?" Bastian asked. "Every one is different. I've showered in ice water and burned my butt—sorry."

"I'll get it." Too intimate standing in this small space with a charismatic giant, especially since he'd be naked in a minute. She turned on the spray and got out fast.

She caught her breath in the dark hall, her back against his bathroom door, and heard him talking to someone named Dewcup. "My name is McKenna," she shouted over the shower. "Did you want something else?" I certainly do.

"No. Sorry. I sing in the shower."

How human of him.

In her own shower, the warm spray soothed and energized her. She listened for more of Bastian's song, but heard nothing.

She wore another of her mother's flowered dresses, a nicer one with a matching sweater and neutral flats. But however feminine she felt, she still had to start a fire in the hearth off the kitchen, in what used to be the keeping room. She planned to remodel around the centerpiece, tall enough to stand in, a hearth once used by her ancestors to cook and heat the house.

Tonight, it would shed light on their spicing and canning.

Bastian's footsteps got closer. "I don't have any clothes up here."

She looked away, fast. "Why not?"

"They're in my bag in the basement."

"I hate to ask, but are you naked?"

"Of course."

"There is no 'of course' about it." This man, apparently, felt comfortable naked. She squeezed her eyes shut. *I will not turn around. I will not.* "Grab a blanket from your bed to wrap around you."

He returned in a blink. Man, he moved fast. "What are you doing?" he asked.

"Trying to start a fire to shed some light on our applesauce project."

He bent down beside her.

"Holy mother of pearl, hold that blanket closed!"

"I'm holding."

"I think I need more tinder," she muttered. "I'll be right back." On the porch, she fanned herself so as not to go up in flames after having the naked stud so close with nothing between them but her favorite quilt.

Great. She'd given him her room but forgot to switch bedding. If she switched now, the quilt would smell like a lemongrass herb garden after a soft rain, like him.

It would remind her of everything she lacked in her life.

SEVENTEEN

❦

Bastian waited to start a fire for McKenna until the porch door bounced closed. He did not want to burn down her house, especially after she had been subjected to Killian's five-fingered lightning drama, not to mention the black-magick hail that might have frozen her apple tree.

He had waited for a thunderclap to silence his fiery tree-warming roar but he accidentally *cooked* her apples in the process. He only hoped he had not killed her tree. Good thing McKenna had not questioned the possibility.

To get the fire in her hearth blazing, he huffed out a small fire streak.

As a dragon, his roar, his fire, and anger, had gone together, but not here, and especially not around McKenna.

The screen door bounced again. "What *was* that weird noise?" she asked, coming back inside. "It sounded like an old car huffing its last."

"What noise?" How dare she insult his beastly huff?

Greater dragons than she had *feared* him. He had a mind to give her a roar that he did not control.

"You got the fire started," she said, arms full of wood, basket of tinder dangling from one. "What did you use, a blowtorch? It looks like it's been burning for hours."

He brushed his nose, to be sure that no smoke lingered. "I have the knack."

"You must have been a dandy Boy Scout. Where did you learn to ride a horse bareback? And what's with the war cry?"

"Do not all boys play at war?"

"I guess they do." She set the wood in a large black ring, tall as her, beside the fireplace. The basket, she placed on the far side away from the fire. "I don't have brothers. I'm the family disappointment," she said. "Not a boy. I broke the family line, I did." She wiped her hands against each other. To remove the wood dust? Or the memory of her failure?

He needed books and a computer to research the new feelings and words she tossed at him today. "I have friends who are *like* brothers," he said to cheer her.

"My friend Lizzie is like a sister, and her husband, Steve, is like a brother. The three of us met in kindergarten. You'll meet them when the weather clears. Are you hungry? You must be. You rode hard."

"Riding Toffee is like riding the wind. All I needed was . . . wings." He had nearly said *my* wings. "I *am* hungry."

"I have a gas stove so electricity's not a problem. But first you need clothes. The basement will be dark by now, and frankly we left too much debris for it to be safe to go down for your bag. Let me get you an old farmhand's clothes. He was a big man so they should fit, though the jeans will be short."

She left him to dress, but when he came back to the

kitchen, she tried not to laugh. The jeans *were* short, the waist big, but he kept them up with a belt that gave him a tail up front, like his man lance, and it hung there long and stiff like a reminder. The shirt fit his shoulders, but it did not have the length to be tucked in.

McKenna worked in the kitchen, slicing something round and white into sticks.

"What is that?"

"A potato," she said.

While she was slicing, a sudden pain shot through his hand as McKenna shouted.

His inner dragon rose up and his hand ached where hers bled, between the thumbs and pointing fingers on their left hands.

"Why'd *you* yell?" she asked, holding a towel on her hand. "I'm the one who cut myself."

"Instinct. I saw what you did and I hurt for you."

"A big brute like you, squeamish?"

"Define squeamish."

"Scared of a little blood," she explained.

Him? A dragon who hunted prey, tore it to bloody shreds, and ate it raw? "Hardly." He might be amused if his dragon magick had not just gone so wrong. He never experienced the physical pain of another. He sensed emotions, like his brother dragons' and Vivica's, though not McKenna's, which she must keep deeply buried. But to feel her physical pain? He'd thought it was his imagination when she bit her lip and his ached, but this? There was no mistaking this.

She washed her hands, dried them, and put something from a "tube" on the cut before she applied what she called a plaster and went back to slicing. After she put the potatoes in a deep pan of liquid that crackled and steamed on the stove, a scent rose from it that made his mouth water. The best earth smell, so far.

He grabbed a crackling potato stick, and snatched his hand from the pan. Fast.

"Bobbing for French fries?" McKenna shouted. "Are you crazy?"

"American food is new to me." He covered his skinless fingertips with his other hand, and the pain receded as he healed. Afterward, he still hurt more where McKenna cut herself than where he burned himself. He wished he could heal her without revealing his magick.

One thing he now knew: he might feel her pain, but she did not feel his. "I guess that was stupid," he said.

"Totally." She tried to take his hand, but he turned away from her to put plasters on his fingertips, so she could not see the new, pink skin.

She set the table. "Are you always that impetuous?"

"I live dangerously." Vivica had told him so, but it would not do to keep quoting his acclimator. Human employment agencies did not normally house people seeking jobs. If he said too much about Works Like Magick, McKenna would wonder why he spent so much time with Vivica, though it had not been enough. Vivica had warned him about leaving before he finished his lessons.

True, he should have listened, but he planned to read before bed every night, all night if he had to, and learn as much as he could. He came here sooner than he should because of his connection to McKenna. His heart connection, he believed.

She filled their plates, salted her fries, as did he, before he dove into them. "This is the best American food I have tasted."

"Thank you."

She cut into her meat. "I hope you don't get sick of eating beef. I raise it. Chickens, too, but plucking's a pain."

"I like beef." Better raw, but he could get used to it this way. He had sometimes roasted his prey on the fly, in order to keep it from running away. Vivica's eating lessons served him well as he wielded his pixie weapons.

They talked, her about her farm. In the way she explained her dream for her family home, he finally understood her plans for her bed-and-breakfast. Her quest—the one he must make his own—encompassed fulfilling a deathbed promise made by her mother to her grandmother, righting the wrong of being born a girl, and honoring her heritage by keeping her home and land in the family.

When they finished eating, and after she cleared the table, she handed him a cloth, showed him how to use it on the dishes she washed, and saw his tattoo.

McKenna took his hand and turned it palm up. "That's unusual," she said. "It looks Greek, like two R's back-to-back with a line in between."

"It is Roman, not Greek."

"Proof that you belong to some type of brotherhood or society?"

He nodded. "A secret society."

She examined his face. "Within the law?"

Bastian relaxed. "Yes. Ask Vivica."

"I might."

Once she let the subject go, an ease of spirit sluiced through him as he worked beside her. This feeling of contentment should *not* disturb him, but it did.

He thought of Vivica's huge feline, half tame domestic and half wild, like him. Did Isis hide its wild nature to keep Vivica happy? Or did keeping Vivica happy subdue its feral nature?

Could subduing his alpha tendencies diminish his warrior strength?

If so, he could lose his ability to fight Killian.

Killian ate "tame" for breakfast.

EIGHTEEN

"Are you all right?" McKenna asked. *"Did you shiver?*
Maybe you caught a chill in that ice storm. An ice storm in
August. How crazy is that?"

Not a chill, he thought, concerned for his brothers' and
Andra's sakes. Worry.

After they finished in the kitchen, she tried to light a
fire in her back parlor. Brick, beautiful, not with a hearth to
cook in but with one to sit beside, the parlor fireplace had
a wood-carved topper that made him go for a closer look.
"This shelf is being held up by a sleeping dragon."

"It's called a mantel. One of my ancestors carved it from
an old oak tree that came down in a hurricane."

"Your ancestors liked dragons."

"I guess they did."

The mantel welcomed him in a way that enlarged his
belief in Andra's and Vivica's magick. His belief that he
belonged here with McKenna. "Amazing, as you say."

The room itself also radiated warmth, with a red sofa

that he would like to sink into, McKenna in his arms, a high-backed chair of red and dark blue stripes, and a small, dark blue chair. The carpet in the middle had a splash of flowers in the same colors and made the room cozier than a cave.

Home, it said, and welcome.

McKenna struggled with the fire in her dragon hearth. He could have started it faster, but he liked watching her move.

"I have another cure for your chills," she said after she got a small flame going. "My mother swore by it. I'll be right back. It'll warm you to your bones."

She could warm him with her body, he thought, making his inner dragon raise its head, but he was able to fight his inner beast. Ah, like his inner dragon, his alpha drive slept when not needed. It would not disappear, he understood now.

Of course, he also knew that his dragon would roar to life when he *least* needed it, during sexual arousal and especially during intercourse. He wanted no fight when his man lance was happy, but a fight was what he would get.

Bastian sighed, lowered himself to the floor, and leaned against the blue-striped chair behind him.

McKenna returned with glasses and a bottle of something dark and red, like blood, on a large, flat silver plate.

"You'll warm from the inside out, drinking this," she said, setting the tray on the small table near them in front of the sofa.

"What is it?" he asked as she poured, the sweet scent of the drink calling to him. Not blood but fruit.

"It's wine. Cherry Manischewitz to be precise, the sweetest wine out there, and the tastiest, as far as I'm concerned. My mom loved it, too. It'll make anyone with a sweet tooth smile and can be both medicinal and calming."

He would not refuse a bit more calm. "I am addicted to anything sweet."

"I know. You told me." She poured them each a glass.

Bastian took a sip and the taste did indeed make his sweet tooth happy. "This is like nectar from the gods."

"Didn't I say?"

Bastian refilled his glass while McKenna went to the kitchen.

"Have you ever tasted key lime pie?" she asked, returning with two plates of green food.

He finished his second glass of wine. "Never." In his experience, green prey bore a pungent flavor and a kick like slime-jumpers in a dragon's belly. True, this did not smell as bad, but he did not look forward to the kick.

"You're in for another treat." She winked and his man lance twitched. "It's tart and sweet at the same time."

Tart and sweet, like McKenna. "Good, because my sweet tooth is as big as a dragon's tooth."

She sat facing him, and when she did, her ruddy swirled feline, still wearing its silly hat, curled in her lap. Freaky faery hopped on the silly-looking snack's back, and when McKenna ran her hand down Jaunty's fur, she sent Dewcup flying face-first into green slime pie.

With a sucking sound, Dewcup freed herself and rose into the air, spitting slime and scraping it off her eyes, until she looked at him through wide rounds of blinking blue in a froth of green. "May it rot your innards as you swallow!" Dewcup snapped when she caught his amusement.

Bastian coughed, and Dewcup's chin came up. "Laugh and I will grind your man parts into dragon meatballs!" She flapped her wings in fury, splattering his face and clothes with bits of green glop. McKenna's, too.

He caught her watching him and sobered. "I apologize," he said, knowing better than to react to a faery no one else could see. He poured himself another glass of wine and drank it right down so he would not have to answer questions.

"You can laugh at my cat all you want. I do. Most don't wear tissue boxes on their heads, though I don't know how she managed to splash us with pie filling." She checked her snack's paws, then its swishing tail, and shrugged. "Guess she already licked them clean, and I don't blame her."

"Nice cat," he said, and by that he meant tasty-looking.

"You called her a snack when you first saw her. I find that worrying. You stuck your hand in hot grease, and ate Popsicle sticks. What did you eat in your country?"

Anything that moved? Best not say so.

"Never mind," she said. "I don't want to know. First rule of the house: My cat is not for eating. She's for petting, companionship, and sleeping at the foot of my bed."

"Lucky cat."

Bastian thought McKenna's reaction to his words revealed a bit of surprised interest.

Shaking her reaction almost visibly away, she, too, drank another glass of wine. "You may call her Jaunty," she said, petting her cat, "if she's agreeable."

"I would be honored." He would feel foolish, but that was earth for you, and keeping McKenna happy counted for more than looking foolish.

Dewcup recovered and, somewhat cleaner, made a beeline for the cat, whispered in its ear, and made it shake its head. Then the flutterbrat tweaked the poor cat's whiskers till it meowed and paw-swatted his faery into the ashes. Could Jaunty *see* Dewcup? Or was that a lucky smack?

"Cat," Dewcup snapped. "Consider the battle lines drawn." The flutterbrat made fast work of snuffing the glowing embers clinging to her clothes and hair, until she looked like a sorry bit of dragon bait. But like any otherworldly immortal, she would soon look like new. Having halted incineration, she chose retribution and climbed on

the feline's back to ride her the way he had ridden Toffee.
Hard.

Speaking of which . . . The more wine he drank, the
more his man lance prepared for battle, and the more easily
he could imagine sparring with McKenna.

NINETEEN

McKenna shook her head as Jaunty howled and disappeared around a corner. "I don't know what's gotten into her," McKenna said, "but she seems to be having a good time."

She picked up her piece of pie and tilted her head at the faery shape in her piece. "Hmm. Looks like a big bizarro bug landed in it, but it got away, and I'm not wasting this." She scooped away that section of green with her little finger, wiped it on the side of her plate, spooned some of the good stuff into her mouth, and made a noise he would like to hear while they tested his man lance. In the event his lance worked with a partner.

"Hello?" McKenna called, pulling him from his thoughts. "Don't you want your pie?"

"Sorry. I got distracted." He tasted it and liked it—a surprising new ambrosia from the goddess served with this earth-type nectar from the gods—though the pie's name made no sense at all. "How do you get keys to look and taste like this? Aren't they normally hard and gold and used for opening doors?"

McKenna set down her pie, sounding like the owl that landed on him. *Hoop. Hoop. Hoop.* She held her chest, as if she had swallowed a gillybulb and could not control her mirth.

Captivated, Bastian took the opportunity to observe her, while he imagined sliding his fingers along her body's curves, outward and inward along every surface—no clothing necessary—to learn her and set in motion the process he believed would lead to mating. As to whether he *should* be mating with his heart mate, Andra had not said.

Sticky question, that. Sticky sweet.

He may not have been a human for as long as he lived as a dragon, but his mating instincts had returned full force. McKenna's lips became another source of distress, or perhaps he meant interest, or both. He wanted them against his lips, his against hers, and against every other inch of her.

With her presence, she *called* to his hands for touching.

He sipped his wine and watched her over the rim of his glass. As much as he could not read her emotions, she must be able to read him, because she focused on him—like prey caught in his dragon claws. Their eyes met.

Hers widened above her glass, but with trembling hands she set it down to lick her lips, and still their gazes held. She attempted to speak, failed, and straightened, bringing her knees up against her enticing front, her flowered dress touching the floor.

She wrapped her arms around her lovely bent legs and stared into the fire.

"I'm glad you do not wear a cape like so many in Salem," he said in the way he would speak to a skittish colt, sensing that need in her to be gentled.

She regarded him from the corner of one eye, lashes lowered. "Do you have something against witches?"

"Not at all."

"Good, because I come from a witch."

"Ciarra, I know."

McKenna looked more closely at him. "How do you know?"

"Vivica does, too. She told me. You both come from Ciarra, though Vivica inherited her magick from Ciarra's brother."

McKenna refilled her glass. "It's capes you dislike, then?"

Bastian nodded and refilled his own glass. "Cloaks and capes, they hide too much. I like your clothes. They show your shape and make you look like a woman."

"You are such a man," she said like that was a bad thing. To prove it, she inched closer to the fire and away from him.

"I did not mean to make you uncomfortable."

"I am the boss."

"Yes."

He followed her lead and took up his pie to finish while the silence became comfortable and they finished the wine between them. The fire about burned itself out before McKenna grabbed a long black metal prodder and leaned forward to push the ashes to the back of the hearth for the night, giving him one last opportunity to admire her backside.

"It's time for bed." She made an attempt at standing.

His man lance prepared for duty. "Bed would be good."

"Help me, grunt. The room won't stop spinning."

Bastian shot to his feet, grabbed his own head, and caught McKenna before she fell. "I've got you."

She made a merry, bubbly sound. "I can tell."

He walked her to her bed. Or she walked him. Or they walked each other, at least one of them tripping along the way.

They had barely reached her bed when his knees gave out and they fell across it, arms and legs tangled. He might have tried to unknot them but McKenna reached for the buttons on his shirt.

Taking that as a sign, Bastian reached for the buttons on her dress.

Clothes flew in every direction, except for his shirt, which he immediately draped across his lap so as not to frighten her with his flaw while she pulled off his jeans. He pointed to her dragon-hardening globes, crowned by dark peaks and wide, rouge red edges, so beautiful they made his mouth water. "Breasts, right?"

"Breasts, ye—" McKenna looked down at herself and grabbed a blanket to hold in front of her. "We're naked!"

"I know."

"Oh, no," she wailed. "I forgot!"

"What? What did you forget?"

"Wine makes me horny."

"Define horny."

"I want to have sex, damn it. With you!"

"That is good, yes?"

"That is good, *no!*"

Apparently, he experienced *all* her physical reactions, not just pain, but pleasure, and the act of being horny, too. "I want sex with you, too, believe me," he said, "and then some."

"Too late," she whispered as she sat and fell forward, her face smashed against his chest, one breast falling into his open palm.

"Another gift from the gods." He looked up. *Thank you.*

McKenna began to sound a bit like a swine. A baby one, maybe. He knew the sound. Since his return to earth, he had awakened from sleep hearing that sound, except that he was the only one in the room. Sleep? "McKenna?" Please no. "Why, why, why?" he shouted to wake her. "Why is it too late?"

She stirred, looked up at him, smiled, snuggled deeper against him, and brought all their naked parts into contact. "Wine," she whispered, "makes me horny *and* sleepy."

"No, wait. I know how to fix—"

TWENTY

Dragons wake with the sun, unless, before sunrise, a breast is being taken from one's hand along with the sweet pressure against one's magnificent morning lance.

Bastian had had a hard night. In every way.

In experiencing McKenna's physical reactions, sleep had also claimed him . . . at the peak of his arousal. Fighting it had not helped. Worse, he dreamed that fiery lava rocks burned the brothers he forgot existed while he took McKenna to his nest.

A magickal warning? Or a threat?

Perhaps he should not mate with her.

He mocked himself with an inner laugh. Tell his man lance that.

He opened his eyes when McKenna's bathroom door clicked softly shut, and he found himself in her bed with a headache, worse than after cracking a tree with his skull.

He placed his hands on his head to heal it, without success. So this must be McKenna's headache. Without relief, in any way, he rose, gathered his clothes, and left her room.

He would need to consider this mating question more carefully before acting on it. He should concentrate on making her quest his own, and find the sign of the crowned dragon, too, though he believed that sharing McKenna's physical reactions *proved* she was his. Still, he would follow Andra's mandate. None of the dragons in Gran's collection were crowned, though the one that looked most like him did have something broken off the top. At any rate, he needed to keep looking.

He had been a crowned dragon, triple horned, two curved toward the sides, his center horn tall and tilting back. The three together resembled a human monarch's crown. He did not miss his crown as much as he missed his wings.

But he was a man now, a sex-starved man.

The weather lashing his window—Killian style—would not allow for searching or working outside today, and he hardly expected to find a crowned dragon in the house, though perhaps he should mention having seen one somewhere. See how McKenna reacted. The dragon carved into the mantel had not been crowned. Were there more dragons hiding in her house?

He stepped beneath his shower. The water hitting his head hurt. He wished he could heal McKenna's headache, but after last night, he did not think she would let him place his hands on her, anywhere. He looked forward to seeing how she reacted to their having slept together, both of them naked.

Anticipation rushed him, but McKenna Greylock was worth biding his time for.

His thick, throbbing lance agreed, and while he washed it, he imagined going alpha on her and doing the deed, with her full and happy compliance, of course. But he would fight his nature here and let his heart mate lead him. An alpha always did what he must to save his men, in this case, his dragon brothers. Besides, knowing now that his alpha tendencies were safe, being led by McKenna did not feel as much a burden as an adventure, with the possibility of a sexual prize for his efforts.

After his shower, an earthside habit he embraced, he wore the clothes she had given him, appreciating the extra room for his "horny" man lance, and made his way to the kitchen, following the scent pulling him toward her.

"Cinnamon rolls," she said, avoiding eye contact.

"Is that a morning greeting, McKenna? You use no enthusiasm."

"No, it's a Greylock breakfast. Would you like coffee?"

Bitter brew. "Milk?" he asked. "I am fond of a cold glass of milk. Dragons do not normally drink—"

"What about dragons?"

He found himself following her around the kitchen. "Your grandmother's collection got me to thinking about dragons. They do not drink milk. Did you know?"

"I know only that dragons are fiercely beautiful."

"Thank you."

"What?"

"How is your hand?" he asked.

"Weird, but it healed practically overnight as if it never happened."

So, after one day in her presence, when McKenna cut herself, he experienced her pain, and when he healed himself, she healed? And when wine made her horny and sleepy, he got horny and sleepy. Their interwoven physicality made no sense. It might point to her as his heart mate. But it might also be a new flaw in his magick, a result of Killian's counter spell.

"May I see your hand?" he asked.

McKenna shook her head, but she stilled, winced, and raised both hands, as if to keep her head from falling off.

He knew exactly how she felt.

"I don't take to pampering well," she admitted. "I'm more likely to mow you down as let you touch me."

Son of a bustard, her maternal ancestors had forgotten to mention that.

She turned pink, probably remembering how she had awakened nearly blanketing him.

He reached out, placed his hands over hers atop her head to heal her, and soon his own headache receded. She did not fight him, which meant she liked his touch, or she embraced a clear head. He took the hand she'd cut without permission, and resisted her attempt to take it back.

A small scar, he saw between her thumb and pointing finger. Satisfied with the way it had healed, he wished he had perfected scar removal. "Looks good. What will be my grunt task, or tasks, today?" He sat and she placed a plate before him. "McKenna, my food is staring at me with big yellow eyes. I do not usually let my food see me."

"Where did Vivica say you came from?" McKenna filled a plate for herself.

"I came from the Island of Stars."

"It sounds lovely, but did you have no eggs on the island?"

Eggs? On the island, he sucked them from their shells.

"They're from my chickens, sunny-side up." She beamed. "This bacon is from the brother of the swine you tried to defend yourself from yesterday."

As a dragon, he would have eaten that swine for dinner. *Nothing* frightened him. Well, except for the depth and speed of his kinship to this woman. "McKenna, I meant to save *you* from the swine, not myself." It had reminded him of a beast from his journey through the planes.

McKenna sat across from him at the table. "The day I need a man to save me is the day I lose my self-respect."

"I see." Another McKenna lesson her ancestors forgot to impart. "So, what animal do cinnamon buns come from?"

Her hair bounced like a horse's tail as she looked up and raised a winged brow. "Cinnamon buns come from ticklish white dough boys."

"Do you raise those here on the farm?"

McKenna slammed her pronged eating weapon on the table. "Are you for real?"

Bastian shooed Dewcup away from his milk glass with a quick hand that he brought up to scratch his nose. His pesky faery had nearly drowned trying to drink. How foolish he would look trying to rescue an invisible faery. He'd leave some milk in the bottom of the glass for the minx. She could have his eggs, too, if she wanted.

"Yes, I am real," he said. "Amazingly so, considering my awkward start and wretched journey. Everything is as it should be with me. Well, almost everything."

"Mysterious, again. Fine. If that's the way you want to play it." She rose from the table, her breakfast half eaten.

"Play it?" He never played, even as a human boy, except at learning how to be a warrior. "You would play with me?"

"Watch it, Casanova! Last night was an aberration. No more wine for you."

For *him*? The wine had affected her more than him, though he would never tell her so. Let her enjoy the wine and him the results.

"I don't trust easily," she said, "and you're not making it any easier. I'm no shrinking violet, whatever your scam. I don't need anybody, including you. If you're not part of the solution, you *are* the problem, and you can be replaced, like this." She snapped two fingers together, yet seemed to doubt her own words.

"My name, I tell you, is Bastian. Not Casanova. Not Buster."

McKenna shook her head and let her arms fall to her sides. "It's still raining so we work in here, today, and every rainy day from here on. After breakfast, bring Toffee an apple. She's pining for you. She pouted when I went to muck her stall without you."

"Muck?"

McKenna's lips curved upward, a rare sight, though she looked anything but pleased, except at some wicked intent, perhaps. "Tomorrow, you, me, and a predawn mucking lesson. I can't wait."

"And today?"

"You'll paint the first of the spackled and sanded rooms. My decorating scheme is early yard sale, so I can work around whatever colors you choose. Cans of bargain paint line the shelves in the shed. After you sweet-talk Toffee, pick whatever paint you want and go to town. No, you're literal. Don't go to town; you'll get lost. Go to the first bedroom off the hall on your right, and paint it. When you finish that one, move on to paint the bedroom next to it. I'm off to the barn."

When McKenna turned to put the rest of her food into the cold box, Bastian inhaled his breakfast, ignoring Vivica's eating lessons, his speed making him able to sprint to the barn in the rain with McKenna—between the raindrops, she said—both of them with apples for her horse.

"Do you use Toffee for anything besides plowing?" he asked as they got to the barn, shaking rain off themselves. "We failed to run between the drops," he remarked.

McKenna laughed. "My plow," she said, pointing to a big green monster with tires half as tall as him, "has a motor."

He pointed to the corner. "But that's a plow."

"Yeah, my great-great-great-granddaddy's. Sometimes, I think you came through a time warp."

Close, he thought.

"I like to grow flowers and plants free-style around the property," she said. "You know, willy-nilly, the more unusual the arrangement, the better. Sometimes I use Toffee to pull up stumps, clear dead trees, and thin out the sun hoggers. Don't tell anyone, but I keep her because I love her and like to ride. She's my one luxury."

Bastian liked McKenna's respect for nature and the way she loved her horse. Free-style flowers, he had never heard of. He should research the expression. "Do you have a computer?" His favorite new earth invention held much information, which he would never tire of absorbing. Not as quick as reading a book but more diverse in offered lessons, plus McKenna kept using words he needed to learn.

"I do my bookkeeping on the computer," she said, "so the answer is yes, I own one. Whether I let you use it is another matter."

"I took lessons," he said. "Extensive lessons from Vivica."

"We'll see. Right now, until the sun shines again, if it ever does, you're painting bedrooms."

"I look forward to it." Yesterday, after making applesauce, he had taken a minute to read a book on painting, and he figured that if Michelangelo could do it, so could he.

TWENTY-ONE

In the shed, Bastian found paint cans with many different and beautiful colors. But so many cans of each? McKenna must plan to paint all the rooms.

Choosing an assortment of paintbrushes, he took a can of each color up to the house, figuring he could return for more as needed.

In the kitchen, he found a note from McKenna. "Gone to town for supplies. You paint. Your lunch is in the fridge."

The fridge? He went to her library, looked up "fridge" in the dictionary, among other new words, and read a few books. He returned to the kitchen a half hour later, opened the fridge, and found his name on a note stuck to a covered dish.

Unable to tame his dragon-sized hunger, he devoured the contents, whatever they were, as fast as he inhaled breakfast. Plates and dishes, he had learned from Vivica, were not for eating.

After three Creamsicles and the last piece of key pie, he went to work.

The white walls called to him. He and his brother dragons may have been trapped on the island as it began to die, but it had once been a vibrant paradise, until lava from the sea mountain boiled the Endless Sea dry, and replaced the water. The lava continued to rise, burning plants and trees on the island's shores, and threatening their existence.

He had gotten away. His brothers had not. Yet.

As he opened paint cans, his brother dragons and centuries of island scenes filled his mind. He picked a favorite scene, and began.

Halfway through the afternoon, Dewcup fell into a can of yellow paint, pulled herself out, and flew blindly around the room, bumping into walls, each bounce leaving her perfect imprint behind. "Thanks for helping," he said as he carried her to his bathroom sink, filled it, and set her on a raft of soap.

She crossed her arms in stubbornness and refused to bathe, so he grabbed her by her wings and dunked her three times.

"May your teeth grow warts," she cursed between dunkings, "and your ears harbor—*gurgle, drumble, slub*—spiderweeds!"

Clean, she tired of taunting him, and he went back to work, adding a bit of color to the wings, and sparkling light to each faery impression, before he continued.

After painting for hours, he heard cars outside and saw McKenna and Vivica arriving together, McKenna in her truck, and Vivica in the car she called her Vette.

Vivica suggested he wait to learn to drive. He agreed. Cars called for roads that went in wrong directions. He would prefer to fly as the crow—or, in his case, the dragon—flew. Though, around McKenna, especially after sleeping naked with her last night, he would most assuredly rather be a man. A man who would get to try last night again and hopefully follow it to its natural conclusion.

He wiped his hands on a cloth and went to meet them as they came up the porch steps. The rain had not stopped or slowed. Killian, he suspected, was continuing to make her presence known.

"Good to see you again, Bastian," Vivica said.

"Why are you here?" he asked his acclimator.

"I wanted to see how you and McKenna are getting along. I try to sense my clients' needs beforehand, but I do like to make sure my placements, and their employers, are happy."

Bastian relaxed. "I am happy. McKenna, are you not happy?"

"I've been confused," McKenna said, "but not unhappy."

"Good. Come see the room I painted." Bastian led the way.

McKenna yelped and stopped walking the minute she stepped inside. "*Now* I'm unhappy."

"I think it's marvelous," Vivica said turning in a circle to see it all. "I've never seen anything so wondrously magickal. Who wouldn't want to sleep in a fairyland like this?"

"Oh, I don't know," McKenna said. "People who are afraid of dragons? I could have nightmares about that big blue beastie."

"Cedrig? He is harmless."

"And the gold dragon?"

"Jaydun. He roars when he does not get enough sleep, but he is a fine figure of a dragon."

McKenna rolled her eyes. "Did you escape from an asylum?"

Vivica cleared her throat. "Bastian speaks his mind always, no matter how fanciful. He's like an actor who gets into his role. This is a work of art and he's in character to create it."

Bastian understood that Vivica's words were spoken as a warning.

"I meant to please you, McKenna," he said. "I read about painting in your library, but I know I have a lot to learn. Please say that you did not bring Vivica to take me back." His chest got tight at the thought of losing McKenna, yet his very attachment to her made him growl inwardly. This need for her frustrated him because it marched beside a loss of control. He could not leave his likely heart mate, because if he did, Andra and his brothers would suffer. Besides, he did not *want* to leave.

Neither did he want to spin out of control.

Vivica looked through her bag. "McKenna and I met by accident, Bastian. She didn't complain, but she did wonder why you thought cinnamon rolls were meat."

"I guess I still have a lot to learn on this . . . America."

"Ya think?" McKenna snapped. "You'll have to start the room over again tomorrow, and stick to one color." McKenna looked out the window. "Vivica, that idiot television journalist who keeps reporting about . . . whatever coming through the veil is parked at the end of my driveway. I thought I saw his car behind us on our way here. Is he following you?"

Vivica shook her head. "He thinks I'll lead him to a story. Don't worry. He'll give up one of these days. Forget about him, and forget about repainting the room, maybe?"

"Are you kidding me?"

"Tourists can sleep in one-color rooms anywhere, any day. Here, they can leave the real world behind, float on clouds, dream of pink skies, green stars, blue trees, and purple swans—" She stepped closer to the wall. "Double-winged purple swans. Bastian's work has depth, light, sparkle, life! It's quite magickal, even the ceiling."

"What's that?" McKenna asked, pointing.

"That is a tigeroon, and there, a porcupig, and in the air, a bustard. All quite prized on the island."

Vivica glanced at him and away as fast. "McKenna, when was the last time you saw three moons in a pink sky, one scarlet, one raspberry, and one paprika? How gorgeous is that?"

"The overall effect is beautiful, I admit, but—" McKenna did not look quite convinced.

Vivica put an arm around McKenna's shoulder, and Bastian wondered how his employer would react if he tried to embrace her.

"Leave it the way it is," Vivica said, "and furnish it right away. Furnish it with plain pieces but not too many. Try a bed with no headboard, so as not to spoil the view. Then before you do another thing, take a picture of it, slap it on a brochure, put it on your website, on the Salem websites, anywhere on the 'Net where tourists would look. Don't forget to use 'magick' and 'enchanting' in your advertising, and mention Ciarra hiding in the caves, historic, hallowed ground, yada yada. And throw in a picture of that giant old tree shaped like a dragon."

"I like that tree," Bastian said. "I noticed it when I rode Toffee."

"Vivica, you really think this is a good idea, don't you? Because you're starting to convince *me* to book a room here." McKenna pulled a notebook and pencil from her pocket. "I haven't even named the B and B yet."

"No time like the present," Vivica said. "You need paying guests yesterday."

McKenna paled. "I have sixty-nine days left to get ready for them. You're scaring me."

"I don't mean to, sweetie. You were blindsided by your mother's death, but you had this mess to clean up. I'm not pushing; I'm encouraging. Bastian, can you paint more scenes like this, with other wild colors and more proud, beautiful dragons?"

"I have an endless supply in my head."

"McKenna, name your B and B." Vivica indicated the room. "Behold the place where dragons live. Picture this room as you name it."

McKenna looked around. "The Dragon's Inn? No, too ordinary. How about the Dragon's Lair?"

"I *like* it," Bastian said.

McKenna hid her pride, but her eyes smiled.

"Magickal," Vivica said, "and perfect, given the family's ancient dragon collection."

"And the back parlor mantel," Bastian added.

"And don't forget the dragon tree," Vivica added.

McKenna looked from one of them to the other. "I used to call it the dragon tree when I wanted my dad to build a tree house in it. The Dragon's Lair. It works better than I expected. We could keep dragon kites in the closet. Families could fly them in the valley. We get a nice breeze there off the old harbor."

"Good," Vivica said. "I know magick when I see it, and when Bastian's finished painting these rooms, your guests will see magick, too."

Bastian's heart about jumped from his chest when McKenna flashed her first true smile. "The Dragon's Lair. That's what it's meant to be called. I'll work on the brochure tonight. When you're finished painting, Bastian, and the walls are dry, you can help me move furniture in, so I can take a digital picture. Cedrig and Jaydun, hey? Do all your dragons have names?"

"Of course."

McKenna raised her arms and let them fall to her sides as she left the room.

"Nice likeness of a faery," Vivica whispered.   •

Bastian washed paprika paint off a brush. "Thank you for saving me."

Vivica winked. "I think you're saving McKenna—well, her family legacy, at least." She slipped him a box of DVDs. "Do these lessons and fast. Getting these to you is why I planned to come out here today. Then I met McKenna and she confirmed my concern."

"I'm glad you came, or she would not have liked my work."

"Fate works its own magick. Your employer needs to make a mortgage payment in time to beat a greedy developer at his own game, but you didn't hear that from me."

"What is a developer?"

"The guy's a builder trying to steal McKenna's land so he can fill it with condos and make a lot of money. You'll meet him soon enough. Judge for yourself."

"Condos are bad?"

"No. In the right place, they're great. On a historic site, on hallowed ground that still belongs to the family that's owned it for centuries, not so much."

"I will protect McKenna from the developer, but tell me what you think of him."

"He's a bit like Killian, but human, unfortunately for the race. When you come face-to-face with him for the first time, don't show your claws, and I mean that literally."

TWENTY-TWO

Bastian woke as all dragons must, ready to do battle.

His attackers screamed.

He roared and smoked up the room, until he realized where he was.

The last time he had an eyelid pried open, he'd nearly lost the eye. His attacker had not been so lucky.

Jock did a quick smoke test on his bite-sized assailants. They passed.

As he expected, the sound of his auto-roar brought McKenna and a woman he did not know into the room, followed by a man in a chair on wheels. "Wyatt! Whitney!" the man snapped, obviously familiar with the dawn invaders.

The tiny hands that pried his eyelids open belonged to two kidlets who had invaded his bed. The bouncing creatures on either side of him were not the least afraid of his roar or his smoke. The girl, with big blue eyes and long, curly blond hair, had a vivid expression that spoke volumes. The other, a boy, had wide, curious brown eyes that spoke of an eagerness to learn the world's secrets.

Bastian sat up in the bed, keeping his blankets to his waist. He had, unfortunately, not awakened in McKenna's bed again during the week and a half he'd spent painting bedrooms. Her very romantic words to him at bedtime last night, as she looked out at the rain, had been, "Only fifty-nine freaking days left!"

The woman he did not know reached over him and snatched her kidlets away as if he might eat them. At one time, he might not have known better, but he now understood the humanness of humanity. Even the humanness of cats. Sad to admit, but creature snacks were losing their appeal.

"Lizzie," McKenna said, "this is Bastian, my handyman."

"Yep," Lizzie said. "He sure looks handy to me. Hello," she said. "These marauders belong to us. This is my husband, Steve."

"Hello," Steve said from his chair.

"I apologize for the shout," Bastian said. "I was in the army. I saw the kind of battle where you stay alive by waking up ready to fight."

"No, we apologize," the husband said. "They move fast and they're comfortable here at McKenna's, which isn't always a good thing."

Lizzie put the children on their father's lap, and McKenna pulled the man's chair from the room. His wife remained like a statue, staring at him in his bed.

Bastian wondered if she could see his claws, wings, or tail.

McKenna came back in a huff and dragged her friend from the room.

It was the first time Bastian had enjoyed his heightened senses, because he could hear the two women talking all the way up the hall.

"I can't believe I had to pry you out of there."

"McKenna, he's gorgeous, a hunk and a half, but taller, broader, and more handsome than any man between here and Hollywood. He's like the best of every hunk in L.A."

"Personally," McKenna said, "I'm thinking he's like a cross between Hugh Jackman and Jeffrey Dean Morgan."

"Yes! Except that he's bigger with wider shoulders, and he puts out an aura of charisma, times, like, thirteen," Lizzie said.

"I hadn't noticed."

"Oh, girl, get a grip, and I'm not *only* talking to myself here. I'm crazy in love with Steve and I'm attracted to your handy hunk. Have you seen him naked yet?"

Silence, Bastian heard.

"McKenna?" her friend said. "You're not answering me. I repeat. Have you seen him naked?"

"Little bit."

"Yes!" Lizzie screamed. "I'll bet he's hung."

"LizBeth!"

"Well, he wasn't hiding a cocktail frank under that blanket."

"I don't know if he's hung, okay? We had wine. I fell asleep, and he got so bored, he did, too. Close call. Survived. Never gonna happen again."

"Liar."

"You think I don't know how yum cakes he is? I wish he was as ugly as the swine he tried to protect me from. He should only protect me from himself."

"What are you talking about? Or maybe I should ask what you're scared of."

"He's too damned perfect. I'm staying the hell away from him. Remind me I said that, will you?"

"He's not perfect; he's scarred. Scary scarred. Did you

see the trails of, I don't know, claw marks, maybe, on his neck and workout abs?"

Abs? Bastian wondered, touching the scars from Cedrig's claws and Devane's dratted teeth marks.

"Are those teeth marks in his side?" Lizzie asked. "How do they feel to the touch?"

"How the hell should I know how they feel or how they got there?"

"I'd sure like to know," Lizzie said.

"You heard him," McKenna said. "He's been in the army."

Lizzie laughed. "Where he fought a T. rex?"

"I think the scars make him look like a beast," McKenna said. "A 'come and eat me' beast, but that doesn't mean I'm letting him near me."

"McKenna Greylock, you're half in lust already. Admit it."

"No way."

Bastian folded his arms behind his head and smiled. McKenna's interest boded well for the possibility of him getting to use his man lance someday soon. If only he could get her to drink wine again.

"Personally," Lizzie said, "I think he's got the hots for you."

"He does not. Why do you think so?"

"The way he keeps track of you with his eyes."

Bastian sat straighter in the bed. He did not, did he?

"You have an imagination and a half, Framingham!"

The women's voices faded at the familiar sound of the porch door bouncing closed. Disappointed that he could no longer hear them, Bastian rose, pleased by Lizzie's view of McKenna's interest in him.

Since everyone else had eaten, he made himself a steak for breakfast, minus the side of yellow eyes, ate it dragon fast, then joined McKenna and her friends outside. "What is my job today, Boss?"

"Steve is your boss today," McKenna said. "You do what he tells you."

"You're roofing today, buddy," Steve said. "First thing you do is get the supplies from the shed."

"My name is Bastian."

"Can I go with him, Dad?" the boy asked.

"I don't know, Wyatt." Steve scratched his ear and looked up. "Do you mind, Bastian?"

Bastian ruffled the boy's hair. "I think I can handle him."

"Wyatt," Steve said with a warning finger, "you wait outside the shed when you get there. Just keep Mr. Dragonelli company on the way to and from, okay?"

"Okay, Dad."

Bastian had no idea how to talk to children. He was trying to think of something to say when the boy looked up. "Wanna know a secret?"

TWENTY-THREE

"Okay," Bastian said, with no idea what he was agreeing to. "I want to know a secret."

"My dad hurts a lot," Wyatt said, "but he doesn't want Mom to know."

Bastian regarded the boy. "Did your dad tell you that?"

"No, but I can see his face when Mom's not looking, and I heard him say he was sick of that chair."

"I guess I can't blame him. I bet you help him every chance you get."

"Yeah, that's why I'm not playing with Whitney in the house, in case Dad needs anything."

"Good for you. Did your dad tell you what hurts most?"

"His knees. He rubs them all the time. And he holds his head, too, sometimes."

"I see. Okay, kidlet, I'm going in the shed but I'll be right out. Don't move."

Wyatt sat on a stump and waited. Bastian handed him a box of roofing nails to carry on the way back.

Steve watched them as they returned. "You're a strong one, Bastian, carrying all those shingles at once."

"I've always been strong. Would you be more comfortable in a different chair?"

"Yes, but I'm stuck in this one."

"I wouldn't say that." Bastian brought out the recliner from the library and set it beneath a tree not far from the house.

Steve shook his head. "You're an optimistic man, but—"

Bastian lifted him in his arms and sat him in the recliner. "From here you can supervise this unhandy handyman and rest, too."

Steve's sigh of relief proved little Wyatt's concern right. Bastian pushed the handle back so the chair raised Steve's useless legs.

"Man, I could get used to this," Steve said.

Bastian leaned down and put a hand on each of Steve's knees. "Your son told me you were uncomfortable. He's worried about you. You should know what a great kid you have. Don't let on that I told you, or how worried he is, though you might give him hope once in a while, tell him you're feeling better, having a good day, stuff like that."

Steve looked at Bastian's hands on his knees, then up at him. "I appreciate your concern. Can you move the chair's lever forward a bit more?"

Bastian hated to remove his healing hands so soon. The tingling in his palms indicated a lot of damage in Steve's knees. A lingering touch would work better, but this was the best he could manage while hiding his gift of healing. He went back to getting the shingles for the roof.

Whitney came running from the house and down the porch steps, her hands on her head. "Barbie's got me! She's got me!"

Bastian looked up from breaking the binding around

a pack of shingles. Could the little one see Dewcup? He caught the little girl and set her in Steve's lap.

Steve chuckled. "How can Barbie be chasing you?"

"She's alive, I tell you. I can prove it. She has wings, an orange flower skirt, and a buttercup hat. She said my hair was like spun silk and could she take a nap in it?"

"Did you say yes?" Steve asked.

"No. I said no. But she's there, anyway."

Bastian checked her hair, and sure enough . . . He raised a brow at Dewcup.

The faery pest raised her chin and turned on her side in the child's soft hair to face away from him.

"What an imagination you have, Whitney," her father said.

"Imagination?" Bastian asked.

"Invisible friends, that kind of thing. It's always something with this one."

What a relief. "Well, Whitney, may I help get her out of your hair?"

"Yes, please, Mr. Bastian, sir."

Something tickled Bastian about her response as he worked to extract the stubborn, clinging faery from Whitney's beautiful curls.

"Ouch!" Whitney yelled. "Ouch, ouch, ouch!"

"My pardon," Bastian said, denying his need to shout as Dewcup wound her arms and legs around a mass of blond curls.

"May you grow limp in your man parts," the faery cursed, "*before* you get to use them."

Bastian rolled his eyes and tried slipping Dewcup down and off the golden strands.

"Boils on your backside. Fur on your tongue!"

"Dewcup, you have no manners," Bastian said . . . out loud, unfortunately.

Steve furrowed his brows. "When you play, you really play."

Whitney's eyes widened. "Is Dewcup her real name?"

"Why, yes, it is." Though since his arrival and the faery's pesky presence, he had wanted to call her the kind of names a little girl should not know.

"I want to be friends with Dewcup," Whitney said. "She can ride my shoulder, or sit in my pocket, but I don't like her in my hair. It hurts, and I can't see her up there."

"Dewcup, do you find that a reasonable request?"

"Eat slug slime," Dewcup said, arms crossed.

He finally got the faery free and deposited the pesky thing into the little girl's pocket. "Feed her honey clover petals and she'll be your friend forever. There's a patch of clover right there beside your father's chair."

Whitney grinned. "Do you want some clover petals, Dewcup?"

Arms crossed, disposition sour, the faery gave him a dirty look, but she relented and gave Whitney a nod.

The little girl slid off her father's lap, and began a conversation with the annoying flutterbrat about dolls and tea parties, and Dewcup's interest sweetened with each tiny petal she devoured.

"Do you have kids?" Steve asked.

Bastian shook his head. "No, but I have a faery I would sell cheap."

TWENTY-FOUR

From the porch, McKenna and Lizzie watched Bastian interact with Wyatt and Whitney.

Lizzie sat on the top step. "I can't get over the way that brute of a man managed to win over my two skeptics. They're hard sells."

"I know. I would have expected him to throw them out of his room this morning when they tried to pry his eyelids open."

Lizzie groaned. "I about had a heart attack when Wyatt admitted that's what he and Whitney were doing."

"Bastian's an enigma," McKenna said. "Big, strong, and fearsome, yes, but he did something about Steve's discomfort that we never thought to do. Okay, he's stronger than we are, but you and I might have managed, if we worked together."

"I've watched my husband wincing and changing positions, but I didn't think to try and get him into something other than his bed or that chair once in a while, I'm ashamed to admit."

Watching Bastian, and going weak at the knees, McKenna sat beside Lizzie. "Look at him stooping down in the grass to play make-believe with a three-year-old as if her imaginary faery is real."

Lizzie wiped the corner of her eye with her apron. "She never had an imaginary friend before."

"It's normal, isn't it? At her age, I mean."

"I don't know, but I'm afraid she's withdrawing into her own world because we have to move and she's about to lose the only home she's ever known."

"Oh, Lizzie, you really are going to lose your house?"

"Done deal. It's not ours anymore. Steve hadn't told me the whole truth, because he didn't want me to worry. Bad for the twins here," she said, rubbing her belly. "Makes me wonder what else he hasn't told me. Anyway, he finally admitted he's been hoping for a miracle, but we didn't get one. We have four weeks to get out."

"You'll move in here with me and Bastian, then."

"And take two bedrooms away from your bed-and-breakfast guests? That would be lost income to you, my generous friend, at a time when you have taxes and mortgage payments hanging over you."

"We'll manage."

"I'm not taking your family legacy down with us. No, sweetie, I don't think so."

"So you'll go where?"

Lizzie shrugged. "Steve's mother lives in senior housing, so that's out."

"Any distant relatives I don't know about?"

"Not by location or kinship." Lizzie leaned against McKenna, shoulder to shoulder, and stayed that way.

McKenna hugged her. "LizBeth, I know you're stubborn, but if you don't find an affordable, and *decent*, place in the next month, I'll send Bastian to abduct the four of you, unless it's six of you by then."

"You'd get the hunk arrested?"

"I'd do it before I let you move into some dilapidated old—" McKenna chuckled. "Okay, so I'd rather have you living in *my* dilapidated old ruin than one up four flights of stairs with neighbors you don't know. And your kids, all four, would be better off here on the farm with people who love them, than in the city with people they know nothing about."

Lizzie's eyes filled. "You think I don't know that?"

TWENTY-FIVE

Bastian left Dewcup in Whitney's care, Steve in Wyatt's, and hefted a load of shingles to bring up the ladder to the roof, though he would rather have jumped than climbed. From the multigabled roof, he enjoyed the view. Swooping bustard, he missed his wings and the exhilaration of flying above the world. He loved this being able to see beyond his nest.

He admired McKenna's property to the sea, while the spirits of her ancestors came out of hiding, all but glowing as they looked toward the porch. McKenna must be coming outside.

Ah, there she was, stopping to talk with Whitney, unaware of the protection and love surrounding her.

He should not be surprised that she brightened their spirit lights. On the inside, he, too, glowed brighter in her presence. Did he?

Making her quest his own was one thing, but did having a heart mate mean giving away his heart? For some reason, he fought the notion, though he surely wanted to give her his body. He wished he had asked Andra more questions about his role, and the rules, where a heart mate was concerned.

McKenna's ancestors surrounded her. A few he had seen when he breached the veil, and others on the day he arrived and rode Toffee for the first time, but right now, when McKenna looked up at him and waved, generations looked up at him as well, as if they expected him to right McKenna's world.

Jock ran interference by swooping down among them and making them smile, as he danced around and smoke-tested each with bright puffs of yellow.

Good people. Not a surprise.

Dewcup came up for a spin around his head. "I'm glad I can't get old," she said, watching them. "I don't like wrinkles."

"They're beautiful. Don't look at their faces; look at their hearts."

Dewcup's wings hummed as she hovered in the air, face-to-face with him. "They don't *all* have beautiful hearts. Look again."

He looked with a more discerning eye this time. A cloaked woman stood back, away from the rest, her heart hidden by the dark shadowy funnel cloud swirling about her. Had she died in a storm and carried her torment to the grave?

Jock flew her way, but she disappeared before he reached her. Spirits did that. Nothing to worry about. She could have misunderstood Jock's intention.

Bastian equated Killian with storms, since she used them as weapons, and McKenna did not need his enemy making life more difficult.

Jock tested the air where the funnel-cloud spirit had stood, and the smoke turned a bright blue green, which did not imply evil, but different. If she had remained, the test would have been more accurate. A putrid green signified evil.

He should read more of McKenna's family history, given her ancestors' presence. He had started with the latest journal to learn about McKenna, her parents, and grandparents. Every night, he took lessons and learned something more about McKenna and her clan.

She disappeared beneath the porch roof and the porch door bounced shut. If he did not know himself that she went inside, the expressions on the faces of her ancestors would tell him. They sobered. The lights went out in their eyes.

How had she become the central figure in a centuries-old family?

They waited for her return with bated breaths.

The shed and barn must have been living quarters at one time or another, given the spirits gathered there, their clothes reflecting the centuries in which each family lived. Women's dresses had risen, and later even the women wore trousers.

Some of McKenna's male ancestors wore swords at their sides, and skirts with crossed colors, purses over them in the general area of their privates. Odd dress for men, skirts.

Closer to the house, McKenna's grandmother looked up at him, and beside her, McKenna's mother, the youngest and most vibrant spirit, likely because she had walked this earth not that long ago.

Overall, the women stood forward in the way of the alpha, as leaders, their men behind them as staunch supporters. McKenna came from strong female stock.

Again he wondered whether being the heart mate of McKenna Greylock called for burying his alpha tendencies. Could he do that? He did not know her well enough to answer yet, but he would help her keep her land to save Andra's magick and his brother dragons' lives. Where McKenna herself was concerned, he would let time give him answers.

As McKenna came out, the spirits cheered like spectators at a joust. Had they remained earthbound only to watch over her? The question unsettled him, as did his odd ability to see them and feel McKenna's pain. Though he did not feel unsettled enough to leave her.

"Bastian," Steve called from his comfortable chair. "How's it going?"

"It is going," Bastian shouted back, kicking a stack of shingles. He supposed he should *act* like a handyman roofer, or be fired by the woman he sought to tame, protect, help, give hope to . . . and care for?

Taking into account his strength and speed, and the size of his work area, he would finish before the day ended. But given Steve's estimated time frame, he could not let anyone know that he finished until tomorrow afternoon at the earliest.

He went to work, glad he read those books on roofing. He got to the point where he thought he had nearly finished when he saw an unexpected extension to McKenna's home off the back.

She had not shown him this part of her house. He wondered why as he lowered himself to the addition's long porch roof, from which he could reach a top-floor window. He slid it open and, with his hands on the window's top edge, raised himself to climb in.

There he found not a shed full of junk, nor a half finished shell, but a room with an ancient bed, more bedrooms, a hall, a bathroom, stairs that split a parlor from a dining room and kitchen. An entire house in better condition than McKenna's. Though, strictly speaking, this, too, must belong to her.

Two spirits appeared at the bottom of the stairs, and Bastian inadvertently roared his surprise, but he held his fire. An older couple, holding hands, faces marked with scars, nodded in greeting. "I am Esther," the woman said. "And this is my husband, Caleb."

"I have never seen you before. Why do you not gather with the rest of your family?"

Esther indicated the lock on the door.

"Did your family lock you in?"

"We were contagious," Esther said. "We locked ourselves in to keep from giving our family the sickness, but we broke their hearts, instead, by cutting ourselves off from them. No one has lived in this house since."

"They never forgave us," Caleb said, "so we stay out of sight like they want."

Bastian's growing understanding of humanity, if not of their language, surprised him. "They wanted to help you, but you wanted to keep them safe. Both good deeds, which I cannot think need forgiving. I will ask McKenna why no one has lived here."

The woman nodded. "Thank you for coming to help her."

Bastian scratched his head. "Did everyone know I was coming?"

"Ciarra, our ancestor, said you would come, that you alone could save McKenna. We spirits watch over her. When she completes her task and is saved, we can all move on."

"My task grows in magnitude and consequence," Bastian said, but the more people who needed him, the more out of reach his own goal appeared. "Without knowing why or how, I seem fated to saving McKenna; you, her ancestors; Andra's magick; and my legion of—"

"Dragons. We know. How can we help?"

A weight lifted from his shoulders at Esther's offer. "If you want to help, look for the spirit among you whose heart is shadowed by a funnel cloud. Tell me if she is one of you. If not, she may plan to hamper my mission, which would by default hamper McKenna's. Put fear into the developer trying to steal your heritage when he comes here. Scare him witless. Have some fun and help McKenna in the process."

Bastian recognized a hint of McKenna's twinkle in the couple's mischievous eyes and, of course, in their beautiful hearts. Like her mother, they, too, had died young.

"We haven't considered fun in a century," Caleb said.

Bastian bowed, a habit from his first human life, he guessed. "I would be in your debt. Can I do anything for you?"

"Get her to use this part of the house. We feel as if we've taken it away from her."

"I will," Bastian said. "She could enlarge her bed-and-breakfast and earn more money to pay her mortgage, whatever that is."

Esther smiled. "Or she could turn it into an apartment for the two of you."

Bastian faltered in his understanding. True, he and McKenna lived beneath the same roof, but their current arrangement was not what the hearts or expressions of these spirits conveyed. "Explain, please."

Caleb rocked on his heels. "We know what is possible."

"And I know," Bastian warned, "that the likelihood of a perfect outcome for any of us has already been compromised by a crone with dark magick. I will do my best, though it could already be too late. Go to your family. I believe you will be welcome." Bastian opened the door to the outside and indicated their way out.

As Caleb and Esther stepped into the sunlight, ancestors and descendents appeared to welcome them, and the funnel cloud around the woman who stood back and apart from the rest darkened. She gave him a nod, like an affirmative answer to his question, raised her hand, and shot lightning into the air from her fingertips.

Killian. Not dangerous yet. But biding her time.

If his being turned back into a man had weakened her, he would not want to see her with her full powers. Killian, the Crone of Chaos, would not make her move until she could strike the blow that would cause his inner dragon to take over his being. That was all she wanted, a vengeance that would destroy Andra's magick, and with that, him and his brother dragons.

Nothing more, nothing less.

McKenna and her family, everyone around him was safe. Only *he* had reason to fear Killian.

When Bastian heard McKenna calling him, he relocked the addition's outside door, ran up the stairs, climbed out the window, and leapt across the adjoining roof toward the front of the house.

As he neared it, he slowed and followed McKenna's call toward the edge. He looked down at her. "Yes, McKenna?"

"Are you hungry?"

"Relentlessly."

Her rare smile pushed her a bit deeper into his heart.

It would be easier to jump to the ground from here, but he put on a show of walking carefully toward the ladder, which meant climbing up and over gabled peaks of all sizes.

As he began his trek, the air cooled, a lightning bolt split the ladder, and a quick and sudden hailstorm covered the roof with a glistening carpet of ice.

Bastian lost his footing.

Steve shouted and McKenna screamed.

Headfirst, he slid toward the edge of the roof, saw his brothers dying in bursts of fiery lava, begged Andra's forgiveness, and called McKenna's name.

There would be no landing on his feet this time.

TWENTY-SIX

The ground hit him fast.

And hard. So hard, he *wished* for a sword bush.

He landed on his side, but the impact broke him.

He saw Steve sitting forward in his chair, but Lizzie and the children were not to be seen. Small blessing.

The sun came out as McKenna knelt beside him despite the carpet of hail. "I'll call an ambulance."

"No! Take my hands, bend my arms so as to rest my hands on my back, and hold them there."

"Are you crazy? That'll hurt like hell. Did you break your brain, too? It looks like your arms are broken."

Steve called Lizzie in the distance as the trees and clouds seemed to spin above him. "Come close, McKenna, and listen."

She came kissing close. He wished he could oblige. "I can heal myself," he said so only she could hear.

She paled. "Sure you can." Her face did not agree with her words.

"Check my hands for the fingers I dipped in hot French fry oil."

McKenna looked at the fingers on both his hands, the movement a painful experience. "I can't tell which ones you burned, except that two of them are pink with new skin."

"I healed them. Help me heal my back so I can move my arms and use my hands to heal my other breaks. Keep my secret?"

"You mean you want to forget that you tried to fly? Were you born in a cuckoo nest?"

"Do as I say!" he shouted through gritted teeth, pain radiating through him, his inner dragon clamoring to overcome his weaker self. "McKenna, just do it. Or all will be lost."

"What do you mean, lost?"

"Do. It. Now!" A roar accompanied the order.

McKenna firmed her spine defensively, but she complied, and as he fought the raging dragon inside him, his crown of horns rose, wings sprouted beneath the hands at his back, and McKenna's tears fell.

Time seemed to stop. Bastian began to lose the battle, because the more he hurt, the stronger and angrier his dragon.

Eventually he realized that the more he focused on McKenna's face, the more he worried about her, the calmer his dragon became.

McKenna was already the center of his heart, he admitted to himself. If he had not fallen, he would never have known that worrying about her was a bit like carrying a shield into battle. A shield against his inner beast.

A shield against Killian.

An unexpected but weak clap of thunder told him that Killian knew it, too, but she would not give up. The crone's feeble response confirmed that having McKenna beside him made him strong and his greatest enemy weak.

He might best Killian yet, except that McKenna's power had just made her the crone's enemy as well.

Killian did not agree or disagree, which he should not take as false hope.

His heart mate had already become his helpmate without either of them realizing it. McKenna's hands soothed him as he healed, soothed his pain in a spiritual way. *She* had the power to heal his heart and his soul as well.

Time no longer seemed important.

When the pain in his back began to recede, so did his wings, horns, spines, and claws. "Enough," he said with unabashed relief. "Remove my hands from my back."

The pain from that move made him roar inwardly, while *she* sobbed openly.

As he palmed the break in his left arm, held, and held longer, another fight with his inner dragon ensued, until he could flex that first hand to use on his other arm. When both arms were healed, he reached around to his back again for a slight adjustment, given his renewed range of reach and the renewed loss of his wings.

After a satisfactory modification, Bastian sat up.

Steve sat forward, his expression one of stunned and silent shock.

Bastian placed his hands on his knees.

McKenna, her expression like Steve's, watched him and calmed. Disbelief fluttered across her own brow to be followed by a range of unspoken questions.

"We will talk later," he said. "After Steve and Lizzie go home. Keep my secret, I beg you. For both our sakes."

"Who *are* you?"

"I am the grunt. You are the boss." He stood and brushed himself off.

Sirens, he heard getting closer. Crazy men jumped from trucks with circling lights of red and orange. McKenna made them examine him.

"Nothing wrong with this guy," the man with the Y-shaped wires hanging from his ears said, removing a hurtful cuff from his arm. "Healthy as a horse. You sure he fell?"

"He fell," Bastian snapped. "But he did not get hurt."

"I apologize for his rudeness," McKenna told them. "Flying makes him cranky."

Flying made him *happy*. Someday he would tell her so.

The truck with the bubble light backed down the drive as if nothing had happened. Because he did *not* want to talk about the fall, Bastian lifted Steve from his chair, carried him into the house, and sat him at the table where Lizzie and the children waited. "I am sorry we are late to lunch."

Lizzie nodded but the quiet held.

Then everyone spoke at once and stopped again as fast.

Silence had a heartbeat. Loud. Questioning.

"Daddy, me and Wyatt like having you at the table like us," Whitney said. "Dewcup, no, that's my milk. Auntie Kenna, do you have a thimble?"

"It's not time to sew, it's time to eat, sweetie," her mother said, eyeing Bastian as if he *had* grown horns.

"No, I want to fill the thimble with milk for Dewcup. She's thirsty and I don't want her to drown in my glass."

Whitney's parents exchanged looks, but McKenna got up, left the room, and returned with a thimble she washed before she gave it to Whitney.

The girl scooped milk from her glass and set it beside her plate while Dewcup clapped her hands and danced around it. Then the flaky faery stuck her tongue out at him and lifted her thimble in both hands, in the way he might lift a gallon of paint to sip from.

"I wanna sit next to Bastian," Wyatt said, drawing attention from the wobbly thimble. Could Wyatt see Dewcup? Had he distracted everyone on purpose?

Bastian wished that McKenna, Lizzie, and Steve would remove their gazes from his person. He supposed he'd shocked them senseless, though *he* should be senseless, not them. Ignoring their stares, he made room for Wyatt beside him, surprised that he enjoyed children.

When that was settled, he tried to eat his lunch but stopped with the fork halfway to his mouth. He set it on his plate and sighed. "I fell because the hail on the roof made it slippery. Steve, did it hail the day you fell off a roof?"

"No hail," Steve said. "But something slippery. You know, I've never heard of anyone falling off a roof and walking away like you did."

Bastian sipped his milk.

McKenna put hers down and stared right at him. "We didn't have any hail this summer, until *you* got here."

"Has it hailed more than in a normal season?" Bastian asked.

McKenna scoffed. "More than in a normal decade." She eyed him and turned to her friends. "You know, I think Mr. Wizard here cooked my apples!"

Steve rubbed his nose. "Please don't share, McKenna. Lizzie and I really don't want to know what you and Bastian do or don't do with each other's apples when you're alone."

TWENTY-SEVEN

McKenna did not seem to appreciate Steve's comment, while Bastian wondered if anyone, human or supernatural, could have wanted, planned, or intended Steve's fall. As McKenna's contractor, Steve had nearly guaranteed her success, until he fell, which nearly guaranteed her failure.

Tonight, Bastian would look up the word "developer."

Killian would not care whether McKenna failed or succeeded. No, for Steve, and for the woman whose house he was supposed to turn into a bed-and-breakfast, a human enemy made more sense.

Finally, McKenna and her friends tired of watching him and turned to their meals.

"You did an awesome job of painting those rooms," Lizzie said as she cut Wyatt's meat. "Where did you learn to paint like that?"

"I learned from a book."

Steve scooped potatoes onto his plate. "You're like

Grandma Moses, just picking up a brush and going to town."

"I have not gone anywhere and I cannot be a grandma, because I am a man."

"I told you," McKenna said. "Literal."

"Well," Steve chuckled. "You may well be a distant Flying Wallenda, but you're also a design genius. You gave McKenna something unique to advertise, a jumping-off point. Oh, sorry. Bad pun. Unintentional. You gave McKenna something unique in the Dragon's Lair, an edge in the tourist trade. I'm glad she found you."

Bastian nodded, not sure what to say. "I am nearly out of paint. McKenna, can we buy more?"

"You're using more than I expected, but I can see why, given the dimensional effect you've achieved."

Lizzie shook her head. "I love the shimmer of the water and the pearlescent scales on the dragons."

"I *love* the dragons," Wyatt said. "They look like they could breathe fire."

"Oh, they can." Bastian faltered as the adults homed in on him again. "Real dragons breathe fire, Wyatt, and I am definitely painting real dragons."

"You looked like a dragon flying off that roof," Wyatt added. "Will you do it again after lunch?"

"No!" his parents shouted.

"You saw me fall?" Bastian asked, looking down at the boy.

"I was hiding behind Dad's chair. I'm the one who ran in the house to get Mom to call the ambliance for you."

"Ambulance," his mother said, correcting him.

"Why, thank you, Wyatt." A close call. Good thing he had healed before the ambulance arrived.

Whitney slurped a French fry, disappearing it into her mouth like a snake into the mouth of a dragon, while Dewcup used both hands to pull globs of catsup off the edge of

Whitney's plate and into her mouth. "I like the pictures of Dewcup on the walls you painted," the little girl said.

Precisely why he would keep Dewcup *away* from his walls until after lunch when he dunked the catsuppy pest in soapsuds.

"What color paint do you need?" McKenna asked.

"It doesn't matter. The colors give me the pictures."

She released her breath. "Fine, then, first chance we get, we'll tour hardware stores and snap up some more bargain paint."

"I would like to see more of Salem." He also looked forward to spending time alone with McKenna.

Lizzie cleared the table. "Steve, you need to take your medicine and stretch out for a while."

"I wish I could fly like you, Bastian. I hate being treated like a kid. Anybody want to take a nap with me?" He wiggled his brows at his wife.

Bastian envied their teasing. He believed that McKenna would cut off something important that he still wanted to use if he teased her about napping together before she invited him to.

"No nap for me," Wyatt said, jumping from his chair to race outside.

Whitney yawned. "I'm too big for a nap."

"Maybe you can sit with Daddy for a while, Whitney," Lizzie suggested, "and read him one of your books until he falls asleep; then you can get up."

Bastian carried Steve to McKenna's bed. "How is your head?"

"It should be better than yours, but it aches, though the chair you brought out helped my knees."

They might have begun to heal if only a bit, Bastian thought. "Glad to hear it. Now, let your daughter take care of your head. Here, Whitney, put your hands on your daddy's head like this to relieve the pressure." Bastian placed the palms of his hands over the little girl's and let his healing flow through her, so his magick would not be noticed. Though after his fall, the lack of questions surprised him.

Too bad their silence would not last long.

Steve fell asleep in less than a minute, Whitney shortly after, which allowed Bastian to keep his healing hands on the man's head, for a while, then on Steve's knees again.

When Bastian heard Wyatt's distinctive step coming down the hall, he left the room and passed Wyatt heading for the bathroom, but Bastian stopped in the hall. From there, he could see and hear Lizzie and McKenna in the kitchen, but they could not see him.

"I'm just saying you can forget it where your handy hunk is concerned," Lizzie said. "I think he's got a thing for Steve."

"Your husband and my handyman?" McKenna raised a hand in the air. "Figures."

"Steve probably hasn't figured it out yet," Lizzie said, "and I could be wrong, but Bastian really seems to worry about Steve's discomfort."

"I need them to work together. I hope Bastian's attention isn't a problem for Steve."

"Don't be silly. Steve's not homophobic. Bastian's handy, strong, paints like an artist, and puts up with our kids. As for me, he's fun to look at."

McKenna elbowed her friend.

"Seriously, my husband's been in pain for weeks, so if Bastian wants to alleviate some of it, let him. I just feel bad for you. I thought this was your shot. I wanted Bastian to fall for you."

"I know you did." McKenna sighed heavily. "Just goes to prove that I—"

"Hired a gay handyman, which means that you can finally let a man get close, without putting up your usual walls."

"I suppose that's a *good* thing," McKenna said.

Bastian did not know why his being happy should upset everyone, but if it meant that McKenna would let him get close to her, he would be gay and happy all the time. He crossed the kitchen and gave them a nod. "I am going back to work on the roof," he said, but he lingered on the porch for a bit.

"Do you think he heard us?" Lizzie asked.

"English isn't his first language, so he might not have understood."

"I hope he didn't. I wouldn't want to hurt his feelings."

McKenna chuckled, a nice sound. "Does that man look fragile to you?"

"Edible. He looks edible," Lizzie said.

"I know." McKenna sighed. "Too bad he's not our flavor. But you're right. I feel like a weight has been lifted from my shoulders. I can enjoy his company without being afraid of getting hurt."

He would never hurt her, Bastian thought with a frown, but at least she wanted to spend time with him.

He left the porch, saluted the spirits, and when he got to the side of the house, he took one satisfying leap to the roof.

He finished shingling that afternoon. Afterward, he read a book about painting the outside of a house and discussed it with Steve after his nap.

Steve said that the blistered paint, especially on the side facing the old harbor, would have to be burned off with a hot-air gun or a gas torch.

Hah, Bastian thought. What he would really need was the cover of darkness.

TWENTY-EIGHT

McKenna relaxed in Bastian's company for the first time since he got here. She didn't mind lingering in the back parlor with him at the end of a day, as long as he didn't drink any wine.

She shivered at the memory of sleeping beside him that first night, the two of them naked and wrapped around each other. "Would you like some wine?" she asked and nearly bit her tongue.

What was wrong with her?

His eyes narrowed as he studied her in the way he might study a chessboard before his next move. "Yes, please," he said, his voice husky.

The implication went against everything Lizzie said about his sexuality. McKenna shrugged and considered his answer as something of a dare from the universe. "I'll be right back."

He followed her into the kitchen to carry the tray to the living room for her.

"My hero. And thank you for carrying Steve down to the basement after his nap, so he could show you how to fix thc wiring. I like having electricity again."

"Steve said it is a temporary fix, until we have time to do it right for the inspection." Bastian set the tray on the floor beside them. "He is a smart man, Steve, though I prefer our evening light coming from the fire alone."

"No fire needed. It's balmy out tonight. Today's hailstorm only lasted long enough to slide you off the roof. Speaking of which, you said we'd talk after Steve and Lizzie left. What happened after you fell? I'm no doctor, but I could have sworn you had broken bones."

He scratched an ear. "Sprained, maybe."

"And you healed yourself? Is that a New Age thing?"

"Okay."

She watched him closely. "Like Reiki?"

Bastian's worry disappeared, she noticed. "Yes," he said. "Reiki."

"Or more like Zwami?" she suggested, testing him with a fake word.

"Exactly!"

She laughed. "That's such a crock."

"A crock of what?"

"Never mind. You'll take the expression literally and we'll be here all night."

"We *will* be here all night, McKenna." He raised his wineglass.

Dangerous territory. She raised her own. Their glasses clinked, and anticipation shot through her. She shivered but came quickly back to sanity. "Tell me what really happened today."

"You saw for yourself. I heal fast. My hands against my wounds make them heal faster. It's a gift. An unusual gift."

Given the fact that he broke through her foundation wall

and carried Steve around like he might carry Whitney, she granted that he did have some unusual qualities. "I reserve the right to question you further," she said.

He nodded. "Reserve away."

She knew him better now and no longer felt the need to put distance between them. As a matter of fact, she inched closer, slowly, so he wouldn't notice. He sat cross-legged, his back against an overstuffed wing chair, she with her legs to the side, her skirt covering them.

The space between them made a perfect aisle for Jaunty to walk through, head high, tissue box at an angle.

Her psycho cat crawled into Bastian's lap, settled in, and began to purr. Bastian stroked the cat exactly the way she tended to. Then her brazen feline rolled onto her back and presented Bastian with her burgeoning belly.

Bastian looked up in dismay. "Is she crazy?"

"She sure is, but right now, she wants you to rub her belly. She's tired from galloping through the house as if she had a firecracker tied to her tail."

Bastian scratched her cat's ears with one hand and rubbed her belly with the other. "I don't know why she likes me."

McKenna cleared her throat as jealousy reared its ridiculous head. Jealous of her own cat? She'd just bypassed Jaunty in the pathetically-starved-for-attention department. Get a grip, she told herself. "Bastian, you're pampering her to within an inch of her life. Second, you're not calling her Snack anymore. Besides, Bast is a goddess who's, like, the patron saint of cats. And you're named for Bast."

Confusion marred the chiseled precision of Bastian's scarred features. "Bast? A patron saint?"

"I know, it sounds blasphemous," she said, "but I'm a halfling, Celtic Scot witch blood on my mother's side and French Canadian Catholic on my father's, and I got both belief systems spoon-fed to me from birth, which makes me sort of a mixed bag religion-wise. I joined the church of rebellion at an early age and I worship there regularly."

"Glad to hear it." He abandoned Jaunty's ears to sip his wine. "My sweet tooth has never been happier. Brownie?" he asked, indicating the plate on the tray.

"Go ahead. More sweets for you."

He bit into one of the thickly frosted treats, Gran's recipe. "I did not think life could get any sweeter," he said.

"Glad to have someone appreciate my baking."

"Is that what you like to do best? Cook and bake? From what I've learned about bed-and-breakfasts, you will be doing both often."

"My guests will need to eat, so I'll cook for them. Lizzie's a better cook. She can make a piece of beef feed an army, and they'll think it's incredible. She cooks and bakes because she likes to. I do it because I have to."

"Then what do you *like*, McKenna, or maybe I should ask you what you want more than anything? Besides opening your bed-and-breakfast, do you have any other quests in life?"

She raised her knees and rested her chin on them. "Funny you should ask. A few days ago, turning my house into a bed-and-breakfast to save the family heritage was all I wanted."

"And today?"

"I still want to save the farm—as cliché as that sounds—but I want something else now. People are more important than houses and farms, aren't they?"

"Though people are blips in a universe bigger than any of us can imagine and of little import to the magickal whole, I have come to believe that, yes, people are everything."

"Steve is under investigation for insurance fraud."

"What does that mean?"

"Bottom line, it means they're going to lose their house.

The insurance company thinks he threw himself off somebody's roof on purpose."

"He should tell them that he did not."

"You sure *don't* come from here. Anyway, he tried. But they'll only talk to his lawyer, and he can't afford a lawyer. Lizzie's twins are due in a few weeks, so she can't be packing up a house and looking for another place in her condition."

"Define twins."

"Two babies who are born together because they were carried by one mother at the same time."

"Oh. Ohhhh. Your friend Lizzie will have *two* new babies?" He used his hand to make an imaginary mound of his stomach. "No wonder she is so . . . full of babies."

Bastian charmed the hell out of her; no other way to describe it. "Right. So how does a family of six find an apartment for peanuts?"

"You can pay with peanuts here?"

McKenna hung her head and sighed. "You should read the dictionary in your spare time."

"I will do that tonight."

The way Bastian watched her over the rim of his wineglass made her self-conscious. "So what you want," he said between sips, "is to invite Steve, Lizzie, and their children to live with you?"

"How did you know that?"

"I know what a generous heart you have."

Her hot face shocked her. Men did not usually compliment her. "I want them here, yes, but if my bed-and-breakfast doesn't get enough paying guests, I'll lose the place, and none of us will have a home."

"You will have guests. You already advertised the Dragon's Lair as Steve suggested, yes?"

"Yes, everywhere I could that didn't cost a fortune. The more paying guests we get, the more likely it is that I can save the farm, and the fewer bedrooms there'll be for family. It's a win/lose situation."

"I do not understand you," Bastian said. "I walked your roofline today. You have another house attached to this one. So many rooms going to waste."

McKenna tipped back her head to finish her wine, refilled her glass, and drank that, too. Being reminded of the family curse threw her. Chilled her. Worried her.

"McKenna?"

"The door to that wing hasn't been opened in years," she admitted. "That house has a dark past. It's haunted, if you must know. When I get enough money, I'm going to have it torn down."

"You would rather tear it down than let your friends live there?"

TWENTY-NINE

McKenna threw a sofa pillow at him. "Bastian Dragonelli, you can be an obnoxious jerk, you know that?"

He removed the pillow from Jaunty's clutches, hefted it, and threw it above her head to the chair behind her. "I do know, yes. My brothers often told me so."

"I care too much about my friends to let them live in—"

"Esther and Caleb's house?" he said, to her surprise. "What exactly is the nature of this curse?" he asked.

Good question. McKenna stood, feeling as betrayed by Bastian's interrogation as the family had felt betrayed by Esther and Caleb's defection. "I was never told why the family felt it was cursed," she admitted—a step toward her own disbelief, she realized as she fidgeted with her dress buttons. "The truth is, when your grandmother warns you at an early age to stay out of a dangerous part of the house, you by damn stay out."

"So," Bastian said, "the whole thing might have been

a misunderstanding that got embellished or made more of over time?"

"I suppose."

"Did anyone explain what would happen if you entered Esther and Caleb's house? An instant case of flesh-eating warts, perhaps, or death by noxious fumes? I know— blindness due to a tendency toward gaudy colors, hunting prints, tinware, or ruffles on even the sinks?"

McKenna nearly laughed. She remembered such a picture from somewhere. "I don't know, okay? I just don't know." Rather than feeling foolish, though, hope was beginning to creep in. "Nobody ever tried to prove or disprove the dreadful stories about the addition, but every generation, I can tell you, did try to find the family treasure. How many places can a casket of gold coins hide, I ask you?"

"Where did the coins supposedly come from?" Bastian asked.

"They were brought from Scotland by Ciarra's father, the first McKenna to set foot on Salem shores. "Why ask, anyway? I thought you knew everything."

"I know what I have read so far about your family."

"How the hell fast can you read? You're smarter today than you were yesterday, and you were smarter yesterday than the day before that, and so on. Your stack of books in my library keeps changing. Read the dictionary tonight, indeed. And when you're done, I suppose you'll read more of my family history? What do you think you know about us?"

"I know that the McKenna clan came here from Scotland. I know about Ciarra. You look like her, by the way."

"Did you find a picture of her? Because I never saw one."

Bastian looked away and became transfixed by a sketch on the wall; then he came back to himself and looked her in the eye. "I will give you her picture."

"Thank you." Sometimes McKenna didn't know what to make of him.

"You were given the clan name as a first name," he continued, "because you are the last, shall we say, to inherit through a McKenna daughter. Ciarra bore an illegitimate son, and after him, sons inherited from their fathers, until your mother inherited from your grandmother, and you inherited from your mother."

"Rub it in, why don't you?"

Suddenly beside her, Bastian ran a finger down her cheek. "What do you wish me to rub?"

"You certainly know how to cheer a girl up," she said, loving his attention and his sweet juniper and pomegranate musk, enhanced by the whiff of cherry wine that brought a wild but treasured memory.

"I know you are frightened, McKenna. Who would not be? Four centuries of stewardship rests on your shoulders." He kissed a shoulder, as if to lighten her burden, and by golly, it was working. "No wonder you are cranky," he whispered.

She pulled away. "Gee, thanks."

"I like your fight. That is what drew me to you from the first day, but you bear a heavy burden, McKenna Greylock, and you are justifiably afraid to fail your clan. I understand how that feels."

He touched her hand, which she liked, despite his mixed compliments, and she appreciated sharing her burdens with someone who tried, at least, to empathize. She liked it too much, in view of what she'd learned from Lizzie about Bastian, except that this nuzzling business—shiver—didn't fit Lizzie's "gay" theory.

McKenna realized that what she knew about men would fit in Whitney's milk thimble. Lizzie must be right. With Bastian, she wouldn't get her feelings trampled. He wouldn't leave her for some skinny— Holy mother of pearl, *that* was why his bubbleheaded followers didn't interest him. Gay. Gay. Gay.

She tried not to let her tears fall but they did anyway. "You can't know how this feels. You can't possibly know." She wasn't talking only about holding on to a centuries-old legacy, but about finding a man to share the burden, who saw the *real* her, who wouldn't toss her away for a stick insect with fake boobs. But a man who liked women. She sure wished Bastian liked women.

He chuckled as if to deny her concern. "I do know of such burdens, but I will save that for a day when we know each other better," he said cryptically, and she didn't have it in her to argue. "I read about the clan treasure, too. We should find it."

She cheered inwardly at knowing, without a doubt, something he didn't. "If that's why you took the job, go home. The treasure doesn't exist. What now?"

He ran a finger up her arm. "Invite Steve, Lizzie, and the children to live in Caleb and Esther's house, and let me look into what happened when Steve fell off that roof. I have a talent for roof walking . . . when it is not hailing. I will walk the roof Steve fell from to see if I can discover how it happened."

"Both improbable ideas, dragon boy."

Bastian shot to his feet and left her without a shoulder to lean on, so she fell over. "Sheesh. Give a girl some warning."

"You called me dragon boy! Why?" Shock transformed his features.

At a disadvantage lying at his feet, McKenna picked herself up and stood nose to chest with him. "I called you dragon boy because you painted dragons in every room, which is also why I named my bed-and-breakfast the Dragon's Lair. Why so touchy?"

"I apologize." Bastian stooped down beside her and lifted a lock of her hair from her shoulder. "I misunderstood."

"Did you think I was calling you names?"

He stroked her face with her own hair. "Why would you ask me that?"

"No need to be embarrassed," she said, trembling inwardly. "I understand. A teen doesn't get called chunky monkey without earning a little scar tissue. I meant no insult."

"None taken."

"Good," she said, mesmerized by the way he tested the texture of her hair against his own cheek, then his lips. She reared back at her reaction to it. "I was thinking."

"Yes?" he asked, looking ready for anything.

"We may be able to solve Steve and Lizzie's housing problem and my family superstitions in one spell."

"How so?" He might be curious, she thought, but not enough to stop toying with her hair.

She felt his every touch radiate through her, but she ignored it. "Vivica's a witch, you know? She could do a cleansing ritual in the addition to remove the negative energy that you believe resides there."

"Vivica is a powerful witch," he said.

"Maybe you could *heal* Esther and Caleb's house."

"*Now* you are mocking me."

She could drown happy in the violet pools of his eyes. "A little bit," she admitted.

"The addition needs less work than this part of the house," he said. "Though it *is* filled with ruffles and hunting prints."

She tried to tug her hair from his hand. "You went inside?"

He pulled her back toward him by tugging on that same handful of hair. "I did. And nothing important fell off. Imagine."

"Who is mocking who?"

He tilted his head. "Now we are even, except that I am still the grunt and you are still the boss."

"Why do I think that we are so *not* even, mystery man?"

His smile was enigmatic. No surprise there. McKenna bit her lip to keep from making an idiot of herself by kissing him. "I guess Caleb and Esther's house is in good shape because it hasn't been used. You think you have all the answers, don't you? I should make *you* live there."

"I would, gladly. I like Esther and Caleb."

"Oh, so you talk to ghosts, too?" McKenna shook her head.

Bastian prodded her bottom lip from her teeth, and she about melted into a puddle of need.

"You are right," he whispered. "The addition is haunted, but so are your house and farm."

Before she could protest, he kissed her, and she lost her knees, so he lifted her in his arms and stood to carry her through the house. She floated and closed her eyes to keep the room from spinning, and realized she'd had enough wine to bypass horny and go straight to "sleep like the dead."

"Let me take your clothes off," Bastian said.

THIRTY

McKenna woke naked and alone.

She fell back against her pillows, disappointed. This time, if Bastian were sleeping beside her, she wouldn't try to escape into her bathroom. She'd wake him up, big-time. But he was gay, or so Lizzie thought.

McKenna never would have thought so last night. She curled on her side. Why did he have to be such a stud, such a turn-on, such a damned . . . know-it-all? She'd suspected all her life that her ancestors weren't as far away as most, but she didn't like having it confirmed. How did Bastian know? How could he be so sure? She huffed. Why believe him?

The knock at her door made her yelp and clutch the covers to her breasts.

"McKenna?" The focus of her thoughts called from the hall. "Are you ready to go and buy more paint?"

"What time is it?"

"Nine."

"Are you kidding me?" She jumped from her bed. "Why did you let me sleep so long?"

"You were sick last night."

She slapped her forehead and winced at the horrific pain that shot through it. Drunk sick. Great, he'd seen her barfing and held her hair, no matter how green his face got. Right now, she wished she could join her ancestors. Did people die of mortification? "I'll meet you at the pickup—"

"What do you want me to pick up?"

"Nothing. Just meet me at my *truck* in twenty minutes. Work on the roof until I'm ready."

"Will do."

She took a quick shower and got dressed. With him in mind—okay, with seducing him in mind—she wore a long flowered skirt that buttoned up the front, but she left the bottom buttons open, while the matching blouse had a nice V-neck. Good for cleavage and to accent her good points.

Beneath the skirt, she slipped on a pair of Bermuda shorts. There was a downside to wearing skirts, especially working a farm, but she found that wearing shorts beneath solved the problem. And sometimes, if she was alone, she hung the skirt on a peg and kept working.

When she looked out at the truck, Bastian wasn't near it, so she wandered in the direction of Caleb and Esther's place, the legendary cursed addition, which these days would be called a mother-in-law apartment.

As she approached the door, she heard the same wail of warning she'd always heard, so she backed up and walked the area again, in the opposite direction. When she heard the wail, she bore down on the same floorboard again. Yep, the warning was a loose old floorboard.

She continued on to the attached house and closed her hand around the knob. As she stood there—waiting for lightning to strike, she supposed—she looked out the window beside her. And there, she saw something amazing.

Bastian jumped from her roof and landed on his feet. He raised an arm in victory and gave one of his body-shivering war cries.

As if he heard her jaw drop, and her libido shift into overdrive, he turned and stared straight at her.

She read his lips, and he hadn't said, "Duck." He learned new words by the minute, that man, and not all from her.

She ran through the house and found him on the porch, hands in his pockets like a kid expecting a spanking, though how he got there before her, she couldn't imagine. As for the spanking? Well, another time, maybe.

He looked better in his own clothes. Black jeans. Black long-sleeved Ts. Masculine. Delicious. Muscular.

"So?" she asked, ignoring his sexual attraction and distraction.

"Special Ops," he said. "I have a lot of weird skills."

"I think you're just plain weird all around and a big crock of horse hockey."

He nodded, hands still in his pockets. "That would be correct."

"Let's go buy paint," she said, marching toward her truck but turning back to him. "I'm warning you, buster. I'm going to figure you out yet."

In the truck, neither of them spoke about anything more important than the weather—though that had been weird, too—as they drove from hardware store to department store buying paint in elaborate colors that nobody else wanted, for the weird artist who would make something magick out of it.

Yes, she had fallen in love with the colorful world he created on the bedroom walls and hallways of her home. Go figure.

The Pied Piper artist had a line of women behind him in every store, the poor deluded things. McKenna liked that he belonged to her, more or less, so she toyed with his entourage by taking his arm and leaning into him. She liked that he played along and put his arm around her waist to pull her closer.

"This is aubergine," she said later, checking a can on the markdown table. "No wonder it's on sale."

"It's almost as purple as Iverus."

"Is Iverus another dragon?"

"Yes, he has the biggest wingspan of any dragon. I can use this aubergine."

"Good, they're practically giving it away. I need bargains."

"What about these cans of paint over here?"

"That's for the outside of the house, not the inside walls. I have to get all the same color for the outside."

"Why? You have so many different sections and porches and trim that would not need to be the same color, but a complementary color."

"The kind of trim my house has is called either wedding cake or gingerbread, I believe."

"I found the painted ladies on the Internet," Bastian said. "It is a row of houses in San Francisco, not actual ladies with face paint as I expected."

McKenna bit her lip so she wouldn't insult him by laughing at his forlorn expression. "Your point?"

"Many have different colors all on one house. We could study them. I found others painted that way. They have what you call charm, those houses."

"A colorful dragon's lair. That would fit the magick theme you've set up. Let me think about it. I've been holding off buying house paint because of the premium price, and because I need so much. We'd still have to paint the basic structure the same color, though, right?"

"Steve could measure and see how much we need for the different sections," Bastian suggested. "Each side could be a shade darker or lighter. Each porch could have its own personality color but they would match overall. Structure changes could be different, like gables, curly designs, peaks—"

"You've been sucking up Victorian house info on the Internet, haven't you?"

"Color speaks to me. Victorian houses fascinate me, probably more than real ladies would have."

Rats, there was her proof. Gay. A decorator at heart. And of course, sensitive and caring. McKenna sighed. "Bargain house paint, hey?"

"How poor are you?"

"Pathetically so. Why?"

"I was worried that you would not be able to feed Lizzie and her family."

"Not a problem. I raise stock and grow vegetables. We lived comfortably enough until Gran got sick. Right now, it's the cost of renovations and starting a new business that's killing me, though I have a little of my mother's life insurance money left."

"I should think your property would have been paid for a long time ago."

"I will not take that as criticism, though that's how it sounds. My mother had no choice but to mortgage the farm to pay Gran's hospital bills. Gran didn't have medical insurance. Neither did my mom. Neither do I, actually. Life can be hard."

Bastian caught her opposite shoulder and pulled her against him. "You are doing great."

She teared up and wallowed in the moment, then she got a quick grip. "I sense that you've known struggle."

"I am the king of struggle. We will get through this," he said. "You are not alone."

How wrong was he? The better she knew him, the more she liked him, the more alone she felt.

In the Home Supply Warehouse, McKenna stopped

short and tugged on Bastian's T-shirt. "That's him, by the registers."

"Who?"

"Elliott Huntley. The developer trying to steal my land."

"The man with the green-striped shirt and tan pants?"

"Yes. Oh, crap, he sees me. Look at that apple-pie smile, as if I'm his best friend." McKenna ditched Bastian and turned down the first aisle she came to.

To her distress, Huntley followed her. "McKenna. Wait."

She fisted her hands and turned to wait for him.

"Sixty days until foreclosure, my friend," he said. "My offer now stands at half a million dollars."

"You can take that offer and shove—"

Huntley held up a hand to stop her, chuckled, and walked away. "Think about it," he called, though he kept walking.

Bastian caught up to her at the back of the store. "McKenna, you're shaking. Are you all right?"

"Huntley made me another offer. It scares me that he's so sure of himself."

"You should be scared. He has a black heart." Bastian clasped her arms. "Listen to me. Stay away from him. I am not kidding. He is evil."

"You're telling me."

Bastian herded her back toward the registers and, for once, she let him be the boss, appreciated it.

"Why did you leave me?" he asked. "I looked around and you were gone."

"I ditched you because I didn't want Huntley to know that I hired a strong and capable man like you."

"That makes sense. Tell me, did Huntley know that Steve was your contractor?"

"Sure. They're both contractors, and Steve had to take out a permit."

"How long after getting the permit did Steve fall off that roof?"

"The next week. Is that Huntley writhing on the floor? What's wrong with him? It looks like he's having some kind of seizure."

Bastian shrugged. "He seems to have gotten some toxic, self-defense type smoke in his eyes."

Jock circled them, trailing a spiral of red celebratory smoke, saluted, and disappeared.

THIRTY-ONE

Bastian helped her put the cans of paint they bought in the back of the truck. "Until we met Huntley," she said, "I enjoyed bargain hunting with you, but now I'm worried about Steve and Lizzie. Are you going to tell them what you suspect about Steve's fall?"

"Not until I have some proof for the insurance company."

"Good. I'd rather not give them false hope."

He followed her to the driver's side to open her door, but pinned her against it instead, leaned in, and kissed her. Not quick, but openmouthed and hungry, his hand riding her hip, her side, then splayed against the edge of a breast, his thumb stroking too close. Not close enough.

Kissed outside in front of God, general contractors, home-goods enthusiasts, and toilet shoppers.

McKenna lost her breath. Sanity fled. She kissed him back, and by the time they were forced to come up for air, she could pretty much admit to herself that she was in trouble.

"You are a good friend to Lizzie and Steve," he whispered against her lips.

And *you* are a good kisser, she didn't say. "Is that why you kissed me?"

"I kissed you because I wanted to."

"Because I'm good to my friends?"

"Because you are you. I like everything about you. True, you are giving your friends a home. But I would not kiss you for that reason alone. I can move their furniture, by the way. I am strong."

"I know. You can 'leap tall buildings in a single bound.' You're *Super* Dragon Boy." She climbed in the truck and shut her door.

"McKenna," he said, climbing into the passenger seat. "I am a man."

And didn't she know it. Her hormone level had volcanic eruption written all over it.

He watched her with such intensity, she had trouble concentrating on the road. "Super Dragon *Man*, then," she said, but her words came out in a telltale whisper of lost breath. Fortunately, he wouldn't understand.

She pulled into her favorite junk-food joint. "Think we have enough paint to finish the job?" she asked to change the subject.

Bastian shrugged. "I hope not. I like to bargain hunt with you, but we will get to shop for other supplies, yes?"

"You are so different from most men—oh, yeah, I suspect why, maybe. Anyway, wait until I take you to your first yard sale."

"Why do you think I am different?"

"You know, guys who like guys and all that."

"I like Steve."

"You understand that he's taken."

"Where? Where has he been taken?"

"Up the aisle—a walk that ended with a big 'I do'? I mean, he's married."

"Good for him. I like Lizzie, too."

McKenna gave him a double take. She couldn't help herself. "You make no sense to me sometimes."

"Ditto. Good word, eh, ditto? Wyatt taught me that."

McKenna chuckled and got out of the truck. Damned if she wasn't heart-sunk and terminally attracted. Hot and getting hotter, though there wasn't a shot in hell—talk about hot—of getting him, for so many reasons. "Welcome to Fried Harry's. Best cholesterol factory in Salem."

"Harry has been fried like your potatoes? Should this not then be French Harry's?"

"Of course it should." She didn't know whether to leave or roll her eyes. "What do you feel like eating?"

"I like corn dogs, Creamsicles, brownies, and cherry wine best," he said, as they sat in a chrome-trimmed raspberry-and-peach plastic booth, "but I have learned the error of my ways. Creamsicle sticks are *not* for eating."

"How do you know?"

"Wyatt was playing with craft sticks. They looked the same, so I ate a few. When he finished rolling on the ground laughing at me, he told me that they were not food. He taught me that pizza rocks and a lot of neat words."

McKenna chuckled. "When you understand the world of Dora and Diego," she said, "you've spent too much time with the rug rats."

The waitress came to see if they were ready to order.

"I am ready," Bastian said, but he hadn't picked up his menu. "I would like a Baloney Sunday, please."

McKenna and the waitress exchanged glances.

"What?" Bastian asked. "Wyatt said I should try one."

"I'll deal with the boy wonder later. Meanwhile, we'll have the appetizer sampler with buffalo wings," she told the waitress.

"Why did she not look at *you* as if you are crazy? Buffalos do not have wings, McKenna. If I had an old nickel, I would show you."

She tried to explain the concept of recipe titles, also known as talking in circles, until their food came.

Bastian asked for the name of each item and picked up a wing. "See? Too small to come from a buffalo."

"It's a chicken wing. There's not much meat on the—"

Bones, McKenna heard breaking as Bastian chewed. The sound made her shiver worse than nails across a chalkboard.

She looked around to see if anyone else noticed Bastian's eating disorder, but the drooling females saw only the hunk du jour himself. She raised a finger to call her waitress. "Can you pack the rest of this to go? We're running a little late." Plus she was embarrassed out of her bleeping mind.

On the way back to the farm, McKenna watched from the corner of her eye as Bastian finished the junk-food sampler, and she shivered in advance every time he picked up a wing. Every crunch made her wince. "Only boneless chicken for you from now on," she snapped.

"Do people put honey on chicken or beef?"

"In some recipes, yes. Why?"

"I've been craving honey. It used to be part of my daily diet."

"So that sweet tooth is inbred."

"Okay."

"How do you feel about water?"

"It's drinkable but not very sweet."

"No. Change of topic. We finally have a sunny summer afternoon. Let's take a swim in my lake . . . with our clothes on," she added. "I can't, in good conscience, let you climb back up on that roof in this heat. Besides, you worked hard carrying everything we bought, a new luxury for me. It would have taken me ten trips at each store to get all those paint cans to the truck."

"I am enchanted by water," Bastian said. He headed for the lake but stopped beneath a tree.

"What's wrong?" she asked, reaching him, the drone of insects a reminder of the beauty in the day.

He pointed upward, his eyes fairly glazing over with glee. "Honey."

"That's a bee's nest."

"That's what I said." He reached into the hive and pulled out a honeycomb crawling with bees.

She ran. He didn't. From a distance, with hands on her hips, she watched the gorgeous idiot start eating the honey, comb, bees, and all, while waiting for him to howl.

"Don't you want a taste?" He waved his prize.

"You're going to get stung!"

"Nah." He practically inhaled the honeycomb as the bees swarmed and charged. Yet he stood there, ignoring them, savoring his treat.

As the bees began to disappear, and the hum died down, McKenna stepped closer, and closer, until she saw the carnage at Bastian's feet.

He licked his fingers and grinned. "Bees are allergic to me."

THIRTY-TWO

Still shaking her head, McKenna shucked her shoes beside her unpretentious spring-fed lake and went in still dressed. "It's freezing, probably from all the hail we've had lately."

Bastian stepped in wearing black boxers—bless him for the view. She appreciated his discretion. Most men would just get naked. But, frankly, she couldn't bear to know what she was missing.

Gorgeous, despite his scars, his bronze body looked as if someone tore at it with teeth, swords, claws, and pitchforks at one time or another. And he didn't have a tan line that she could see.

He did, however, have a tattoo wrapped around his upper arm, and when he reached her, she circled him to see the whole of it. "You have a dragon tat starting on your right shoulder and curling around your arm. I guess we're both hooked on dragons."

He tilted his head. "Hooked on, possessed by. Same difference."

"A sense of humor and a good kisser." After that parking-lot kiss, she was more turned on with every minute in his company, shamelessly so. "The dragon tat is sexy." Not to mention the naked muscles she'd like to explore. Small waist, tight butt, nothing left to the imagination.

Up to her waist in water, which seemed to be warming, likely from the sexual heat she was generating, she took off her skirt beneath the water and threw it to shore, aware that if she were in her right mind, she would never have done it, Bermuda shorts or not.

Was she in her wrong mind?

This was more than a turn-on, much more, given the buzz of molten heat simmering her blood, making her dizzy, her treading water, him swimming around her, putting her in some kind of weird sexual trance, like a mating dance. Foreplay. No hands. "Something weird is happening to me," she said.

"What?"

"I'm tingling, everywhere, with . . . hope, happiness. Joy. Elation. Uber-bliss. Like I'm on drugs. Hallucinogenic drugs. And the water is getting warmer." She blinked and blinked again. "This is bad. I swear that I can see—okay, don't have me committed, but there's a tiny blue dragon hovering above you puffing purple smoke."

Bastian swiped his hand over his face.

"Bastian? You're supposed to be surprised."

"Water magick," he said. "You're in water with me, so my magick is flowing from me to you. I wonder if you will lose your abilities and forget about them once you get out of the water."

He might as well have been speaking in tongues. "Holy mother of pearl, is that Whitney's flying Barbie?

One of my hallucinations has butterfly wings and a buttercup hat."

Bastian waved Barbie away as if he could see her, too. "Dewcup, go take a nap in some clover, and Jock, go smoke-test the pig."

"Bastian?" McKenna said, swimming slowly, as if weighed down by doubt. "You said Dewcup. Whitney called her imaginary friend Dewcup when she gave her a thimble of milk. Who's Jock?"

Bastian came closer, clearly intent on calming her. He reached for her but she stopped treading water, stood, and stepped away.

He raised his hands so she could see them. "Jock is smitten by you, and I do not blame him."

"What the hell are you talking about?"

"Purple is the guardian dragon smoke color for love. Jock is my guardian dragon."

McKenna couldn't move, though Bastian approached her like an animal stalking its prey. Focused. Possessive. Hungry. "Are you planning to eat me?" she asked. "Because if you are, I'm okay with that," which sounded wrong when her words echoed over the water.

She shrugged. "I'm floating, but not on water." On lust, maybe, and she was okay with that, too. She so would have sex with this man. She looked toward shore but didn't want to go there, even though panic swirled along the fringes of her awareness, but not deeply enough to make her move away from Bastian. "What is *wrong* with me?"

"You're perfect," he said.

She laughed, not believing a word of it. "Your eyes are so violet. Darker than usual. Dilated. Ravenous. Like, if you had big teeth, I'd be lunch."

"You would be delicious, McKenna Greylock."

"You frighten me, Bastian Dragonelli, but I don't want you to turn or look away from me. I know I should be worried about the blond pixie and the little blue dragon, but strangely enough I'm not, probably because I have you to protect me."

"Can I touch you?" he asked, his voice a caress skimming through her veins, bringing her womanhood to flower. A simple question, words she thought she'd never want to hear, yet she reeled with elation at hearing them from him.

She wanted his lips, felt her own parting, saw him coming for her. They were both treading water now, getting closer until a kiss would be inevitable.

"You're gay," she whispered, his breath against her lips. Warm breath. Hot. Hot enough to raise her temperature and steam her hair from the roots out, hair she had purposely *not* gotten wet. Too late.

She shivered at the contrast between his heat, the warming water, and the cold air, as the temperatures met, crackled, and upped her lust factor to infinity. "Seriously, what are you doing? I thought you were gay."

"I am gay. I have been ever since I met you."

"Oh, great, I'm so undesirable that I turned you?"

"What is wrong with being happy? Sometimes I don't understand you people."

"No, *gay* as in you're attracted to Steve. Men who like men, are, like, you know, gay."

Bastian's head snapped back as if he'd been socked in the jaw. Awareness changed his expression to disbelief. He'd understood gay to mean the literal happy, she realized. Of course he had.

"I am not that kind of gay. What made you think I was?"

"Your concern about Steve. You touched his knees—for a long time, Bastian. Lizzie saw you. And you're a painter and decorator."

Bastian stood, bringing her up in the water with him. "I

touched my own back for a long time after I fell from the roof, remember, Kenna, to heal myself? I touched Steve's knees to *heal* them. The fact that I love color should not influence your thinking."

"Shame on me for stereotyping," McKenna said. "You really *are* a healer?"

"I will look up stereotyping later, but yes, a happy healer. This is how happy I am," he said, cupping her cheek in one hand, tracing her brows, her nose, the shell of an ear, the length of her neck with a finger, to her pulse, to the V of her blouse.

At every new sensation, McKenna shivered, icy and on fire at the same time.

Bastian slipped his hands beneath her shirt at the waist and skimmed his palms up her torso.

"I should object," she said, throwing her head back. "You'll know my flaws after this."

"As you will know mine," he whispered against her pulse, where he planted small biting kisses, making her shiver.

With his thumbs, he teased her beneath her bra, and he drank from her lips, but not against her will.

By the time he circled her nipples through her bra with both hands, McKenna thought she might jump from her skin. She unhooked it, slipped the straps off her arms, pulled the bra out through her cleavage beneath her blouse, and tossed it to shore.

His head disappeared beneath the water, beneath her blouse. He popped buttons, literally and metaphorically, as he placed hot, slow kisses from her waist upward. "I hope you can't see under there," she said. "Try to keep your eyes closed."

Bubbles rose and released his chuckle.

"I hope you're not laughing at my flaws. Ah, screw

them, you feel too good for me to care. Oh, yes, go there."
With his lips near a nipple, she'd catch fire.

When he closed his lips on her and pulled on an aching
bud, she shouted with shock and pleasure.

Bastian shouted with her, as if he felt the same rush.

Not sex-starved or anything, not her. How embarrassing, and yet, she didn't care. Not yet, anyway.

She nearly came knowing they were sharing pleasure.
"Keep doing that. Wait. How can you stay down there so
long and not drown?"

He resurfaced with a twinkle in his eyes. "I would appreciate making love to you without the comedy routine," he
said. "Yes, I have been doing my language homework . . .
as well as my sex lessons."

"You did read the dictionary last night, didn't you? What
kind of sex lessons?"

"On DVD. Instructional lessons. I'm a bit . . . rusty. And
there was nothing better to do. From now on, you can only
have enough wine to make you horny. I learned that word,
too."

When she opened her mouth to deny her reaction, he
closed his own over hers. Desire quickened and jarred her
with the surge of an active volcano. Lava flowed through
her veins. His, too, it seemed. She half expected the lake to
take to boiling. His mouth was so hot. *He* was hot.

The phrase making love had never made so much
sense.

His sex prodded her entrance, and she wished, despite
being outdoors, that she was naked with this man.

Something slithered against her and up her thigh.
"Snake!" she screamed, taking a fast swim for shore.
"Snake, snake, snake! Come out, Bastian, or it'll get you."

He swam her way, his breath coming fast, but he stopped
and stood up where the water met his waist and bent over

double for a long time, his hands on his knees, while he took deep, deep breaths.

When he straightened, he shook his head. "For one blissful minute, McKenna Greylock, I thought that snake was going to get you."

THIRTY-THREE

"I hate snakes," McKenna *shouted. "But you wanted it* to get me?"

Bastian's man lance wept and grew smaller as McKenna grabbed her skirt, slipped it on over her shorts, and walked away. "McKenna, there are a few things you should know," he called after her.

She stopped and turned back to him. "Yeah, well, there are a few things you should know, too. Like, now that I'm looking at you from a distance, it does look like—" She hesitated and crossed her arms. "I'm probably hungover from that buzz I felt in the water, but it still looks like there are creatures flying around your head."

"Your hallucinations are from being in the water with me. Remember when I said that I find water enchanting? Well, that thing I have that makes me a healer, it seeps out my pores, and if you're in the water with me, you are apt to feel light-headed. Buzzed."

She raised a brow. "You're lying through your perfect

white teeth. And I don't think that was enchantment I was feeling."

"How can you tell?"

"Your nose is growing."

And that wasn't all, considering the way her wet clothes clung to her incredible figure—an hourglass figure, he'd learned. He wanted them off her. Now.

"Come out of the damned water so we can talk," she ordered.

"I am not quite ready."

"I am the boss, remember. I order you to come out of that water and tell me the truth."

He started walking toward her very, very slowly. "Okay, the truth is that I used to be a dragon, and the murals in your bedrooms are scenes from the island I left to come here, and now I am a man again, but I still have dragon magick. That is what you felt in the water with me. My magick."

"You're certifiable," she snapped as she walked away, and who could blame her?

"Dewcup," he shouted, "the faery who came through the veil with me—who Whitney *did* see—has been tormenting your cat. Riding her. That's why Jaunty races around the house so much lately."

McKenna let her hands fall to her side and faced him. "Came through the veil?"

"From a parallel plane of existence, on an uncharted island, known as the Island of Stars."

"Can you be out in an hour?"

"Out of the water?"

"Out of my life."

"I could leave your employ, but I do not want to leave *you*. The truth is, I have wanted you since I set eyes on you at Vivica's the morning you came looking for a handyman." Perhaps he could equate heart mate with "the female one wants to mate with." Because, now, it fit.

He did not know if one used a man lance with a heart mate, but he desperately wanted to use his with McKenna. Andra had not said to make his heart mate's body his own, just her quest.

"Don't be stupid," she snapped. "You can't want me. If you've been marooned on an island, you don't know what you're missing."

"Surely you do not mean that I should want a string-bean creature like those who follow me?"

McKenna disappeared inside the house.

Bastian left the water, put on his shirt and jeans, and sat on the porch steps. Everyone would lose if he left, especially him, because he would lose McKenna, the first important person in his world. Andra belonged to him and his brothers.

McKenna belonged to him alone. Did wanting a woman to belong to him make her his heart mate? He had not yet found the sign of the crowned dragon. But he must be right about McKenna.

Confusion taunted him. If he lost her, everyone stood to lose. Andra would lose her magick and the good she could do. His brothers could lose their lives. McKenna, her farm. Her ancestors, their legacy. McKenna's friends, their home.

The only winners would be Killian and a blackhearted developer.

"McKenna!" he called, going inside. "You have to see reason."

"No," she said, standing in her living room with a towel over her clothes and the television on. "Despite your wild, borderline-schizo personality and imagination, here is the truth that matters." She indicated the television. "Sit yourself down and enjoy the fashion show, then you tell me that this"—she indicated herself with scorn—"is what you want."

To please her, he accepted a towel as well, folded it on a leather ottoman, sat, and looked at the television. He could not believe what he saw. He pulled the ottoman closer, heard McKenna's mumbled "I told you," and could not take his eyes from the sight. "Goddess help them," he whispered. "They need feeding more than the women who follow me."

McKenna looked up. "What did you say?"

"They are dying. Look at them. You can see their bones beneath their skin. It is savage, parading them around this way. I mean, I thought the women who followed me were pitiable, but these women should be put in a hospital. I expected more compassion on the earthen plane."

McKenna placed a hand against the far side of his face, a touch he savored, for fear it would be the last, but she turned his gaze her way. "Bastian, do you have tears in your eyes?"

"I would for any living creature so abused."

"You've been calling my cat 'snack.'"

He covered her hand with his to keep her there. "When I was a dragon, she would have been a snack. No, do not give up on me. I have been evolving by the day. I see your devotion to Jaunty with her silly hat and tissue worship."

McKenna pulled against his hold. "You tell too many fairy tales," she said. "I would prefer the truth."

He held firm, and she stopped fighting. "Sit down," he said, "and let me tell you about my life. About why I care for you. Why my body screams for a connection with yours."

For a minute, he thought she had softened, but then she looked like a frightened earth animal. "You don't care for me," she said. "In the lake, that was magick. You said so yourself."

"The wonder was you experiencing my magick and me experiencing your pleasure. My emotions, my very being, is transformed when I enter a body of water, and evidently my magick can be absorbed by those who are in the water with me. Earth is new to me. I am finding my way, and my magick changed and evolved with my transformation."

"So, now I have a magick lake?" she snapped. "And if a duck stops in for a swim on its way south for the winter, it's going to fall in love with me? Will a love-struck purple swan start following me around the yard the way women follow you?"

"When I leave the water, so does my magick . . . I believe." He hoped. "As for the trail of women, I have no explanation for it. None."

"Don't you?" McKenna laughed. "There's a lot of clueless male in you for a former dragon."

"Then you believe me?"

"No. Not your story. Not your declaration of caring. You and I, we're beauty and the beast."

"I know I am a beast," he said, "but if you could find it in your heart to—"

"Uh, Clueless? You're the beauty."

"You are wrong. Listen well," he said, taking her hand. "I can restrain you if I want to, make you listen to me. I am that strong. But I prefer you hear my story because you want to."

McKenna pulled her hand from his. "Can we get into dry clothes first? We'll catch pneumonia like this. The temperature seems to be dropping from hot as hell to cold as a snowman's toes."

"You have men made of snow, here on earth? Are they magickal supernatural ancients like me?"

McKenna tilted her head and hesitated. "Okay, dry clothes, then back here for shock therapy."

Bastian sensed her indecision. "I am warning you," he

said. "If you run out that door, get in your truck, and drive as fast as possible, I can catch you."

McKenna laughed, not a compliment. "You have a terrible sense of direction, remember? You said so yourself."

"Perhaps, but my sense of smell is remarkably keen."

She placed her hands on her hips. "You think I smell?"

"Your scent is unique, like ripe berries, exotic spices, and rare island flowers. Being near you drives me wild, and you were doubly intoxicating when we were kissing in the lake. You smell like the woman I ache to have in my bed."

She sat quickly, as if her legs refused to hold her. "I shouldn't believe a word you say."

"Meet me back here in five minutes and I will change your mind." He took her by the hand and she let him lead her to her bedroom. Good sign.

Until she closed the door in his face.

THIRTY-FOUR

"You take my breath away," Bastian said when McKenna returned to the living room.

"In a caftan made to hide my body?"

"Your flaws are nothing to mine."

"I seriously doubt that."

"You show me yours, and I will show you mine?"

"Your story," she said, sitting on the sofa. "Talk. I'm listening."

"Fire?" he asked, indicating the hearth. "It is cold because it hailed again a few minutes ago."

"Sure. A fire. Why not. At least it's September now. I'll get us a snack, and I don't mean my cat."

Bastian caught her arm. "No food until you watch me start the fire."

She regarded his encroaching hand. "You gonna use magick? Or force?"

He let her go with reluctance. "Dragon magick," he said. "Watch."

She rolled her eyes but she watched as the fire he . . . *breathed*? Did he? Yes, and it enveloped the logs, which roared into a blaze on the instant.

Bastian sat back on his heels and looked at her. "Do you know any humans who can do that?"

She frowned and lowered herself to the ottoman. "You're not human?"

"I am, once again, but I retained several of my dragon characteristics despite my transformation, like my fire and my magick. They are likely important to my purpose here, but I do not know if I will keep them once I fulfill it."

"Human . . . *again*?"

He sat on the striped chair to face her. "One minute my legion was trying to help establish the Romans as a military force in Britain; the next we were dragons banished to an island plane surrounded by an endless sea. You see, our enemy had a sorceress on the payroll—Killian, Crone of Chaos. Her trademark is hail and lightning. Sound familiar?"

"You mean she followed you here? But why?"

"Because I escaped her banishment, though not by myself. Andra, Goddess of Hope, set herself up as our protectress. She taught us to adapt and survive. She's Killian's polar opposite. Her magick is white to Killian's black."

McKenna firmed her spine. "Your story is ridiculous."

"You don't know the half of it. Try scratching your nose with a wing claw. You asked about my scars? Dragon fights. Those suckers bite!"

Bastian could tell that despite herself, McKenna could not hide her interest. "So this Killian is angry because you got away?"

"Yes, and my brother dragons are still on the island. Andra can only send one at each phase of the moons, a phase you would call an eclipse. I came first to make way for the rest, and to prove that we can survive here. If I do not succeed, my brothers will die with the island, and Andra will lose her magick. She risked it all to get me here."

"Killian isn't helping your cause, is she?"

"Thank you for understanding."

"I'm not certain I do, but for some unearthly reason, I have a paradoxical belief in you, if not in your words."

He took her hands in his. "I appreciate your candor."

"Is that really your island painted on my walls? That fantastic beauty exists?"

A fantastic beauty existed in this wide-eyed woman before him, he thought. "The Island of Stars exists to the smallest details, bustards, faeries, dragons, and all." He wanted to tell McKenna everything, but he dared not reveal *her* part in this, because if she knew that his success depended on a connection between them, she would never believe that his feelings for her were real.

"So, you're not Special Ops?" she asked after a doubtful silence.

"The Roman army did not have special forces. In this country's army, believe me, I would be." He showed her his left palm. "This tattoo proves that I belonged to the Roman army."

"Tats are a dime a dozen," she said, indicating that it proved nothing, he supposed. "And the dragon curling around your arm?"

"When I came through the veil, I got the dragon to keep me humble."

"Keep eating Popsicle sticks. You'll stay humble."

He liked the way her eyes danced when she teased him.

"Your vocabulary is getting better by the day," she said, almost changing the subject.

"I have been on your computer every night, else how would I know about Special Ops? I read and learn quite fast."

"Seriously," she said, "how do I know that you're not delusional?"

"You saw me leap from your roof. And the day I arrived, I dragon-leapt into your basement. Back then, I could not yet control my leap."

"You were like a leaping lizard?"

"Is that a joke, like Wyatt tells?"

"No good? I'm trying to teach you to laugh."

A positive sign, he thought. He would have to stay for her to do that. He bared his teeth in a mock grin, so she would think she had a challenge on her hands.

She shrugged. "I didn't say it would be easy. So, the *Roman* army? Is that why you speak so formally?"

"I learn your words, but I cannot seem to string them together as you do. I expect that has to do with my early language skills."

"How old are you, exactly?"

"I have no idea. I lost track of time. Dragons live for centuries. Humans do not, of course, but I would rather be here with you for one human life than live for centuries without you."

"Especially because your island is dying."

"No, especially because *you* are here."

McKenna sighed. "I always feared that I'd end up with some ancient dude who couldn't perform."

"Define perform. Because I cannot dance, or act, or play an instrument."

"I mean 'do the deed.'"

Bastian blanked.

"You're annoyingly literal, aren't you? In bed, I mean, during sex. Does everything work? I'm especially impressed by the remarkable size of your package."

"Package?" He held his hands, palm up. "I have no package."

McKenna sighed heavily. "You are determined to make

me blush, aren't you? You appear to be extraordinarily endowed in the sex-organ department, and I've wondered if it all works, especially now that I know you're so old."

"Ah."

"Wow, that put a gleam in your eye."

"I would greatly anticipate the opportunity to wield my man lance."

"Have you never used your, uh, man lance before?"

"Possibly, when I was a man. Never as a dragon. We were an army of men."

"I'm glad you told me the truth about your sexual preference earlier, because learning you spent centuries with only men for company would have made me certain you were gay. I'm so glad you're not. And I do hope performance isn't a problem." McKenna covered her rosy cheeks with her hands. "Did I say that out loud?"

"I am glad you did. My man spike has been going to waste for centuries. I am so ready to 'perform' that our kiss in the lake nearly ended my first performance too soon."

"Your mouth on my breasts nearly did that to me."

He adored the gleam in her eyes and vowed to put it there often. "So you believe me about my past?"

Her outright laugh charmed and aroused him. "Not a word," she said.

So much for arousal. "But I breathed fire for you!"

"A parlor trick. Jumping off the roof, not such a big deal. You chose a deep-pitched section where the foundation is totally underground."

He lifted her in his arms. "Come. I will show you more proof."

THIRTY-FIVE

Bastian carried her out the kitchen door with no intention of putting her down. "Are we going to the lake for more magick? The hail's turned to an icy rain. It's also dark out. I think I'd like to be able to see you when you prove—"

"So impatient, my Kenna."

"What did you call me?"

"Kenna, I called you, and I claimed you at the same time. Does that displease you?"

"My mother used to call me Kenna. I like it. I like the sound of it in your voice. You do have a bit of a foreign accent. The kind women fall for."

"I will keep my voice and accent in mind when trying to seduce you." He would not push for her reaction to his claiming her. He could be patient. "What about your father and grandfather?" he asked. "You speak little of them."

"My grandfather abandoned my grandmother when my mom was a kid. Midlife crisis. My father died in a car accident when I was five. I still miss him. His flannel shirt smelled of leather and spice—I remember it against my cheek as he rocked me to sleep at night. I still choke up if I hear the French Canadian lullaby he sang to me. I felt safe in his arms."

"I'm glad you had a good father, and I hope that you feel safe in my arms, too."

"In a former dragon's arms? The jury's still out on that. Where are we going?" she asked as she wove her arms tighter around his neck.

"I am going to the backyard, here, where the addition meets the main house."

"This is where I saw you jump off the roof."

"Yes. The ground is even here. No bushes to fall into."

"And it's lower—Eek!" She screamed as he leapt from the ground to the roof.

"Okay," she said. "That doesn't seem so normal in reverse, easy pitch or not."

"Why, thank you, my Kenna."

Having suffered Killian's wrath from up here, he did not want to take a chance with McKenna's safety, so he settled them, her on his lap, in a nook between one of the gables and her chimney. The chimney would be warm from the fire, and he could hook it with his arm, in the event of a hail-slide. Also, the gable protected them from the elements.

"Now we're both going to fall," she said, holding tighter.

He liked that part best, her hanging on to him. Her trust, he liked. "I leapt upward to prove a point. Pay attention, Kenna, and behold the spectacular view of your farm from here."

"It's beautiful, but too dark to see."

"I see well in the dark. I forgot that you could not. There is a full moon. Too bad you only have one moon. Our nights on the island were triple bright."

"Tell me more about your island."

"Ah," he said. "Like your trees change colors with the seasons, our sky, moons, and suns also change with our seasons."

"What happens?"

"I will tell you sometime when our heads are on the same pillow, shall I?" He waited for her answer. "McKenna?"

"I'm thinking about it."

"Think hard," he whispered, inhaling the scent of her hair, like a mix of the trees on her property and the wild-flowers scattered among them. "In your opinion, Kenna, what would be the role of a heart mate?"

"A heart mate? Given the sci-fi nature of the word, I suspect it means mate of the heart. Someone you love."

"Define love."

"Bastian, writers, scholars, philosophers, and the every-day Joes of the world have been trying forever to define love. I'm not sure I have a definition."

He inhaled her musk, keener in the crisp night air. "Try, Kenna, please. For me."

"Mmm." She sighed and snuggled against him. "If I loved someone, I would love him for his faults—"

"Like flaws?"

"Yes, I would love him for his good points and bad, unconditionally."

"And what would you *do* with a heart mate?"

"Share a home, have children, work the farm, run the Dragon's Lair, grow old together."

Having children meant sex. His man lance grew in anticipation. Bastian shifted her so McKenna rested against his leg, not his lance, because he did not want to frighten her with his large enthusiasm. "So you would sleep with your heart mate?"

She looked at him as if his tri-horns were visible. "In a word, der."

"Define der."

She kissed his ear, her breath warm like a blessing. "Of course I would sleep with him."

"Have sex with him, you mean?"

"The whole enchilada."

"You eat Mexican food while you have sex?"

"I would do everything with my heart mate, including having great sex with him. Wondrous sex, and often—screaming, sticky, healthy, making-love kind of sex. We'd get into bed on either side every night and meet in the middle, and then we'd occupy the middle together, me on top, or my man, and—"

McKenna's whole body shivered, and her heart beat fast against his.

"And?" he asked.

"I'm sorry," she said. "I got carried away."

"No, you answered my question quite well. Are you cold?"

She gathered her wits with a whole-body tremble. "The rain is icy. Yes, I'm cold."

How could she be cold when she warmed him so thoroughly? "I can fix cold." He breathed warm air against her face, hands, neck, down her blouse—his favorite part. "If we weren't on the peak of a roof, I'd try to warm your legs, but I think that could get us into trouble."

McKenna buried her warm, pink face in his shirt.

"Jock," he said, "we need a protective smoke cloud above us to keep the rain away, if you please."

Jock constructed a purple cloud above their heads large enough to protect them from rain falling from any direction. "Better?" Bastian asked the woman curled into a ball against him, her proximity growing his heart.

"I appreciate not being rained on, but the air is still cold."

"Warm air, coming up. Watch." He breathed fire around them to warm the air in a circle.

"Do it again," she said. "That was amazing."

He fired the air once more, showing off a bit when he allowed his fire to go the distance where possible.

"I don't know about you," she said, "but I'm so toasty, I'm beginning to like being up here. I feel . . . powerful. Like a giant. Queen of my kingdom."

Judging by her ancestors watching from around the farm, she already ruled her kingdom. She simply did not know it yet. "I feel toasty, too," he said, "especially where your body meets mine."

She leaned forward, or he did, or they both did, and their lips met, though he kept their precarious position in mind. When he pulled back, the green of her eyes had brightened. "Are you warm enough?" he asked.

"Mmm. For what?"

He wanted to kiss her, again, and more. He wanted everything kissing led to, but first she must believe in him.

"Jock, please smoke the spirits from behind, one by one, head to toe, so McKenna can see her ancestors watching over her and understand the depth of their love for her."

"You know," McKenna said. "I just realized that when you get to thinking that the man holding you hostage on the peak of a roof must be a lunatic, you don't have a lot of options."

THIRTY-SIX

"McKenna, I would never let you fall."

"You let yourself fall."

"That was Killian, remember?"

"Oh, right."

"Look, Kenna, on top of the caves," he said to distract her, as Ciarra slowly appeared, Jock's yellow smoke backlighting her, from her ancient cloak and gown to the wild mane of her red fire hair blowing in the breeze.

McKenna sat forward. "Who *is* that?"

"With the leadership in her stance, and the hands on her hips, she claims the caves as well as all she sees. Who do you think she might be?"

"Not Ciarra? Is she? The matriarch of our clan? Seriously, Bastian, is that the spirit of the woman who hid in the caves and survived the hanging times? She's extraordinarily beautiful."

The shadowy spirit at the top of the caves tilted her head in thanks.

"Can you hear me?" McKenna whispered.

Ciarra nodded.

"I didn't know you were still here."

"I am here to protect you." Ciarra's response came like a whisper on the wind.

"I'm honored to be your descendent and to have your protection, but I'm distressed that the prophesied champion of the McKenna clan never appeared. Even so, I will work very hard to save your legacy."

From the tilt of Ciarra's head as she nodded, and the way the matriarch, and McKenna's descendents, focused on her, Bastian believed that he held in his arms the long-awaited champion of the clan, but to burden McKenna with that weighty knowledge at this difficult time would only frighten her.

Ciarra began to fade but not before McKenna waved. "Thank you for saving us," she said. "Thank you for giving us life."

"Thank you," came Ciarra's echoing whisper.

McKenna turned to him. "Did she thank me?"

"Seems so."

"Odd, but, oh, thank you for showing me my famous ancestor. Wait until I tell Vivica. Can I tell Vivica?"

"*Only* Vivica. No one else will believe you."

"Of course. Bastian, I met the family leader, sort of."

"Kenna, Ciarra is not the only ancestor here."

Jock worked fast, highlighting spirit families, the first outline already fading, but McKenna got the idea. Their Celtic blessings and cheers warmed the air and came with raised hands, bows, curtseys, and air-kisses. Before their eyes appeared elders, babies, men in kilts—Scot male dress, Bastian had learned—the men who worked this farm and the women who bore children and shouldered family burdens.

"There," Bastian said, pointing. "There are Esther and

Caleb. They left the addition and have been accepted with love. There are no curses or negative spirits in the addition, but you might want to get Vivica to do a health-and-prosperity ritual for Lizzie and Steve, and the same for your house before you open the Dragon's Lair."

"You believe in magick, then?"

"Kenna, darling, I am magick."

"I'll be the judge of that," she said with a wink.

Teasing him? If she teased him, could he not retaliate and tease her?

But McKenna forgot his tease in view of her ancestors' rousing cheers. She turned to him with tears on her cheeks. "My family. They're my past and, in a way, the inspiration for my future. I have to save this land for them."

Bastian stole her tears with kisses. She was beginning to understand her role without being told, though the impact of her responsibilities had not yet hit her.

"Look closer to your porch," Bastian said. "Jock saved the best for last. Who knew that Jock had a flair for the dramatic?"

Close to the house, a cluster of spirits materialized, and McKenna caught her breath. "Gran. Mom!" She wiped her eyes with a sleeve. "Sorry for crying," she told him, "but my mom; the wound is still raw."

Bastian loved the way Kenna loved. "I understand."

"Daddy?" Kenna tried to stand, but Bastian held her firm. "It's been too long. See, Bastian, how handsome he is?"

"Kenna, shh. Listen."

"Oh, he's singing that French lullaby I love. Daddy, I'm coming. Don't stop." She fought Bastian's hold to turn in his arms, and he was afraid she might knock them both off the roof. He grasped her, so if they fell, he would land on his feet. "Bastian, I want to see him—them—all of them, up close. Now. Can I touch them?"

"No touching. They're spirits, shadows made of energy,

but you should be able to see them in the morning and perhaps even talk to them if you absorbed enough of my magick."

"If I don't retain enough, can we go back in the water together, until I can see them?"

"You learn fast, my Kenna, but they will still be here in the morning. They are always with you."

Bastian stroked her hair. According to Caleb and Esther, saving her heritage would be a bittersweet success for McKenna, because her ancestors would be free to go on to their eternal rewards, or to reincarnate, whatever their destiny or varied beliefs mandated. Since he did not know whether they would have a choice as to whether they stayed or moved on, no need to distress McKenna with the knowledge.

"Bastian, they're fading." McKenna threw quick kisses in every direction, focused on her parents, who lasted the longest, and wiped her eyes by pulling up his shirt and using the edge. "Can Jock show them to me again?" Her voice trembled.

"Jock is that lump on the ground near your father's feet, sound asleep. He will need to rest for some time after this night's work. He loves you, or he would never have taxed his energy so mightily. Now do you believe that I was a dragon?"

McKenna's eyes danced. "Well, I believe that Jock is. Don't you think he's a little young to smoke?"

"But . . . but, but . . ."

"You sound like a dragon whose engine won't start." She threw her arms around him, a first, and so deliciously sweet, he wanted to take her to her bed on the instant. "Let's go for a swim," she said.

"What?"

"I need to spend the rest of the night in the water with

you, so I can soak up enough magick to talk to my family in the morning."

Bastian sighed, his sex dream dissolving in a smoke puff of disappointment. "You want to swim *now*?"

"You heat the water with your magickal and sexual energy, remember? Of course now."

THIRTY-SEVEN

McKenna floated, warm and toasty, not only in the water but in her elation as a result of seeing her family. The full moon cast a silver path through which she and her handy hunk swam. "Handyman, hell," she said, treading water to face him, "you're a flippin' miracle worker. Bastian, they're together, watching over me, Mom, Dad, and Gran. Thank you for showing me. I can't wait to talk to them in the morning."

"While we wait for morning," he suggested, "may I interest you in a few moves you might not yet have experienced in water?"

"Are you talking about that . . . snake?"

"You know what it was, do you?"

She wasn't stupid, though it had taken her a few hours to figure it out. "Was it a . . . trouser snake?"

"Ah, Kenna, you spoiled the surprise. C'mere. Give us a kiss."

"Us, meaning you and your zipper brain? Which, I

might add, seems to cavort like a long and bendy jock-sock puppet."

"Let me show you what this puppet can do."

When he came for her, she remembered her relatives, smacked him in the chest with the palm of her hand, and held him at arm's length. "My ancestors are watching! Take one more step, bozo, and you're turkey meat."

"Bozo is an endearment, yes?"

"Sure it is."

"Your relatives have left. I have your mother's permission to court you."

"You've spoken to my mother? About me?"

"She and your grandmother approve of me."

"Hah! Well, maybe I don't approve."

"Let me rephrase that."

"I don't see how you can speak at all with both feet in your mouth." Her eyes were adjusting to the darkness, because she saw his face as he tried to figure out, literally, why she might think his feet were in his mouth. His thought processes amused her. "It's an expression," she explained.

The furrows on his brow eased. "I see. Your mother and Gran said they approved of me, but you might not, because you are stubborn, though the decision is yours."

"How politically correct of them."

He tipped his head magnanimously. "You might be inflexible, bossy, opinionated, and a wee bit of a shrew, but I still want you. Do you want me?"

"Oh, sure, who wouldn't want a fugitive from the Lizard of Oz Funny Farm with delusions of dragon deeds?"

"What does that mean?"

"It means, Bastardon, that I'm ticked off."

"I was not a dinosaur, Kenna; I was a dragon."

"I rest my case."

"Thinking time is over," Bastian said as he warmed the

air around them to match the water and pulled her over him. And though she should fight, she didn't want to.

In using a man raft, one's female parts fell into mating mode and thrummed against all said raft's huge manly parts. She especially enjoyed his undulating trouser snake, which gave her a wet, hot shot of orgasmic promise and melted her at her core.

"Talk about buoyant. I didn't think this was possible."

"You'll find that a lot of new and different exercises are possible with me."

"Are you bragging?"

"I may have flaws, but they seem to work in my favor, as they will work in yours, I believe."

"Not all things are possible with you."

"Name one thing that I cannot do well."

"You said yourself that you have a dragon's sense of direction, which is useless here, and you can't eat appetizers without an instruction manual."

He dunked her and kissed her beneath the water, stealing her breath but replacing it with his own so she could stay under longer.

They popped up together. "Did you turn me into a mermaid?"

"Nearly, but none are as effervescent as you, nor do they hold my heart the way you do. Do not even bother to protest; just know that I am moving toward a night of wet and wetter foreplay."

"Foreplay," she squeaked, despite her best efforts not to act like a schoolgirl. "You're just all over the place with your education, aren't you? Sounds intriguing." *She was gonna get la-aid.*

This was all new to her, this lust for a man, one man, a god who permeated her senses as he stood before her, sexy and lickable. His hot, talented lips grazed her ear, melted her. He turned her and tread water for them both, her bottom against his lance, while he slowly nibbled her nape, fine-tuning her yearning, stepping up her eagerness, and causing a slow burn in all the right places. Scary places that she tried to ignore but couldn't.

Spirals of need licked at her inner thighs while the water lapped about them, tangible in its sensuality, like a living, stroking presence, warming her, as it sensitized her nerve endings.

Bastian's lips tasted of salt and sweat. Man and beast. His arms, like welcome vises, held her in place, molding her against him, while he inhaled her essence, his body growing taut and aroused. She liked his package better than any she'd ever found under her Christmas tree.

She wanted him. Inside her. Yesterday if not sooner.

Her eyes popped open out of sheer guilt. She looked around. Too still. Too silent. "Are you sure my ancestors can't see us?"

"Jock," Bastian called, and that small blue head rose, dragon eyes blinking sleepily. "Jock, a quick smoky turn about the farm, my friend? Just one."

Jock's blink became cranky. He closed one eye, but the open one looked hostile.

"For me, Jock," McKenna said. "Please?"

That did it. Jock shot into the air and swirled around the farm, his yellow test smoke like the light of a sparkler on the Fourth of July, bright but disappearing nearly as fast as he flew.

The yard was empty.

McKenna sighed with relief. "Thank you, my sweet blue friend."

Jock snuffled purple smoke and landed by the water to sleep again.

"He's lovesick, our Jock."

McKenna sighed inwardly. He might not be the only one.

THIRTY-EIGHT

She was losing her irritable edge, McKenna feared, her strength and ability to say, "No," dissolving with it. Probably due to the magick in the water. Or Bastian's magick, or were they one and the same? "Did you use your magick on the water so it would stroke me in nearly as gratifying a way as you do?"

"Do you like it?"

Her heart pounding with insecurity, McKenna slipped away from the source of her yearning, but not for long. He came up beneath her and curled his body around hers as if he were a snake and she his prey.

Why did being eaten alive feel so damned good?

The comparison should scare her, but it didn't. She'd never water danced. This felt like romance, but it was probably only lust. They were wound so tight around each other that Bastian's man lance knocked at her door, throbbing and abrading her in that spot where it was most likely to spear her, fill her throbbing sheath, and bring her terminal pleasure.

Despite her best intentions, she opened like a flower to receive her lover.

She'd known him for no more than a month, but she could get stupid for this man. Allow herself to *feel*. Reveal her flaws. Lower her walls.

No, she wouldn't let herself go that far. She'd satisfy her lust. Have sex. Live for the moment. She'd never done that before.

For his good as well as hers, she'd keep the fortress locked, but she'd open the drawbridge.

Bastian nuzzled her hair, and she loved it, but . . . "You do realize that my hair is the prettiest thing about me?"

"*You*, my Kenna, are the prettiest thing about you. You show the world a beautiful heart and a lush body sculpted by a master. These breasts," he said, peaking a nipple with his thumb, through her dress, and making her open further. "They fill my dreams. I would like a pillow made of breasts like yours. Though yours belong where they are." He stroked her hips and bottom and slid his hand between her legs.

McKenna swallowed an involuntary moan.

"You have a woman's body made to cradle the man who loves you, perfect for bringing him comfort."

Had he said love?

Not love; lust. English wasn't his first language.

She would consider this night's play a prelude to pleasure. Foreplay at its finest.

And if this was foreplay, what would the deed be like?

McKenna slapped the flat of her hand against the water at either side of them to splash some sense into herself. Bastian jumped and she fell away from him, but he caught her and water danced around her in slow, swirling circles, his eyes mirroring pinpricks of moonlight, his wet hair lying rakishly on his brow, his angular features predatory.

A cool breeze zephyred through her as their waltz became more intimate. Her hips in his capable hands, he held her near the center of his need, controlling her. Controlling himself, she believed.

This was a man with a fire in his belly, intense, beastly, precise in every move, his gaze hot, hungry. Voracious.

Why could she see so much better in the dark tonight than ever before?

She half expected his heat to bring the lake to a simmer, while their desire collided and sparked, like flint against steel, which seemed actually to be happening, because sparks flew from between them, like pale, fluorescent blue fireflies flitting around them.

Stars of their own making. Magick!

Despite her best efforts, tentacles of desire changed her, and the slightest abrasion, like Bastian's lips at the crown of her breasts, raised her high with desire, molten and pulsing.

When had he come so inexorably close?

When had this raging physical awareness overtaken her?

She lost her breath to a rush of longing. Without permission, her breasts tightened, her nipples pebbled, and she slipped the palm of his hand inside her blouse—bold creature that she'd become—and Bastian knew exactly what to do.

She closed her eyes and gasped from the bliss of his touch.

How much tighter could she be wound, before she climaxed without him?

The magickal jock-sock puppet beneath his jeans danced under her hand, and he hissed. Trying to get closer, she learned that zippers did not slide well against wet denim.

Bastian's determination, however, won the day. Their clothes came off so fast, he might have used magick on them, too. Or he broke the damned zipper.

Then again, maybe he'd used magick on her. Who cared?

He raised her in his arms and put his mouth to her breasts.

She shivered. She screamed. Arched into him, and abraded his mammoth man lance with her heat-seeking body.

Her legs parted.

Bastian found his way there, caressed her with the back of a hand, sending shock waves through her, but he stopped abruptly. "McKenna, a confession."

Open and ready for more, she pulled from her own pleasure and focused on his words.

"I remember nothing of women," he confessed. "I do not remember how to pleasure one."

Her interest peaked like his dragon lance, but he owned enough doubt for them both. "You've got great instincts, then. Put your hands where they were, and if you go wrong, I'll guide you," she said, simply *not* herself tonight.

Bastian relaxed and went with his instincts, and with a talented hand, he pleasured her, making her body sing, no guidance needed. She floated, partly in the water, partly in his arms, but mostly among the stars, definitely under his spell.

Perfection, his touch. Tender and gentle, slow, sweet, scarcely stroking. Stunning in his precision, he made her slicker than the water, raised her to heights that took her breath. She came, and came again.

After years of celibacy, she thanked the universe for this man, a dragon with a magick touch.

She lost track of how many times she came. "I'm sorry," she said. "I'm afraid I'll pass out before you get yours."

"This is for you, just you. One more time. Once more, my Kenna."

When she thought she might die of satisfaction, he let her catch her breath, then made her come once more.

"I can't," she said. "No more."

He slid her down his body, and what did she find? Heaven between his legs. "Holy mother of pearl. This is enormous." Her limbs shook as she fondled him, her knees like jelly. She could drop from exhaustion any minute, yet she couldn't stop exploring him beneath the water. "There's more here than meets the eye, buster."

"It's ugly," he said. "You should know before you see it. Buster is another pet name?"

"Sure, pet. Ugly or not, every man should have such size. Better yet, every woman should have a man with such size. Bastian," she said, opening her eyes." I'm not sure this will fit. I think it's too big."

He covered her hand. "We will take it slow, then, make your reception of my flawed man lance easy. But not here. On your bed where we can play all night and sleep in between, my Kenna. And you need to see my lance first and approve."

Or disapprove? Not bloody likely. "You're a good man, Bastian Dragonelli. Better not catch *me* in your net."

"I am already caught in yours."

She supposed she was caught, too, but she'd learn to get over him when the time came.

Bastian shook his mane of wet black curls and splashed her with common sense. "Bastian, I came, like, eleventy-seven times and you didn't come once."

"Come where?"

Not an issue, then. She refused to feel guilty and stepped away from him.

He allowed her to.

How dare he allow it!

THIRTY-NINE

McKenna wanted more of . . . everything, and Bastian acted as though they were done for the night. She stamped her foot in frustration and caught something sharp.

He shouted with her, and carried her from the water. Dawn teased them with its presence as he sat her on the bench beside the lake, and turned to put on the sandy jeans he'd tossed to shore. Ouch.

"My dress, get my dress. Don't look," she said, crossing her arms and legs, trying to cover everything. "Hand the dress back before you turn around."

"We are a pair," he said, sitting beside her and lifting her foot to his lap.

She tried to tease his package with her toes.

"Kenna, stop that. I am trying to examine you."

"I was trying to examine you." She batted her lashes and attempted an innocent look.

"Your foot is not bleeding," he said, warming and rubbing it with his talented hands—hands better suited to making her come her brains out, she believed.

The pain in her foot vanished, and they both breathed easier. Her other discomfort, however, lingered. "What kind of a pair are we?" she asked.

"The kind who are uncomfortable in their bodies. Mine does not fit right and I am embarrassed about my flaw."

"My body should be smaller," she admitted.

"Smaller?" he asked. "I feel like a big clumsy oaf when I am near you."

"You do?"

"I do. You said you thought Ciarra was beautiful, did you not?"

"Stunning," she said. "Ciarra is stunning."

"Keep that in mind," he said, cryptically. "Me, I am, how do you say, turned off, when I see a girl's bones beneath her stretched skin. While *your* bones are beautifully covered."

"Your perception is skewed, but I rather like the way you think." Was he for real? "Never mind that. Listen, when I hurt my foot, you shouted *with* me. Why? And how did you know which foot hurt, because you checked the right one?"

"When you hurt yourself, I feel pain in the same place. Probably because you are my heart mate."

"Get out of town! I am so *not* your heart mate."

"You want me to leave town?"

"No, it's an expression. Like . . . you're bananas, bugsy."

"You are joking with me. I can tell."

About damned time.

"When you cut your hand making French fries, McKenna, I shouted, too, remember? Because I felt your pain."

"Holy guacamole, I remember that. Wait, so you're taking care of me to ease your own pain?"

"I care about you, McKenna."

"But you feel better when I feel better?"

"Well, yes. Is that not the definition of caring?"

He was undeniably trying to think through his answers as he spoke.

"Pain is nothing to me," he said. "I have been run though by warriors bearing the finest spears, bitten by the vilest of dragons, sword-sliced, battle-axed, wing-clawed, and slam-dunked by tail spades." He made a clawing action with his hand against the claw scars on his neck. "Often to within an inch of my life." He kissed her nose, and didn't she love it.

"I can assure you that when it comes to stepping on a sharp stone, I care more for your pain than my own."

"Why don't I believe you? Oh, I know. You're a *man*."

"A man who made you pant with sexual pleasure not long ago. The man who will do so again."

The husky promise shivered beneath her skin and licked a trail to her center like warm molasses on a hot summer day, skimming, slithering, shivering her nerve endings, inch by happy inch. Anticipation times a trillion.

"You have no idea how beautiful you are," he whispered, his breath hot against her ear.

More shivers, a series of them, like small earthquakes. "I know how blind you are."

"My eyesight is keen, day and night. You do not know, do you, what you do to me?"

"I suppose I do; you having been stuck on a desert island without a woman for centuries. I'm sure I seem attractive enough, until you find someone better. And you will."

Bastian stood over her, his back straight, fists clenched. "You anger me when you belittle your worth and beauty. Do not say such things about my heart mate."

Unsteady emotional walls called for laughter as a distraction, but McKenna couldn't work up a chuckle. He'd touched her, body and soul, and she might never be the same. Where were those self-defense mechanisms when you needed them?

Bastian began to undo the buttons on her wet dress, beneath which she hadn't replaced her underwear, and when her blouse lay open, he boldly examined her breasts, his violet eyes bright. No doubt about it. No faking. He liked what he saw.

He kept his gaze on them as he carried her back in the water, and there he continued his magick as he took to laving a nipple, scattering shock waves, like mini orgasms, raging quivers, and breathless gasps.

"It should be your turn now," she said.

"Not until you *see* what you are getting yourself into with me."

"Sounds ominous."

"Define ominous."

"Scary."

"Ah. That is for you to judge. If you do not want that ugly part of me inside you, I will go back to my own bed, and we will never speak of it again."

"Are you kidding me?"

"I am not, believe me."

"Did your Andra Goddess teach you to be gallant to the ladies?"

"No, Vivica did."

McKenna chuckled. "Trust Vivica to get to the heart of what needs fixing. That explains so much, you polite little devil." Lust with Bastian, she decided, she could probably survive. He, if no other, would understand her quirks. She could do lust with a gallant dragon. But never love. Love hurt.

She kissed him, because she didn't want him to see her disappointment. Stupid her. She wanted love. Lust was less than, but, just once, couldn't she have *more than*?

He kissed her tears, the ones he wasn't supposed to see,

and her damned emotion overflowed at his tenderness. She wanted more from him. Yes, she would accept what he offered, though she should fire him. She'd send him away after Halloween. No, she wanted to make his first Christmas special. And he *could* help with spring planting. Summer and fall would bring more guests than usual in Salem; a handyman would be . . . handy.

Okay, so she needed him, but not necessarily in her bed.

He whispered his concern, apologized for making her cry, didn't want her to hurt. Good thing he couldn't see in her head. She was a lunatic, so spooked by her feelings for him, she could talk herself out of, or into, anything.

Despite all the right words, she saw a lifetime of wild need in his eyes. The eyes of a fire-breathing dragon, claws bared, wings spread, ready to fight for or mate with her.

"Bastian," she whispered. "Should I be able to see your wings? Holy mother of pearl, you have wings. You *are* a dragon!"

"I am fighting my inner beast," he said through clenched teeth, "a beast who does not want love to win."

That word again. Love. He didn't know what he was saying. "What can I do to help you?"

"Let me look at you. When I fought my inner beast after I fell, I discovered that you can become like a shield against my demon dragon."

She stroked his brow and didn't take her gaze from his. "Watch me. Use me as your shield. I'm honored."

The telltale signs of his struggle stood out in stark relief, clenched teeth, delineated muscles, pain twisting his features. The way he looked the day he broke through her foundation.

Lightbulb moment. He'd been fighting his inner beast when she came down the stairs that first time. "Who's winning? You or the beast?"

His silence made her nervous, until he sighed and shuddered. "I won. This time."

"Shall I test the dragon?" She teased his warrior lance with her body, moved against it, teasing him and herself, and finally, she boldly cupped it through his jeans once more. "Big," she said.

"Afraid so."

"Bigger than the norm?"

"I've seen pictures, so yes, I rather think so."

"Bastian, play the game to keep me safe. Say it's small, tiny even, so I don't want it. Tell me it's not good for me. I won't like it. You can't possibly satisfy me. Say it."

A grin split his face, wider than she'd seen on the rare occasions he smiled. Had he smiled before this, beyond the first day, other than to the children? "Oh, but, my Kenna, you are in for the biggest, largest, longest, most unique pleasure of your life . . . if you would but let this poor dragon into your bed."

She swam away.

He swam after her.

The water, warm from his body heat, added to their buoyant play, pleasure a goal for them both, yet he kept allowing her to push him away, to keep the ultimate battering ram at bay so as to keep her walls intact, more or less.

Bless him and curse him, too.

"Now really, can it possibly be as big as a battering ram?"

His warm breath tickled her ear. "McKenna Greylock," he said. "I have in my shorts *one* resourceful, multitalented, prehensile dragon lance. *And*, in its own magnificent way, it very nearly does breathe fire."

FORTY

When Bastian opened his eyes, he expected to find McKenna sleeping beside him at the edge of the water, but he found Lizzie on the nearby bench, Steve in his wheelchair, and the sun high in the sky.

How long had he slept? "What time is it?"

"Half past lunch," Lizzie said. "Did McKenna throw you out last night?"

Steve chuckled.

Bastian looked over the property behind them for McKenna but saw neither her nor her ancestors. "Where did everyone go?"

"What everyone?" Lizzie said. "*We're* here."

That was when Bastian heard the children behind him and pulled his feet from the water, too late. Wyatt tossed Jock, curled into a happy ball, to Whitney, while his docile guardian emitted tiny purple puffs.

"Hey, Uncle Bastian. Look at our fun new beach ball."

Bastian nodded.

Dewcup hovered about them, applauding. At least Whitney had sweetened his faery's disposition. He hadn't been cursed in a week. Both entities had fallen for the children, as the children for them.

Bastian regarded Lizzie and Steve. "Did either of *you* go in the water?"

Lizzie shook her head. "I'm too close to my due date and Steve can't get out of his chair. We felt safe letting the kids play close to shore, because you're here. We would've sent you in, if they were in trouble."

"I am honored you felt you could count on me." Bastian dusted the sand off his jeans and looked for his shirt. "Is McKenna in the house?"

Lizzie shook her head. "She must be doing errands. We thought she beat you up and left you for dead, but when we saw you breathing, we let you sleep. Is that McKenna's bra floating near the shore?"

This could mean trouble, Bastian thought.

"Uh, you wanna move it before my kids see it?" Lizzie asked.

Bastian picked it up and put it in his pocket. "Shout if you need me for the children. I have good hearing," he said and headed toward the side of the big house, the side facing the old harbor, around to the addition out back.

Furniture filled the addition's front yard, its doors and windows open. There, he found the spirits talking and laughing, some inside, some out, a first-ever family reunion of the centuries.

He cut through the crowd, accepting congratulations, though not sure why, and found McKenna cleaning house while talking to her mother and grandmother, her dad to the side, supervising every move.

Bastian saw their relationships more clearly now. Men who married into this clan took the lead in such an unremarkable way, their women didn't realize they were doing it.

"Bastian, you're up!" McKenna said. "Telephone Steve and Lizzie at home and ask them to come over today, will you? I want to show them their new home."

"I don't need a telephone. They're sitting out by the lake waiting for you to get home from running errands. I'll get them."

"Thank you."

Bastian stopped McKenna's father outside. "Sir, can you teach me that French lullaby McKenna loves, in the event that I have babies to rock and sing to sleep someday?"

McKenna's father, eternally young, looked over at his daughter with love in his expression. He cleared his throat. "I'd be honored."

Bastian made his way back to the lake, remembering what Lizzie said about Steve not being able to go in the water. He could fix that.

A few minutes later, Bastian pushed Steve's chair toward the back of the house, the children hitching rides, while Jock and Dewcup entertained them.

A good, uplifting sound, a child's giggle.

"What's this?" Steve asked as they rounded the corner facing the addition, but he wasn't talking about the milling spirits because he couldn't see them.

"Oooh," Lizzie said, "it's the haunted, forbidden addition. Never opened . . . until today. McKenna? Are you in there?" Lizzie questioned him with a look. "She can't be in there."

"Can't she?"

McKenna popped into the doorway, beaming, dress dusty, nose smudged. She never looked more beautiful. "Okay, don't freak," she told her friends, "but Bastian found a volume of the family history I never saw, and guess what? This place *isn't* haunted. Everyone has misunderstood for years but we never knew. So, anyway, I wanted to say, welcome home."

"What?" Lizzie placed a hand on her baby belly, soothing her little ones, telling them, and herself, that everything would be fine.

"McKenna," Steve said. "I don't understand."

"You don't have to move here if you don't want to," McKenna explained. "The house only has one bathroom, and that's old, but we can update. Three bedrooms upstairs and one down, a good-sized living area, and it's yours. The family record says it's sixteen hundred square feet. Think you can live in a house this size?"

"We're crying about losing twelve hundred," Lizzie said, a bit like a sleepwalker.

McKenna shooed her invisible relatives aside. What must that look like to Steve and Lizzie? "Come in and look around."

"Mama, who are all these people?" Whitney asked, but Lizzie didn't hear her.

McKenna whipped around to him. "You let the kids go in the water?"

He pulled her aside. "They're kids. They'll forget. Children see spirits easily, but they'll learn to stop because it's not accepted, or the magick from the water will wear off, whichever comes first."

"At least you weren't in the water with them."

"My feet were, but I was asleep. I didn't know Lizzie had let them go in."

"Great."

Bastian lifted Steve's chair up the steps to set him down in the forties living room. "You can tell me what to do to fix it up for you," Bastian said.

"McKenna," Steve said. "While this is enormously generous, weren't you planning to sleep in your basement after you opened the B and B? I should think you'd want these rooms for yourself or for paying customers. We can't mooch."

"You're the contractor who gave me a rock-bottom price to renovate my house, because I might lose it. You were saving me. Keeping a roof over my head. I don't know how *that's* gonna work out, but as long as I have a roof, you do, too. I won't accept no for an answer. While you're getting better, you'll continue telling Bastian how to fix the place. He's already finished the roof, painted six bedrooms, helped me spackle the rest, and painted the inside trim."

"He's fast," Steve said.

McKenna raised a brow his way. "You don't know the half of it."

"What do you want me to do here, Boss?" Bastian asked Steve.

"No," Lizzie said. "Stop trying to change the subject. We can't accept the house."

McKenna looked around. "It's old, I know."

"It's bright and has a water view. Age is not the issue. Self-reliance is. The house's age only makes it homey and charming. But, McKenna, Steve and I, we pay our own way. We'll find a place we can afford. That's the end of it. We won't take charity, not even from you."

"Become an employee of the Dragon's Lair, then."

Lizzie placed a hand on her back, belly forward. "I'm listening."

FORTY-ONE

"I'd like to hire you as the Dragon's Lair's cook, Lizzie. I've thought this through. Get Steve's mother to come mornings for the kids while you make breakfast and lunch for my guests. You said she likes to get up and out of the house every day."

"Mom does," Steve said.

"I plan to offer dinner at a separate charge to my guests. You can cook that, too, after the kids are in bed. Heck, LizBeth, you went to cooking school; you might as well make the Dragon's Lair famous for its chef as well as for its enchanting bedrooms."

Steve slammed the arms of his chair. "Damn it, I want to carry my own weight. I hate the thought of Lizzie working when I can't."

"You'll be our full-time consultant. Bastian will be your arms and legs."

"You're going to get better, Steve," Lizzie said, but Bastian didn't think Steve believed it, or he knew better and hadn't shared the news with his wife yet.

"Steve, let's go for a walk," Bastian said, "while Mc-Kenna and Lizzie talk. Without getting an answer, he picked up Steve's chair and put it back outside. "Lizzie," Bastian called back, "it's settled. I will pack and move everything. Take a look around the inside. I will paint the children's rooms however they want."

Whitney and Wyatt cheered as he took Steve outside and back to the lake. Bastian sat on the bench to face Steve. "First, let me clear up a mistake. I am not gay."

Steve cupped the back of his neck. "I wouldn't want to disappoint you, so I'm glad to hear it."

Bastian raised his hands and held them palms up for Steve to see. "In these hands, I have a gift for healing. Wyatt told me how much you hurt so I placed my hands on your knees to help heal them, and later, with Whitney's help, I tried to ease your headache."

"You did?" Steve sat forward. "You did."

"I would like to think so. Now you come clean with me. How much better do the doctors say you are going to get?"

"They say that if I don't have a series of surgeries, I might be in this chair for some time, if not for the rest of my life. With no health insurance, the surgeries are out for now, but I didn't want Lizzie to know until after she has the babies. I'm not paralyzed, but I am in pain."

"Do you believe that I have healing skills?"

"Bastian, no one can change the truth of what the doctors have told me. And pardon me for being crude, but I hurt in places where I don't want your hands."

"Want to go for a swim?"

"Do I look like I can swim?"

"I can carry your chair into the water."

"What's the point?"

"Mine is a whole-body healing power that is carried through water like . . . electricity." He would settle for a half-truth for obvious reasons. "Some might call it magick."

Steve shook his head. "So if I'm in the water with you, I might heal? Do you really believe this crap?"

"You can do it without believing, for your family. Let me take you into the water for a little while every day and see what happens. I will tell Lizzie it is therapy, which it is, in its own way."

"So you'll exercise my legs in the water, like my therapist used to do when I had health insurance?"

"Yes, and I will hold you in your chair in deeper water."

"This isn't so bad," Steve said, as water covered him. "It'll keep me cool, anyway."

"It will warm up from my body heat. Sorry, it can't be helped. Tell me," Bastian said, swishing Steve's chair through the water. "How many roofs have you shingled?"

"A hundred, maybe."

"How many have you fallen from?"

"None, but the second I stepped on the last one, I went flying."

"Where can I find this house with the slippery roof?"

Bastian didn't know how long they'd been talking in the water when Lizzie came out to the kitchen porch, hands on her big belly. "Spaghetti and meatballs?"

"Let's go," Steve said. "Whitney, Wyatt, dinner," he called to the children beneath the tree. "Your favorite."

"Yay," they shouted, running toward the house, Dewcup, Jock, and Jaunty behind them, Jaunty wearing a dress, and flowers in her tissue-box hat.

Steve questioned Bastian with a look. "Whitney must have had a tea party, but her stuffed animals don't usually fly around under their own power like that."

"I can explain," Bastian said as they left the water. "Later. What are we eating?"

"The nectar of the Italian gods."

"I am familiar with Italy, Rome especially, and the Roman gods, but I have never heard of spaghetti and meatballs."

FORTY-TWO

McKenna set the table for their celebratory dinner while the men dried off and changed clothes. It had taken Lizzie half the afternoon to stop being stubborn and accept Caleb and Esther's house and the job as the Dragon's Lair cook.

When McKenna's phone rang, she answered in the way she'd been doing since she went live with her website. "The Dragon's Lair. Innkeeper speaking."

This time, finally, pay dirt. "Yes, we have rooms available for Halloween week. How many?" She did some quick math. "As a matter of fact, we've had a cancellation, and we *can* accommodate a party that size. A week, yes." She made a crazy happy face at Lizzie, settled the price and the down payment, one night in advance per room, something else Steve set up on her website for her.

When she got off the phone, she screamed and screamed, Lizzie smacking her with a dish towel. "What? What?" Lizzie snapped. "Tell me."

By then Bastian and Steve had returned to the kitchen.

"I booked a family reunion! Lizzie and Steve, I hate to be a pesky neighbor so soon, but can we sleep at your house out back starting on October twenty-sixth? There'll be no rooms for us here. Ack!"

The kids jumped up and down with her. Lizzie applauded. Steve's eyes looked suspiciously bright, and McKenna would remember Bastian's grin forever.

As everyone served themselves salad, they made a timetable to finish work on the house, including scraping and painting outside. "Bastian, you have to paint the third-floor bedrooms sooner rather than later," she said. "We'll need them for our full house. Steve, do you think the elevator you put in when Gran was sick is up to code?"

"It was then, but I'll check for recent code changes."

"Third-floor bathrooms. You boys up to doing some plumbing?"

Their excitement carried them to the main course.

McKenna challenged Bastian to a spaghetti fork-swirling contest, but he accidentally shot spaghetti across the room and it stuck to the wallpaper.

A giggling Whitney bet Bastian two meatballs that he couldn't slurp spaghetti as fast as she could.

Sauce splashed him, and his eyes blinked against it, but he kept going, despite the laughter. He lost. "No fair. I had a never-ending noodle!"

McKenna dabbed at his face with a napkin. A man. *She* had a man in her life. And paying guests. And she'd spent time with her mother and father, and Gran, again. Her heart was so full, she was afraid it couldn't be true. "A toast," she said, raising her milk glass. "To family."

Lizzie nodded. "Family to come home to, the Dragon's Lair, and plenty of guests."

"Family," Bastian said, clicking her glass, his gaze stealing her breath.

The prospect of running the B and B suddenly seemed less frightening with a family to share the tasks. Having Lizzie, Steve, and the kids around would also help ease the tension between her and Bastian.

Maybe they needed a time-out. Last night in the water had been something wild.

"McKenna?" Lizzie said, trying to tug the empty plate from her hand. "Where did you go?"

"Oh, sorry. Overwhelmed, I think."

Lizzie winked. "If Bastian watched me the way he watches you, I'd be overwhelmed, too. Go for a walk. Steve will help me with the dishes."

"Where's Bastian?"

"He took Whitney and Wyatt to bring Toffee an apple."

McKenna walked in the opposite direction from the barn and into the woods for a bit of time to think. She'd awakened before Bastian this morning, glad she wouldn't have to face him before she went looking for her family.

He had become so much handier than a handyman, a magnificent hunk of sex and sensuality who cured her loneliness.

She was already too attached. Could she chance lowering her walls and getting hurt again? Even a sturdy farm girl like her could reach the breaking point. It would hurt more when this man left.

With Bastian, everything seemed grander, yet more fragile, more brazen, more sensitive, sensational, the whole man/woman thing exaggerated. More physical.

More anticipation. She had a habit of glancing at his package, imagining it through one of those mirrors in which things seemed larger than they appeared. Or was that closer than they appeared?

Either way, *yikes*, and bring it on. The titillating threat spoke with a come-hither voice, husky and hopeful. Oh, the promise in that dragon voice.

He said he wouldn't hurt her, but he most assuredly would, him being so beastly, and so "lay me on the table and take me now" gorgeous.

As if her angst called him to her, Bastian fell into place beside her, keeping pace, respecting her silence, stroking her arm with a finger, admiring a flower here and there.

She could almost hear her heart pick up speed. Without warning, he took her hand, clasped their fingers together, and continued beside her in silence.

"I'll phone you in the morning," Lizzie called from beside her van, Steve and the kids inside.

McKenna waved. "Have a good night. Thanks!"

"Congratulations!" the four Framinghams shouted as they drove away.

McKenna turned to Bastian. "Paying guests!"

He caught her up and twirled her. When he stopped, he kept his arms around her. "Ready to investigate Steve's accident?"

"How?"

"I have the address and the owner's name, but Steve said nobody ever sees the owner. Apparently she's a shut-in."

"Playing sleuth makes me nervous," McKenna admitted.

"You do not have to come, Kenna."

Oh, she wanted to come, all right. "Can you read my thoughts or emotions?"

"Not yours. I never came across a set of emotions so tightly guarded as yours. I read every dragon on the island, Vivica, Lizzie, Steve, but not you."

"Thank the stars."

"McKenna, I think we both want a closer physical connection," he said baldly, and rather accurately for someone who couldn't read her, "but right now we need to think about getting Steve his insurance money."

They *were* thinking along the same lines. "Right, let's

go jump a roof." Holy mother of pearl, even that sounded sexy.

"Afterward, maybe I can jump *you*?"

Oy vey Maria. Yes.

They held hands as Bastian continued through the woods.

"Why don't we take my truck?" she asked, pulling him up short.

"We can approach the house more quietly if we're walking. It is not far."

"Says the directionally challenged dragon boy."

He faked a smile, though his eyes crinkled at the corners. "You take the address, then."

Given Bastian's stride, McKenna had to hurry at first, until he slowed so she could keep up. Did this make her like the women who followed him? Probably. "No, don't turn here," she said. "Keep going straight."

He looked back at her and scooped her into his arms. "Tell me when you catch your breath," he said, without breaking a sweat, which couldn't be said for her, hot and getting horny with her bottom now bouncing off his remarkable package.

"You are a distraction, McKenna Greylock."

"Glad to hear it, but I am also the map in your head. Turn right."

"Thank you."

"If you didn't stick your dragon lance out there, my hips wouldn't keep bouncing off it."

"If your hips weren't bouncing off it, my lance would not be sticking out half so far. I like it. I wish we were headed for a bed of any kind."

"How many kinds are there?"

"A bed of flowers, sweetgrass, clover, a cozy cave, moss in a forest, or a bouncy human-type bed."

She had never imagined making love in all those places, and now this man—from whom she should run—made her want to experience all of it with him.

"Unfortunately," he said, "any kind of bed must wait." He set her down beneath a cover of trees. "There."

"The house looks deserted," she whispered.

"It is dark, but it might not be empty. Follow me so I can protect you."

She didn't *need* anyone to protect her, but she sure wanted Bastian beside her.

They avoided getting caught in moonlight by creeping from shadow to shadow, her behind the great wall of Bastian. "Cue the crescendo of danger," she said softly. "Set the drums to beating in sync with our hearts, the wolves to howling, the earth to trembling . . ."

Bastian turned to face her. "Are you out of your mind?"

McKenna straightened. "I'm setting the scene. Music. Sound effects. You know?"

"I do not. *You* are a nutcase."

"Did you learn that from Wyatt?"

"McKenna, shh."

"So you use McKenna when you're annoyed with me, and Kenna when you're horny. Good to know." She'd failed to make him smile. "Okay, so I've never done anything like this before. I'm shivering in my pink lace panties."

"This is exciting," Bastian said. "As is the thought of your panties."

She was pleased to distract him, especially now.

"Let me look in the garage window to see if there is a car."

McKenna caught his arm. "Why don't we knock on the door and ask if we can check their roof?"

"Because this way, if we are caught, we can pretend

to be lost. If we ask and they say no, we will be boldly trespassing."

"We are trespassing."

"But they will *know* it, if we introduce ourselves. Another thing, suppose the owner knows what happened to Steve and has been paid to be quiet."

"You're into this intrigue, aren't you? Did somebody do you wrong?"

"Only if you count being turned into a dragon and banished from earth."

"Right. You don't have a reason to trust, either. You really think Steve was ambushed? Why? Who'd want to hurt Steve?"

"Whoever wanted to stop him."

"From doing what?"

"Helping you succeed."

"Bastian, that's—I can be so naive."

"That is why we strike such a good balance between us," Bastian said. "The garage is empty. We should make our move now."

He took her into his arms and with barely a spring to his step, he carried her up to the roof in one leap, but as he did, the house and yard lit up like a Christmas tree.

"Motion detectors," McKenna said. And they *were* in motion. Bastian slipped the minute he stepped on the roof, but he held her tighter. He also tried to get a handhold as they slid, caught at a shingle, but tore it, and took the piece with them. As they fell, he twisted to take the brunt of the fall, giving her an idea of the control he might have wielded as a winged creature.

They landed behind the backyard shrubs, her on top of him. "You make a great mattress," she said. "Lumpy, but comfy."

He stiffened beneath her. Had his inner dragon been

awakened by the impact? "Bastian, look at me," she said. "Concentrate on my face. Let me be your shield."

He opened his eyes, caught her gaze, and within seconds, his shoulders relaxed, his expression became less feral and more like a man in pain. "My back," he said, as the sirens in the distance registered.

Not an ambulance, she presumed.

FORTY-THREE

"Are you all right?" Bastian asked.

"You hurt your back and you're asking me?"

"I am putting off the inevitable. I know how it will feel when you stretch my arm to reach my back."

"Give me your hand," McKenna said. "I have an idea."

He gave her his hand. "And you think I am a lunatic."

"I've been in the water with you. Maybe I can conduct your magick through my body. You hold my right hand, and I'll slip my left hand beneath you against your back."

His inner dragon raised its head again when she jostled him to reach his back, but it calmed quickly because he refused to take his gaze from her.

The motion lights went out at about the same time the police cars arrived. "Shh," McKenna whispered near his ear, and he gave her a nod. While they remained hidden behind the shrubs, the glow of flashlights danced around them. The investigating policemen set off the motion detectors, and before they left, they checked the grounds and made sure the doors to the house were locked, but nobody checked behind the bushes, probably because it was so obvious a place to hide.

It took a bit longer for his back to heal with McKenna as a conduit, but it worked, and with much less pain.

She reacted to his sigh. "Better?" she asked.

"Better."

"Why didn't you ask me to do this the first time you fell? It would have been so much less painful for you."

"You have to *believe* to be a conduit of magick. You weren't ready then." He flexed his back, sat up, then stood and took her hand.

"I healed you," she crowed, as he pulled her along.

As they crossed the street, what looked like heat lightning lit the sky and illuminated them.

At nearly the same time, a siren startled them.

They ran.

The police car that had been parked in front of the shut-in's house pulled into traffic.

"Maybe we should split up," Bastian said, as the siren came closer and they scooted into the woods.

"You'll get lost if we do," she pointed out, and rightly so, the bossy thing. "You can't travel as the crow flies in these woods."

"As the dragon flies," he said, correcting her. "*That* is how I traveled the direct route, with my own wings."

"Don't you wish you could work up some wing power now?"

"I got close when you crushed my man globes on landing."

"Man globes?" She giggled and tripped over a branch.

He stood her up and managed to get himself a handful of breast, lucky him. "The rough translation from man globes in dragon speak is brains," he said.

She stopped running. "Goodness, that explains so much."

He grabbed her hand and kept running.

She pulled him up short when she fell against a tree. "I can't go as fast as you. I'm sorry, but I'm cramping here."

More lightning, then hail, just to make this easier, he thought.

He threw McKenna over his shoulder like a sack of grain.

"Thanks," she said. "Bouncing on my belly makes the cramps so much better. So does the hail. Cold, wet, crampy, and upside down. Nice."

"Glad I can help."

"Such a man," she muttered, but every other turn, she made him change direction. "You could tell me ahead of time," he snapped.

"I'm seeing where we went, dragon boy, not where we're going. Try not to slip on the ice, will you? The only thing I'm missing is a concussion."

"You can be a bit twitchy, you know."

McKenna gasped. "Are you saying I annoy you? That I'm bitchy?"

"If the snark fits."

"You learned a new word. Snark. Good little dragon."

"I rest my point. We are running from the law and you are being prickly about what route we take."

"Your *case*. You rest your misdirected case? Do you know your way back to my house?"

"I think we should hide," Bastian said.

"We could go to Lizzie and Steve's old house, since they haven't moved to our place yet."

"We should not involve them. That was the house where Steve fell. They might think to ask him questions and would find us more easily. If that evil contractor has friends in high places, as you said, you might be a suspect."

"Boy, you lap up the details, don't you?"

"Where can we hide?" Bastian asked.

"The caves on my property?"

"Seems obvious. Are they deep enough for us to lose ourselves inside?"

"Huge and shaped like a pitchfork. The prongs are well charted but no one will step foot in the whispering cave, which begins the handle of the pitchfork. Even if they did, they'd come up against what looks like a stone wall. We'll be hiding behind that wall."

"The lights through the trees are police cars," Bastian said. "How long until we get there?"

"These are the woods where we started. You really do have a bad sense of direction, don't you? The police are like the wolves I imagine nipping at our heels," she said. "This is the far entrance to the caves. We can only be seen from the old harbor here, which is unlikely. Follow me."

He stood her on her feet, followed her into the caves, and felt homesick for the island. "They're big, your caves. I hear someone or something nearby."

"It's the whispering cave. Some say it's the wind; others say it's the spirit of Ciarra warning her enemies away. Who knows? The opening to the handle is here and it's small. Do you think you can get through?"

"As a dragon, I had the ability to fit through small spaces that often seemed impossible."

"Like a cat." The tunnel became pitch-black. Bastian pulled McKenna to his side to protect her, and though he could see, he sent a fire stream to illuminate her way. The wall, which he thought closed the cave, was an overlapping wall with a narrow entry, behind and between.

He watched McKenna slip easily through, but he took a minute. It opened to a large furnished room. As broken and bug-ridden as it appeared, someone had once lived here.

"This," McKenna said with reverence, "was Ciarra's home during the hanging times."

Ciarra appeared in spirit form as if out of the ether. "Welcome." As she spoke, the fire in the old hearth came to life, as did the flames on candles in wall sconces. Their combined light revealed a wood-plank table, several chairs, some broken, and an ancient wall tapestry of many colors.

"You are safe here," Ciarra said. "And dry now, too."

She was right. Their clothes had dried on the instant, thanks to her magick.

McKenna stepped her ancestor's way, but not too close. "You *knew* we would come, didn't you?"

"For centuries, I have waited." Ciarra smiled a secret smile. "Bastian, I gathered sweetgrass, your favorite, and made with it a bed for you and McKenna. Tonight I will keep watch up above."

"We thank you," Bastian said with a bow.

"Before you rest, look behind the tapestry. I believe you will find what you seek, in addition to our McKenna, that is." Ciarra vanished, leaving them with a fire to warm them, a place to rest, an oil lamp beside a sweetgrass bed, and a wooden bowl of apples and pears.

After running so far, they drank with cupped hands from the spring pool in a corner of the room.

"This is the spring that feeds my lake," McKenna said, using the water to wash her face.

Bastian went to examine the tapestry.

"You have pasty white lines on your jeans," McKenna said.

He tried to see them. "It could be streaks of whatever is stuck to the downside of this shingle I tore off. I felt something on it when I slipped it in my pocket." He took the shingle out.

"Evidence?" she asked, touching it. "It's hard and waxy."

Bastian shook his head. "What now? How do we do the most good with this?"

"We can always turn the evidence over to Vivica," McKenna suggested, "if it is evidence. My cousin knows everyone in town. Surely some chemist can tell us what that shingle is caked with. Whatever it is or was, it does retain a bit of a greasy quality that could have made Steve slip and fall. Before we can make any accusations, we need to know, without a doubt, what this is and where it came from."

"Vivica, the perfect solution." For Steve's sake, Bastian was ashamed that he hardly heard McKenna's detailed response beyond Vivica's name, falling as he was into the wonder of his love's bright eyes, stirred by the knowledge that they would be spending the night together on a pallet of fresh sweetgrass in a warm, dry cave. Yes, perhaps he had been a dragon for too long, but this was like a dream come true for him. Except that the woman was more desirable than he could have imagined.

He reached for her hand to lead her to his bed.

"The tapestry." She stopped to remind him. "You should look beneath the tapestry."

Examining furnishings was not primary in his mind, or his zipper brain, as McKenna often called it, and rightly, he now understood. But since Ciarra had been so generous as to prepare for their comfort, he would do as she suggested. Taking McKenna to the best of dragon beds could wait a minute longer. Complying with his hostess's suggestion could not.

He expected nothing as he lifted the tapestry aside, but absorbing the sight behind it felt rather like being clawed, slap-winged, and tale-spaded—all three at the same time.

Though he reeled from the sight, Bastian had man sense enough to understand that the amazing sight before him put period to any doubt he might have harbored about the choices he had made since breaching the veil and arriving here on earth.

A simple cave drawing. Antiquated. Crude. A treasure to an archaeological team, perhaps, but nothing to the average man. Except to him. And, hopefully, to Kenna. Because the sight could change her life as well.

Bastian's heart raced, and his hand trembled as he raised it toward the magickal prize. His emotions shivered, too. Dreams more lasting than a bed of sweetgrass, more powerful, life-altering, impossible dreams, seemed suddenly possible.

"Is that a cave drawing of a dragon?" McKenna asked.

He pulled her against his side. "Not just any dragon. A crowned dragon. Andra, the sorceress who transformed me, said that my heart mate would lead me to the sign of the crowned dragon. You, Kenna, are, without doubt, my heart mate. This is the final proof. Call it destiny or karma, but you are meant to be mine."

"Unless I don't want to be yours."

FORTY-FOUR

"What nonsense is this? You are my heart mate, my contrary Kenna. You cannot deny that."

No, she couldn't deny it, damn him. "You think some old cave drawing can decide for me? I don't think so. I'd like to be wanted for myself, thank you very much. Love, I believe it's called. I don't like your assumption, as if I'm some kind of magickal prize. A done deal. Decided on a parallel plane by some goddess I never met? I'm so easy, you just have to announce that I'm yours and I'm supposed to do what, say thank you? Fall at your feet, or into your bed?"

Bastian scratched his nose but he failed to hide his amusement. And why that should make him look so damned charming, she didn't know, but it ticked her off even more.

"My heart wants yours, my Kenna," he whispered against her neck. "You know that. Where you are, I am home. I wanted you, loved you, before I found the sign of the crowned dragon."

"You mean that your body wants my body," she said. Let him get out of that one.

"As you can plainly see, but I never tried to hide my sexual interest, not from the first day, did I? I have also said I loved you, a sentiment at which you scoffed. But I did not wait for the sign of the crowned dragon to declare myself. Please take that into consideration."

"I'm not easy."

"No, you are not."

"What's that supposed to mean?"

"That I enjoy a challenge, especially when you are the woman presenting it, whether it involves words, emotions, sex, or home repair. Did I cover everything?"

McKenna sighed. She wanted to pout but more than that, she wanted to lie beside him and sleep, and so much more. She ached . . . in so many ways. "Well," she said. "That's better, but you have to work on that attitude, buster. I won't be taken for granted."

His eyes smiled, sexy as hell, and damn it, she *wanted* to be his heart mate more than she wanted her next breath. So why was she fighting him?

"Come to bed?" he coaxed.

Could he read her emotions now? Had he torn down her walls already? *That* wasn't a possibility to entertain tonight. But tomorrow. Now she was just too tired to panic. "Just for sleep," she said. "Out of respect for Ciarra's hospitality."

"I will hold you in sleep. Yes. Keep you safe."

She was Bastian's for the night, at least, McKenna granted, though any further sexual exploration would have to wait until they got home. Out of respect for their hostess? Or out of fear for the turn they'd just taken? That sign of proof, that crowned dragon, made her feel like his heart mate. Like she belonged to him suddenly, no turning back. "Cold feet," she said, diagnosing her problem.

Bastian pulled her toward the sweetgrass. "Come, then, and I will warm them while I protect you."

"Leave it to you to come up with the right answer."

Serenity she found in Bastian's arms, in Ciarra's warm, cozy home, amid the fresh scent of sweetgrass, her quick-to-sleep dragon beside her, the beat of his heart beneath her ear, her leg over his, her knee nearly teasing his lance but not quite, his hand cupping a breast. Who was protecting whom, here?

For her to let down her guard enough to climb into bed with a man, without the aid of too much wine, to feel safe in his embrace, close her eyes and relax enough to sleep, meant that she had learned to trust . . . one man.

For Bastian Dragonelli, she had fallen, and hard.

He would leave someday—everybody did—but right now, she trusted him.

During the night, they changed positions in tandem and slept like spoons in a kitchen drawer. Bastian spoke her name in his sleep—wonder of wonders—as he pulled her close. She kissed him and drifted, wondering if she'd gone off the deep end, putting her trust in a family ghost, a dragon, his sorceress. In magick and love. Destiny.

She woke to find Ciarra standing beside their bed, looking down at them, her hands raised in a blessing. Love for her ancestor welled up in her, their kinship deep and abiding. "Thank you," McKenna whispered.

Ciarra's love radiated from her in warm, soothing waves, and McKenna slept again.

She and Bastian stayed at the cave until late the next morning, because she loved spending time with the matriarch of their clan, learning family history, about the hanging times, how Ciarra survived, and Bastian waited patiently as they talked.

"No one came looking for you in the night," Ciarra said. "You are safe."

McKenna felt herself welling up. "I wish I could hug you."

"I feel your embrace and return it."

McKenna nodded. "Good-bye." She didn't look back. She couldn't. Loss did not need to be confirmed. She knew it well.

Bastian squeezed her hand. An altogether sublime night, McKenna thought as they walked toward the house.

Goddess help her, she didn't want to go back to life before Bastian. Alone. Lonely. How long did a former dragon stay with his heart mate?

Their night together had been perfect, her and the man she loved, placing full trust in each other.

As they made their way to the house, her cramps returned, but she went right to the truck. "Let's get that slimy shingle to Vivica."

The ride took no more than a few minutes. Works Like Magick had barely opened, but Vivica stood in her office, watching as they approached. "I knew you were coming," she said. "My psychic visions have been running rampant. You met Ciarra, you lucky girl. What I wouldn't give." Vivica turned to Bastian. "You have evidence?"

He gave her the shingle.

Vivica accepted it. "I'll get this into the right hands. McKenna, about your suspicions. The building inspector never played cards with Elliott Huntley. He doesn't know him, so you have an honest chance of succeeding. I sensed that to warn Huntley away would cause you more trouble, so he's still a loose cannon, though he isn't aware that you know he was bluffing about knowing the building inspector."

"I trust your instincts," McKenna said.

"This doesn't mean you'll have an easy road, but the surface is pitched evenly now. Just don't forget that Huntley probably *owns* the road."

"Gotcha."

Vivica kissed them both before they left.

In the car on the way home, McKenna realized how badly she needed to shower. She wasn't ready, either, to bare her body to Bastian in daylight, yet. "Suppose we take separate showers and meet in my bed afterward?"

His grin swelled her heart and other places, too. Horny hardly described her anticipation.

The shower didn't help her shake her lethargy, discomfort, or fuzzy head, though. Her hands, she saw when she toweled off, were swollen. As she was bloated. What day was it, damn it?

She checked her calendar. Bingo! Just her luck.

From her bed, she heard Bastian's moan before he appeared in her doorway.

"I think I am dying," he said. "Something must have broken when I fell that I did not heal. I am bleeding internally, I am sure of it. I will not live out the day, I tell you."

"Are you one of those guys looking for equal sympathy? The kind who has to feel lousy because their significant other does?"

"Are you admitting to being my significant other? Wait. Do you not feel well, my Kenna?" He crawled into her bed behind her and spooned her, his arms coming around her in a protective gesture. "Perhaps Killian's counter spell during my transformation is slowly killing me. I am done for, McKenna. One cannot feel this kind of pain and live."

She turned to face him and rest her head on his chest. "Tell me your symptoms."

"I am tired after a good night's sleep, edgy and uncomfortable in my skin. I had a fight with the shower curtain, and it won! I am swelling. Look at my hands, my ankles; touch my puffy stomach. No, don't. It is cramping. I miss my brother dragons—how foolish is that with you beside me? My head aches, and I am craving a mound of very salty French fries. This is very weird, McKenna."

She got up and went to her bathroom.

"Where are you going? How can you leave me in my hour of need?"

When she got back to her bedroom, she found him in the fetal position, holding his stomach. "I must be dying," he whispered.

"I have the perfect medicine for you," she said.

"No medicine could cure this. I am done for. I would prefer sword thrusts, battle-axes, or dragon claws to this all-over misery."

"You're not dying," she said.

"I am, I tell you."

"Midol's the cure." She wiggled a glass of water and showed him a pill in the open palm of her hand. "As soon as I take this, *you'll* begin to feel better."

"As soon as *you* take it? You mean that I am feeling your pain? Poor Kenna."

"I guess this puts period to your 'pain is nothing to me' theory?"

"There is no pain like this, not in the Roman army nor as a dragon warrior."

"I'm almost glad to hear a man say that. Fact is, I go through this every month. I promise, it won't kill you."

"Every month! Who could live with this?"

"Every woman on earth," she said, to his slack-jawed dismay. "I always suspected that PMS could debilitate a man." She chuckled. "Fortunately for you, as soon as I feel better, you will, too. I'm calling Lizzie to tell her we're not up to working today."

"Bless you."

After she telephoned Lizzie, she plugged in a heating pad, which they shared, belly to belly.

Bastian rubbed her brow to soothe her head.

She smiled and they napped side by side.

When she woke, Bastian needed more pampering and she needed another Midol. "This is going to be a detriment to our making use of your dragon lance any day soon. A woman can't . . ." Dare she say make love? No, of course not. "You do remember that a woman can't mate when in this condition?"

"Condition? What condition? Remember from when? I looked up the Roman invasion of Britain. It took place in 43 AD. Vivica told me that I am now in the twenty-first century. What would you remember this many centuries later if you had stopped being human for that length of time?"

"Not much. Do you remember nothing of women?"

"I am ashamed to admit that I remember what I dreamed about as a dragon: the pleasure of dipping my lance into a woman. Before you, I might have said, 'What else is there?' but I know better now, because there are so many facets to our relationship. Still, please explain why women cannot mate with this malaise, besides the fact that it must lessen their pleasure. And forgive me for skipping the lesson on a woman's reproductive cycle. I am afraid that I jumped straight to men and sex."

"You and every man out there." McKenna explained in detail what happened to women once a month.

"You bleed for days and do not die? I am glad you survive, but what you describe sounds like science fiction."

McKenna chuckled. "This from a Roman warrior turned dragon, who breached the veil from a parallel plane of existence."

Bastian shook his head. "Stick to the point, McKenna. Are you saying that I will feel like this once a month? Always?"

He was thinking they'd be together *always*? A thrill ran through her, but she cautioned herself to take it slow. A good word, always. It smacked of commitment. She wondered if Bastian knew that. "If you stay, you will feel this way once a month until I'm old and gray, or unless I'm pregnant." Let's see if that scared him away.

"Like Lizzie is, you mean? I am afraid that I skipped that lesson, too. The pregnancy and birth lesson was bundled up with a woman's reproductive cycle. Why would you not bleed if you were pregnant?"

"Because the growing baby would need it for protection inside me. You can look it up on the 'Net for the proper terms."

"I will borrow the lesson from Vivica," he said. "It sounds like something I should learn."

McKenna bit the side of her lip. "If I were pregnant, we would have morning sickness."

"Define morning sickness."

She'd barely started when he sat straight up. "You mean like we barfed the night you drank too much wine? *Quelle horreur.*"

"Are you taking French lessons?"

"I have already mastered English."

"Sure you have." She raised the setting on the heating pad. "Anyway, most men think that having sex during this time of the month is fine, but it's uncomfortable and messy, and not at all romantic."

"Who could blame you? I would never put you through such discomfort."

"Bastian, you may well be the most understanding man on earth."

"How long does this affliction last?"

"Three to five days. Sometimes longer."

"You suffer every month for one or two babies in a lifetime? It sounds like an inefficient system to me."

"Doesn't it, though? But them's the facts."

Bastian groaned and fell back against her pillows. "The

unending brutality of it. I am used to healing quickly, you understand. But with this, I have no choice, no control."

"Welcome to my world." She lay beside him, hiding her smile, and he gave *her* the heating pad, pulled her into the crook of his neck, and stroked her tummy over the pad, because . . . let's face it . . . the sooner she felt better, the sooner he would, too.

She pampered him for three days—Lizzie was sure she was, to quote her friend, "getting laid" —but to be fair, McKenna got her share of pampering, as well, until their touches turned to kisses and explorations of the most titillating nature.

Once her period started, and their PMS abated, they left her bed to work on the house, and every time Bastian saw her, he wanted to hold her. "I am so glad that I *cannot* bleed for days on end," he whispered. "I do not care about PMS pain any longer, as long as I do not have to—"

"I get it."

"I am here if you need me."

"I need you. The clock is ticking. Forty days until the house gets inspected and is mine for good, or not, and forty-one until my guests check in, unless I get a booking for the week before. Either way, we have to hustle."

They met Lizzie and Steve downtown to go shopping for bargain paint. Steve brought the house plans so he could tell them how much paint any specific section needed. Bastian's eye for color paid off. She ended up getting her paint for a fraction of the expected cost.

When McKenna woke up the morning after their paint shopping expedition, the blistered paint had been scraped clean. "Bastian, do you have something to tell me?"

"Yes," he said, looking proudly up at the house. "I torched the blistered paint during the night, dragon style, no heat gun or scraping needed."

When Steve and Lizzie arrived a short while later, Steve whistled. "Hey, the house is ready to paint. *That's* what you two have been up to for the past week. See, Lizzie, they weren't—"

His wife shoved his arm.

"Ouch," Steve said. "You know; I mean, they were scraping the house."

"Hard work," Bastian said with a nod.

"Yeah," McKenna said, thinking of Bastian's lance. "Hard."

Once they began, the kids painted the lowest levels. Lizzie painted wherever she could reach from an office chair that moved up and down. Mostly, however, she cooked and directed the children.

Vivica came on Saturday with boxes of pizza and friends from her employment agency.

Days later, when the house looked like a Victorian confection, in lavenders and greens, with hints of purple, blue, and mauve, the most enchanting house McKenna could imagine, they took pictures to replace the black-and-whites on her website.

"With the outside finished," she told Bastian, after Lizzie and Steve left one night, "we can put all our efforts into getting the inside up to code. We have thirty days."

"We made a good start on the inside," Bastian said as he directed her to her bedroom with a hand to her back. He sat on her bed first, pulled her down on his lap, and kissed her with enthusiastic skill. They had practiced foreplay a lot during PMS week.

This, however, was a trouser-friendly kiss. Yes, his dragon lance was getting antsy. "Your period is finished?"

She nodded. "Period finished."

"You are well after painting the house?"

"Well and up for a celebration." She stroked him through his jeans.

"I hope the sight will not send you screaming into the night."

"There's one way to find out. I finally get to see you with your boxers off. Take it out. Take it out. No, I changed my mind. Let *me* take it out."

"You will not scream and run from me?"

"Wait!" McKenna raised a brow. "That was a joke, right, that silly thing you said once about your lance being prehensile and fire breathing?"

Bastian set his jaw. "It does *not* breathe fire."

FORTY-FIVE

More than anything, McKenna wanted to get naked with this man—no, correct that; in a perfect world, he would get naked while she stayed under wraps.

Maybe if she took charge, made it into a game, and relaxed, she could enjoy herself. Sex, pure and unadulterated.

She sat on her bed, but that wasn't right, so she raised herself to her knees on the mattress, then she backed up to her headboard, gave an imperious but silent command with her hand, the king of Siam gesturing his subjects forward . . . or in her case, to make her come, damn it. "So get naked, already. Naked, naked, naked!"

"Should we not be taking each other's clothes off?"

"We can play by your rules tomorrow," she said, still not sure there'd be a tomorrow once he saw the bare truth. She put a hand out to stop him as he started to kneel on the bed.

"No kissing, no foreplay?" he asked.

McKenna couldn't stop her grin. "I remember how good

you are at foreplay. Thank you for your patience for the past week and a half."

"I have liked holding you in sleep."

"Your lance has been impatient."

He nodded. "It has a mind of its own."

"Right, a zipper brain. Did you say you studied sex?"

"I studied it often."

"Did it require practice?"

"Solo practice, which made my other lessons pale in comparison."

"Yet you thought you didn't know how to pleasure a woman."

"I have no memory of doing so, but since I dreamed for years about having sex with a woman, I imagine that I did have some experience. I became a dragon at the age I seem now."

"This discussion is not foreplay; you know that, right?"

"Andra never told me that my heart mate would be officious."

"I *am* the boss."

"And I was the alpha dragon. The leader of my kind."

"So, you were like the Lizard of Oz?"

"Joke, right? But dragons are not lizards, McKenna. To dragons, lizards are like popcorn."

"Hey, I just realized, there's a dragon in my bed."

His lids lowered over his hot, smoldering bedroom eyes. "A *naughty* dragon."

"How bold of you to admit it. Pretend, then, that I'm your plaything and you're my . . . pool boy—"

"Please tell me that you do not wish to mate with a water creature."

"No, I wish to mate with you." McKenna clapped a hand over her mouth. "Did I say that out loud?"

His eyes turned the deepest violet she'd seen yet. They nearly glowed.

"Forget the pool boy," she said. "Be my dragon boy and obey me at all times, especially now, when, judging by the activity beneath your jeans, your lance wants out, and bad. Have I told you how much I admire your package?" She nodded toward his zipper—be still her heart.

"Often, actually." He bowed like a loyal subject, as if he'd had practice. In the Roman army, maybe.

McKenna uncoiled, or that was how she felt when she moved from kneeling to sitting against her headboard, hands behind her head, ankles crossed. "I could get used to playing the royal in the bedroom."

"I will adore you, my queen, with every inch of my body, and I have *many* inches." His rough voice promised heaven while his look turned her into a useless puddle of need.

"Take off your pants."

"If I must get naked without your help," he said, "I will remove my clothing in the order I choose. If you wish to come and take matters into your own hands"—he winked—"feel free."

She sat forward on the bed, glad to have an equal playing field despite her royal commands. "Should we have music? I've never had my own personal stripper before, which means: he who strips away his clothes." She raised a royal finger. "Strip, strip, strip!"

He started with his shirt buttons and slowly revealed his scarred but perfect chest.

"Do you exercise those muscles?"

"I flew around the Island of Stars, above its endless lava sea, until the heat of it scorched my scales. I should think that carrying one's enormous weight on one's wings strengthens one's chest muscles."

"Are you putting me on?"

"Soon, I will wear you like a glove."

A sizzling streak of liquid heat rushed through her as he turned his back to unzip his jeans.

"Hey, no fair," she said, raising herself on her knees. "Face me. I want to see that puppy."

"I'd prefer you get the full view all at once."

"Wait, what is that on your back?"

"On my shoulder? The dragon tat. You saw that."

"I don't mean the tat, though it's gorgeous in the light. I mean at the base of your spine." She knelt forward to trace the curved areas. "They're curved," she said, explaining the indentations. "Like parentheses about ten inches long."

Bastian looked puzzled, so she brought one of his hands around to trace an indentation with his own fingers.

"Oh," he said. "That's where my wings were connected, where they emerge when my inner beast is winning, and into which they withdraw when I ultimately win."

That knowledge, more than anything, jarred McKenna. A dragon . . . with wings. She lowered herself to sit on the bed because her prickling legs would no longer hold her. Pinpricks attacked her arms as well. "Will you always ultimately win, Bastian?"

"My hope does not always overcome my fear, Kenna. Killian wants me to fail you, Andra, and my brothers."

McKenna held her chest. "You're giving me heart palpitations."

Bastian cupped her face in his hands. "Our time together is not guaranteed, I am sorry to say."

"Then let's make the most of it," she whispered as she met his lips with hers.

As he stepped away from her, an aura of sexuality poured from him, an imperative to beat time at its own game. "I know what is happening with your body," he said. "I feel you opening for me, as my lance readies itself to fill you." He turned away from her and stepped from his jeans.

"Black boxers," she said, still worried, but she fell back against her pillows, because this was their time, and the provocative light in his eyes a minute before had nearly undone her. "I might need reviving."

"You might when you see me. Are you ready?"

She supposed she had to be, but she didn't think she could take another shock.

She sat on the edge of the bed for a better view. The rest of Bastian's body was such a temple of perfection, despite his scars. It could have been sculpted in bronze by Rodin. How bad could his flaw be? "Ready," she said.

Naked, Bastian turned to face her.

She saw but did not believe.

Her heart raced. Pinpricks attacked her limbs.

The floor rushed up to meet her.

FORTY-SIX

Bastian's heart stopped as he lifted McKenna off the
floor and placed her on the bed.

She opened her eyes. "I'm sorry."

"You scared me."

"Funny," she said. "I was thinking the same thing."

He stepped away from her. He knew now that this would
not work. He picked up his jeans.

She sat up and tried to get a better look at his erect
flaw.

Despite her fear, he caught the change in her musk,
the scent of her sex in his nostrils. She might have been
shocked senseless by the sight of him, but arousal marched
beside interest.

Damn. His inner dragon rose in thrumming cadence to
his ready lance.

He caught McKenna's changing expressions, her glance,
wary, exhilarated . . . unsure.

He knelt beside the bed. "I apologize for frightening you."

"I won't kid you. It's not what I expected. For one thing, it isn't shaped like any penis I've ever seen, pictures included. It's like a pulsing, living sex toy." She raised herself to a kneeling position, then sat on her legs, and pointed behind her hand to his flaw, like she didn't want to hurt his lance's feelings. "I think the average woman would pay big bucks for that, or a copy of it," she whispered.

Did she fear waking it up? News flash. It was awake and roaring to go. Still, he could say nothing, do nothing, except beg her silently to accept him, flaw and all.

He tried to cover the embarrassing erection with his hands, but it had a mind of its own.

As she examined it, McKenna caught her breath. Her breasts appeared to rise toward him, her nipples to pebble. She lowered her lashes, to hide her eagerness? And she shifted her hips, which aroused him the more.

She mirrored his unease in the face of his blatant arousal, but if she moved her hips that way again, he might explode. He could not look away and touched a lock of her hair, red as the paprika sun. He loved the way it curled in waves and tumbled from her shoulders to her breasts. He had seen in the water, when they shed their clothes, that her woman's center was the same red—the color of passion.

He could not conceal his body's reaction, his hunger and yearning. "Forgive me, but you are like sweet cherry wine and honey from the hive, combined. I yearn for you. I want to taste you."

She shook her head. "You sound like you mean that."

"What can I say to convince you?" Perhaps he had not mastered the English language after all.

She leaned toward his lance and it surged to meet her.

"Beneath its skin, my lance has scales, I believe," he said, "which other men's do not, and the appendage itself, especially in this erect state, resembles a dragon tail, you may have noticed."

McKenna ran her stroking gaze up its length.

"Touch me," he rasped.

"Come," she said, "sit beside me."

At her invitation, he placed a knee on the bed, expecting her to change her mind. Expecting and dreading.

McKenna lay back, her clothes in disarray, blouse open, mostly covering her, except for the peach silk excellence of her skin and the inviting red bra beneath her blouse.

When she reached for him but hesitated, he caught his breath, his heart pounding from his chest, echoing in his head, making him dizzy.

Finally, she closed her hand around him, and he hissed and bucked while she tested his lance, moved it, played it, a torment of the most exquisite nature.

He rode the high and tried to control himself, despite an eternity of celibacy, but he needed a distraction and she needed to say something. "I believe this could be pleasurable for us both, in its current adaptation," he said. Foolish statement.

"Yes. Sorry. I'm . . . speechless."

"A rare occurrence."

"If the women who follow you *knew* what you kept beneath your zipper," she said, "*you* could die of pleasure."

"Will you be telling them?"

"I think not."

She liked it? Odd way of showing it. "I could only die of pleasure if you were the woman slaying me," he admitted.

"Bastian?"

"Yes?"

"Your penis has curled itself around my hand."

"It has been pining for you, and now I guess it is greedy for your attention."

"I guess it *is* freaking prehensile."

"I told you in the lake. Did you not listen?" Bastian removed himself from her hand with difficulty and sat a distance away. "I apologize," he said as he began to zip his lance back into his jeans, except that there was not as much room in them now.

He settled for pulling a corner of the blanket over himself.

"No, no, no." She tugged it away to reveal the flaw trying to make its way back to her. "You know, you might be the only man alive who *does* have a brain beneath your zipper."

"It's never been so out of control."

"Bastian, you're embarrassed."

"What was your first clue?"

"You're getting good at snark."

"Snark, yes, *that* is my great concern at this moment."

FORTY-SEVEN

McKenna's amusement eased the anxiety binding his chest tight.

"Bastian, I'm fascinated by it, not repelled, and I'm not blacking out anymore. It's amazing, actually, something every woman would want if she knew it existed. You'd be a gazillionnaire if you made one of plastic and added batteries."

He stopped trying to keep the hungry thing in check and looked down at himself in some surprise. "This is good, then?"

"It's extraordinary, and it's mine. Well, yours," she countered, "but you're willing to share, which I appreciate, and we get to play with it together, right? How does it work?"

"You tell me."

He caught her arousal as she leaned kissing-close to it, a woman made of earth and stars, an elemental goddess without pretense. "Does this puppy have—I mean, are these really *scales* beneath the skin? Whatever they are, they seem flexible, and . . . Oh, I like this—they fan back and forth, or up and down, depending on your perspective, or where your lance might be, like inside me. That must feel nice."

Her whole body shivered, from anticipation, he hoped, since he felt like a volcano near to erupting.

She closed her hand around him, firm finally, no hesitation, her only goal pleasure, sending white-hot lightning through him, the good kind, fast pumping his heart.

Her brows arched as her interest piqued. With her top buttons open, her blouse off one shoulder, he imagined her nipples, ruddy, hard, and ready for his touch, or his lips. He had suckled her in the lake, but this first real time for them was different. Planned. Desired.

Mutual desire. Finally. A near thing.

He cupped her head, pulled her toward him, and as they kissed, fell together to the bed, their hands seeking, hers and his. Mouths, too. In quest of pleasure, silk skin, new territory, uncharted, every inch.

Her lips tasted better than honey. Sweeter, more inspiring, addicting. A driving obsession overtook him, as surely as his inner dragon woke. He wanted to kiss her more deeply, know her more intimately.

She slipped a leg between them, against his need, and his lance jumped to attention, drawing a moan from his lips. She raised her hips in invitation and spoke his name.

His hands trembling with lust and love, he began unbuttoning her clothes and caught his breath. The red bra, he remembered from that first day. Her top came off over her head. He pointed to the center of the bra between her breasts and it fell open.

Her head came up.

"Magick." He wiggled his brows.

"So you could have done that anytime?"

"Anytime you were ready." The matching panties might have put him over the edge, if she hadn't pulled them down and away so fast.

He explored her skin, every surface. Luscious curves. Sweet hidden places. Layers and layers of secrets to explore.

She slipped beneath him, or he rose over her, difficult to say, but before he made the next move, she stopped him.

Alphas, he told himself, did not cry.

"I bought these for us," she said, reaching into her nightstand. "Yes, I have had the hots for you for some time. Get over it. Gloating is not permitted."

Her words made no sense. "What is this you are holding?" He took the box from her hand to examine the contents. "Candy?"

"Better than candy."

"Are you are as eager for this mating as I am?" he asked. "Say yes."

"Jiminy, I didn't have to confess my lust, did I?"

"Confession is good for the soul. I read that somewhere. I like that you are breathless. It feeds my hunger for you."

She took a packet from the box and tore it open. "Berries," he said at the scent, as he examined the contents. "What is it?"

"You took sex lessons at Vivica's, yet you learned nothing about birth control or protecting your partner?"

"I fast-forwarded to the good part. Did I miss something?"

"I'll say. We slip this on over your dragon lance."

"Are you sure we need this?"

"Just like a man."

"A man who is shrinking as you speak."

"Listen, buddy, I don't want to wake up one morning to discover that I'm about to lay a dragon's egg, all right?"

"I am human, again, I tell you, but go ahead, put it on me."

She tried. "I should have bought python supremes." She attempted to slide it on him, a pleasure all its own, he discovered, but the sheath stretched only halfway. "I suppose it'll cover you where it counts," McKenna said.

He looked down at himself. "Looks fine to me. Are we done playing now?"

"Oh, baby," she said, wrapping her legs around him. "We've just begun."

His lance rose to the occasion.

She taught him new variations on foreplay.

He taught her staying power. And together they learned that a dragon-tail penis could handle foreplay on its own. His arrowed tip worked her clit until she wept and cried out and begged him to come inside her. He granted her wish and together they sought heaven.

"Bastian!" she shouted as he filled her.

"Scales," she purred.

"Magick," she gasped as she approached one of many orgasmic peaks.

He felt each orgasm, as if it were his own, which made him pump more energetically, his love for McKenna growing by the beat. Again, they sparked their own stars, pale blue and fluorescent dancing in the air around them. Manifestations of sex and satisfaction. Love.

She raised her hips, grew taut, milked him from the inside, once again, pulling him deeper and deeper inside her. And when she called his name loud enough to wake her ancestors, he was lost, and Bastian followed her to that place beyond suns.

They collapsed together, trying to catch their breaths.

"I never," McKenna said, "*never* imagined."

After a short nap, she rode the dragon, to quote her, then he rode her, and they switched, again, with the same delightful outcome, though the force of each orgasm grew bolder, brighter, and more life affirming.

"Impossible," she said, catching her breath. "Men can't have multiple orgasms."

"This man can," he said. "I feel what you feel. You hurt, I hurt."

"I come, you come?"

He grinned, reached into the nightstand, pulled out that box, and turned it upside down. "Oh, no!"

McKenna could barely raise her head. "What?"

"We are out of condoms."

"I didn't expect you to be so greedy."

"It's been centuries, woman. We have to buy more. Are the stores open now?"

"No. They're not. But tomorrow, we'll buy a pack of super giant deluxe."

"Good, because I kept overflowing these."

"You what!"

FORTY-EIGHT

When the cock crowed, the one in the yard, McKenna
snuggled up to the one who'd made her come all night,
and she was sore, everywhere, especially between her legs,
where his big, giant dragon pecker had been.

Not a dragon. A man. He said he had blood tests to prove
it. Human. His penis was an anomaly. A defect. He would
take her to the doctor who told him so, if she wanted.

Hell yes, she wanted. He'd overflowed a dozen damned
condoms and didn't say so until they'd used the whole
blasted box.

Oh, hell, if she didn't get dressed before he woke up,
he'd actually see her fully naked in daylight, not just bits
here and there, and the jig would be up.

She'd barely turned on the shower when she heard a familiar growl. "Good morning, Kenna."

"I guess that wasn't a one-night stand, then," she said,
trying to cover herself with the shower curtain, but Bastian
pulled it from her hands and stepped in to join her.

"I tasted every inch of you. I love every inch. Let me see you."

"Why would you want to?"

"I worship you, McKenna Greylock, not only your heart, but your amazing body. You inspire my dragon lance to rise, yes, but your body is the grail that holds your heart."

She went limp against him. "Do you really think that skinny girls need feeding?"

"They're a disgrace to earth."

This man could make her laugh at her own insecurities.

"Besides, you like my flaw. You enjoy it, too. Want to give it a morning jog?"

She winced. "I'm sore. Aren't you?"

He tipped his head. "Tender, maybe." He cupped her between her legs and she stiffened.

"Kenna, I'm healing you."

"You're like mister freaking perfect, aren't you, except for being directionally challenged."

"Perfect? Except for my flaw and the dragon inside me roaring to be free. I cannot let it out, you understand, under penalty of death, and not necessarily my own."

"But your death as a dragon is a possibility?" She stopped lathering his chest. "You really could turn back?"

"I will not let it happen. Too much depends on my being strong. If I succeed in my quest, Andra gets her magick back, and my brother dragons will be transformed and come here, one at a time. I hope you do not mind."

She shrugged. If they were coming to him here, that meant he was staying. "Where else but to the Dragon's Lair would they come?"

"Good point."

"Cedrig will probably be transformed next. Or Jaydun. They are both strong. If all goes well, you will meet them."

"What would happen to *you*, if you turned back into a dragon?"

"On this plane, I would not survive. But that is not what worries me."

"It worries me," she said.

He kissed her nose. "Thank you. As for transforming, I worry more about my brothers."

"You mentioned a quest. Can I help?"

"I love your heart." He gave her breasts a one-handed wash. "My quest is to make your quest my own."

"I don't see how that'll help your brothers."

"It's all part of some master plan. Fate. Destiny. Kismet. I was expected here. You saw Ciarra's cave drawings."

"You've graduated to the *Oxford English Dictionary*, haven't you? Kismet, indeed." She gave him a quick kiss. "I feel better now, down there, but don't stop."

She heard his inner chuckle and wondered, if she listened closely, could she hear the roar of his inner beast?

As they dried each other off, she threw a towel around his shoulders and rubbed her nose against the mat of hair on his chest.

"Itchy nose means you're coming into money," he said, his lips against her brow.

She stretched like a cat with one purpose in mind, to harden his lance, and she proudly accomplished her goal in record time.

"That towel keeps my back warm. Come closer and warm my . . . front."

FORTY-NINE

A week later, after Vivica blessed both houses, charging them with health and prosperity, love and bright blessings, they started moving Steve, Lizzie, and the kids into the addition. McKenna appreciated the distraction, because she had the raging hots for Bastian—and he for her—and if it wasn't for the Framingham family, they'd never get any work done in the house.

She should be running, McKenna supposed, from the emotional dartboard she'd made of her heart, which she put out there for dragon target practice, but she liked having Bastian in her life. She liked it so much, she couldn't stop grinning, which Lizzie noticed, especially when McKenna bought that pack of python supremes at the drugstore.

"Dish," Lizzie said, unable to hide her grin, and well, it was really hard not to brag about an especially gifted lover, but McKenna wasn't the type to kiss and tell.

"I'll take whatever it is Bastian and I have, for however

long we have it," she said. "And damn the consequences for once in my life."

"Good. I'm happy for you."

"I'm happy for me, too."

"I know Bastian is . . . unusual," Lizzie admitted, "but the kids love him, and Steve can wiggle his toes without pain, which his doctors said would never happen. He sincerely believes that Bastian is healing him."

"Bastian *is* a healer, Lizzie. He's different, yes. But he's a good man." McKenna pulled her truck into her driveway. Whose car is that?"

"I don't recognize it, but it has kid seats in the back."

"Don't lift the grocery bags, Lizzie. I'll send Bastian out."

"Thanks."

The pregnant woman on her porch looked familiar but McKenna couldn't place her. "Hi," the woman said. "My name is Melody Seabright—"

"The Kitchen Witch!" Lizzie gasped. "I watch your cooking show all the time. I'm Lizzie Framingham, and this is McKenna Greylock. She owns the Dragon's Lair."

"Won't you come in?" McKenna asked.

They went inside, which really made McKenna wish her kitchen didn't look so faded seventies.

"Let me come to the point," Melody Seabright said. "I'm in a bind. I've lost my Halloween location and I saw your ad. I love the paint job outside. Talk about gorgeous. I love your hook: the Dragon's Lair. You're a local business, and I try to feature locals whenever I can. I'd like to shoot my Halloween Kitchen Witch cooking show from here. It'd be free publicity?"

"But my kitchen sucks," McKenna said. "Seriously, I'm embarrassed to have you see it."

"That's not as much of a problem as you think. We have a location budget for cabinet fronts, countertops, standard, but you choose colors. I'll throw in wallpaper or paint. Your choice. It's a bit more than usual but we go international on Halloween."

"Are you kidding me? Free publicity and a new kitchen?"

"That's the *location* budget. Do you do the cooking yourself?"

"Uh, no," Lizzie said, raising a finger. "That would be me."

"Then I'd like you both to be on my Halloween show, if you're interested. Lizzie, we'll pay you. McKenna, care to take your pay in new appliances? Standard white?"

"As much as I'd like to," McKenna said. "I could use the pay with setting up the business. Is that ungrateful of me? I feel like a jerk taking money *and* free publicity, but if I have a choice . . ."

"No, you'll both get the stipend. Lizzie, do you have any special Dragon's Lair meals that you plan to serve your guests?"

"Yes, I make a great dragon stew."

Melody raised a brow. "How do you make a dragon stew?"

"You make him wait," McKenna said.

FIFTY

Melody Seabright chuckled. "A dragon joke and a recipe? Say yes. Because if you have the recipe, we're using both on the show."

"I do have a recipe," Lizzie said, "of my own creation. It's a stew of beef and pork, with New England fall and winter vegetables, tomatoes are key, and thirteen secret herbs and spices that we grow right here. I call it dragon stew because it makes a roaring good meal."

"Perfect. Any signature desserts?"

Bastian came into the room, a frazzled plumber looking like he'd had another run-in with an electrical panel. She introduced him to Melody.

"Someone is driving into the yard," Bastian said. "I saw the car from upstairs, parked out front, and a man taking pictures of your house, Kenna."

McKenna looked beyond the kitchen porch. "Huntley, damn it." She locked the screen door and waited on the kitchen side. "Melody. I'm sorry," she barely had time to say before the dirtbag appeared on her porch.

"You don't have any business here," McKenna said when they stood face-to-face with the screen between them.

"A nice paint job doesn't mean you have the house up to code or the money to pay your back taxes, McKenna. I'll give you two hundred and fifty thousand dollars for the place, *today*. That's my final offer. If you wait two weeks, it's mine."

She shook her head. "Huntley, I know that you *don't* play poker with the building inspector. But I do believe that you're as dishonest as you imply. My land will never be yours. Never. I intend to pay everything on time." She shut both doors and turned to her guest. "Melody, I'm sorry you had to witness that," McKenna said. "He's trying to force my hand."

"That *was* a bit of a drive-by," Melody said.

Huntley knocked and called her name. "I have a better idea," he shouted. "If you don't open the door, I'll shout it so the world can hear."

"Feel free to shout your head off."

"Marry me," Huntley shouted through the door.

McKenna whipped it open. "Shut up!"

Huntley grinned, the picture of innocence. "You know we had fun together when we dated."

"Two damned dates because you wanted my land. You're proposing for the same reason."

"No, I want to marry you because you're . . . you're—"

"Beautiful. She's beautiful," Bastian snapped, coming up behind her, "and she has a heart to match." He moved her to the side and slammed the door in Huntley's face. Then he rounded on her. "You dated that blackheart? How could you?"

"I didn't see his evil until the second date, so shoot me. I poured a mojito over his head and walked."

"I still can't believe you dated him. I thought you had better judgment than that."

Bastian was angry enough for her to see the beginnings of claws and wings. "Look at me," she said, cupping his face so his inner beast would calm. "I *was* stupid," she admitted, "but not for long."

His beast receded.

Melody cleared her throat. "I know I'm an outsider, but give a girl a break. We've all dated our share of frogs. Didn't you, Bastian? Be honest."

Bastian crossed his arms. "Dragons do not consort with frogs."

"Dragons?" Melody asked.

Steve had rolled in during the embarrassing scene. "Bastian painted the rooms with the dragon scenes," Steve said, "so McKenna made him her resident dragon, for the guests, you understand. Lizzie's making him a scaled cloak."

"A red one," Bastian said, relaxing.

Thank goodness he was calming, McKenna thought. "We'll bring the dragon out for certain celebrations," McKenna said, "like for Christmas and the Summer Solstice, to keep the spirits of both my parents happy, the Catholic and the Celtic."

"I plan original menus for each," Lizzie said. "Maybe you'd like to come, Melody? Bring your husband? I mean as a guest, not to tape a show."

"Do come," McKenna said.

"The Christmas event sounds fun, but I'd love to shoot a program around your Summer Solstice celebration. It's something I've never done, but this *is* Salem."

"Great," Lizzie said.

Yes, great, McKenna thought, *if* she kept the place long enough to celebrate anything. Talk about a save. Lizzie and Steve carried it so far, they came up with two more events to bring in guests and locals.

Bastian had calmed, but to be fair, he didn't understand how dating worked here. She'd explain later. "Again, Melody, I'm sorry you had to witness that scene with Huntley. He's been browbeating me on a regular basis, but a marriage proposal? That was desperation. At least you understand now why I need to get paid more than I need new appliances, though I'd rather it not be commonly known."

"When do you get your first paying guests?"

"On October twenty-sixth, the day after my possible foreclosure, but it's a family reunion, so I'll have a full house. A couple of days from now, the deposit will be mine, because it'll be past the cancellation date. If the slop hits the fan, however, and I do lose the place, I *can* pay their deposits back with the money I've been hoarding for the mortgage and taxes."

"Maybe if you go to the bank, they'll accept the *promise* of your guests' full week's stay when you give them the deposit," Steve said.

"Will my paychecks help, McKenna?" Bastian asked. "I never cashed any. Take the money for taxes."

"That's a generous offer, Bastian. Thank you, but you should keep the money."

"No, I want it to be my investment in the Dragon's Lair."

"Your investment already exceeds any paychecks I might be able to afford."

"Melody, make out the check for my stipend from *The Kitchen Witch* show to McKenna," Lizzie said.

"No," McKenna snapped, putting her foot down. "You need that money for the babies."

"I needed a roof over my babies' heads. You gave us one."

"Listen to Lizzie," Steve agreed. "You know she's always right."

McKenna's eyes filled as she looked down at her blurry

cat for a minute. She picked up Jaunty, her heart overflowing with her friends' generosity. "I feel like such a loser."

"Because your friends care so much about you?" Melody asked. "You should be celebrating your good fortune. McKenna, I spent a lot of time *not* taking money from my father. I know what a waste of time it is. Stubborn isn't necessarily the right way to go, and, Lizzie, did you say babies, plural?"

"T-twins," Lizzie said. "You?"

"Twins. Our fifth, a surprise—well, a shock—turned into our fifth and sixth. Logan has been a zombie since we found out. My doctor says that we *mature* moms release more than one egg at a time."

"We sure do," Lizzie said with a sigh.

"I'll end up with an even number of boys and girls. What about you?"

"Yep," Lizzie said. "That's what we should have, too."

"Lucky us," Melody said, a bit distracted by the keeping room fireplace. "Possible new shoot plan." She walked over to the keeping room hearth and sat in one of the rockers in front of it. "Lizzie, can you cook your stew on the hearth, here?"

"Absolutely. It'll taste better."

"It'd give us more vintage nostalgia and all we'll need are Halloween decorations. This hearth definitely says dragon's lair, doesn't it? We can set up a plank table beside it as a work space for the shoot."

"We have one of those," McKenna said, thinking of the one in Ciarra's cave, which seemed only fitting to use, since she started all this. "It belonged to one of my ancestors."

"Yes!" Melody said. "Then we'll chat about your ancestor during the show. This way, McKenna, I'll give you the location budget with your stipend."

"Melody Seabright, something tells me that you're bending over backward here after Huntley's maniacal visit."

Melody rubbed her baby belly. "Something tells me, McKenna Greylock, that I couldn't bend over backward if my life depended on it right now." She'd eased the tension, snap, like that.

"Lizzie, what else can you cook on the hearth here?"

"Yankee cornbread to go with the stew, and the Dragon's Lair special apple upside-down pumpkin cake, fresh from our apple orchard and pumpkin patch."

"Melody," McKenna said, sliding her arm through Melody's. "Would you care for a tour of the Lair?"

"After the pictures I saw on the 'Net? Absolutely. Where's that purple dragon?"

"Iverus. Right this way."

FIFTY-ONE

McKenna and Bastian occupied the parlor sofa, him with his head in her lap.

"I can't believe that a television crew is coming to shoot an episode of *The Kitchen Witch* from my bed-and-breakfast," McKenna said. "Talk about a gift from the universe."

"I cannot believe that plumbing is such a pain in the dragon rump."

"Have Whitney and Wyatt been helping you?"

"As much as Jock and Dewcup do. Where is Jaunty?"

"I think she's hiding from Dewcup."

"Is Lizzie feeling all right? Steve has been getting nervous."

"Lizzie is tired of carrying those babies around, which won't last much longer."

"Speaking of things not lasting," he said, raising his head. "Did you buy what we needed?"

"Impatient dragon. Yes, we have condoms. Take me to bed?"

"You do not have to ask twice."

McKenna stood beside her bed as Bastian knelt to remove each shoe as if they were Cinderella's, instead of serviceable farm boots. Then he watched her as he slid his hands up her legs, before his head disappeared beneath her dress.

McKenna squeaked and pulled the dress up, holding it so she could see him, her face growing warmer than his fiery breath as he kissed her and pleasured her there with his mouth.

He looked up, violet eyes dancing, his mane of sooty hair endearingly messy, and she'd swear that her heart pounded from her chest and lay at his feet.

She'd be foolish to give him her heart. Yet, every day, there went another piece of it, and wasn't Bastian the one to catch it?

She'd take him any way she could have him. Yes, something was missing, the love she'd never dare share with him, and not having it made her sad, like falling a long distance and enjoying the thrill, though you know you'll hit bottom, eventually, but you don't care.

Despite that, her gratification swelled, as only Bastian could expand it.

He kissed her through her practical cotton panties, rushing warmth to pool there, and he rested his cheek in that very spot, before he turned his head and opened his mouth against her, whispering her name like a prayer, his hot breath permeating the fabric against the wet lips of her sex.

McKenna caught her breath, closed her eyes, and wove her fingers through his long, thick hair.

Sliding his palms up beneath her panties, he cupped her

bottom, skin to skin, and splayed his hands to stroke and tease her with his thumbs, near her center, but not near enough, which didn't keep pleasure from rising—sweet, subtle, slow—a pure and elemental ascension, in harmony with the thrum of her heating blood.

With a shuddering sigh McKenna gasped her pleasure and rode the wave he created until the hungry dragon rose up to face her, looking like the vengeful angel she imagined on the day of his arrival, wings poised to embrace her, as he took her mouth once more.

He swallowed her sighs of satisfaction, drew more, until he was so much a part of her, heart and soul, she might bleed if he moved away.

While her knees threatened to buckle under her, he opened her bodice, adoring the tender skin there with his magick touch, freed her arms from her sleeves, and slid her dress down her body, the palms of his hands skimming, arousing, until her dress pooled at her feet.

Nuzzling her neck, he took her hand to help her step over the dress to face him—her lover. Yes, *she* had a lover.

Wearing only her bra and panties, McKenna wished they were lace or silk, or even new, and not Rubenesque, yet Bastian regarded her with a dark fire hunger that seared her to the deepest recesses of her soul.

He stepped back to regard her like a connoisseur and she waited for disappointment, for the light in his eyes to dim, but they got brighter.

She shook her head. "Damn it, Bastian, are your eyes as bad as your hearing is good?"

"Kenna, I saw the spirits in the night. Jock lit them for *you*, not me. My vision is better than most magickal creatures."

"Then what's this? Don't you see what I see when you look at me?"

"The question is, when you see yourself, why do you *not* see the beauty I do? Wait here. I have something for you."

She sat on the bed as he left, and she wondered if he'd ever be back.

If he did return, she'd soon stand naked, no shower spray to blur the view, before the man she lo—liked a whole lot. To her surprise, he did come back, and he handed her a sketch.

"It's Ciarra," she whispered. "Bastian, the sketch beautiful. She's beautiful."

"As Ciarra is beautiful, you said, and I agree. One of the most beautiful women you have ever seen."

"She's stunning." McKenna couldn't get over her ancestor's beauty.

"Here," he said. "Another."

"This one's good, too. There's something different about it, though." McKenna compared the two. "Her eyebrows, maybe. No, not the brows. Bastian, you gave her green eyes in the first sketch and blue in the second. Ciarra's eyes are blue."

"No," he said. "The most beautiful woman I know has green eyes."

"No, I remember they're—"

"You see it now, do you not, the uncanny resemblance between you? You look more like Ciarra than any of her descendents, more even than her granddaughters. You, my Kenna, are beautiful, by your own admission. No arguing. I will not hear another word to the contrary."

"Bastian—"

He crossed her lips with a finger. "I am a big clumsy oaf, and you are a stunner with a heart to match."

FIFTY-TWO

"Real women, Kenna," Bastian tried to make her understand, "wholesome, healthy, lusciously sexy women, do not look like Creamsicle sticks, nor would they taste as sweet, because the lush has been sucked out of them. They are dry, bony caricatures of women. They suffer daily. They starve. Did you see that program where the girl wanted to be sick to lose weight? She ate a skinny pill when she felt faint? That is life? I do not think so."

His Kenna sighed, and he liked the way it raised her breasts. "I suppose," she whispered.

"Now maybe you will see what I do when I look at you. A beautiful woman with a heart to match."

McKenna cupped his neck beneath his hair. "And to think that Vivica just happened to send you to apply for my handyman job."

Hardly, but he would not tell Kenna that yet. She needed to believe that he loved her first.

He worshipped her boldly with his hands. "You have

a heart that speaks to mine and a shape I find desirable. It lifts and strengthens my lance in a way that makes me heavy with wanting."

He used his magick to unhook her bra. He liked that she leaned her back against his front as he plumped her breasts like pillows, pebbling her nipples and whispering his adoration, using his breath and kisses to warm her neck, ears, and shoulders.

Bastian turned her and lifted her, with one arm, to suckle a breast. With his other hand, he reacquainted himself with the heat of her beneath her panties. Soon, they, too, were gone.

She released his dragon lance, circled him, to keep him tense and guessing, then she grabbed that part of him, so it stroked her hand. Thick and supple, it pulsed against her, and she petted it, to smooth the scales one way, then the next, up and back, and Bastian nearly lost his ability to wait for her.

She seemed intent on tormenting him as she knelt on the floor and cupped his man sacs, surprising him and making him shout.

Wielding and celebrating her power, she made him throw back his head and roar. And she made him beg and buck and plead for her to stop, then more, and faster, and, "No more!" He caught her hands. "I have an idea." He took the gown she called a caftan and slipped it on her over her head.

"See," she said. "You want to cover me up."

He laughed as he worked to zip his lance back into its confinement, but his jeans had shrunk and it wasn't easy. "Time for an adventure, my Kenna."

"Now?" she wailed.

He chuckled as he dropped condoms from the box, slipped a handful in his pocket, then picked her up and carried her out the kitchen door.

"Where are we going?"

"For a ride on Toffee."

"With condoms?"

He grinned and set her down to take the horse from its stall.

"Wait," she said. "Toffee needs a saddle blanket and we need that bareback pad I got, so we don't get horsehair and horse sweat all over us."

"Smart girl," Bastian said as he fastened it and mounted, stroking Toffee first, then the suede bareback pad, before he brought McKenna up to face him. With a word from Bastian, Toffee trotted dutifully away from the barn. "Now, McKenna. Unzip my jeans."

"What?" She looked back at her horse. "Toffee girl, you just look straight ahead, don't mind us, and hum so you don't hear anything."

That said, McKenna unzipped him and accepted the condom he handed her.

She slipped the largest-size condom she could find over him, making him hiss and rise to her expectations.

"This is still a bit short, but long enough for the over-flow," she said, "though that's *another* horse that's left the barn."

"This is not the time for jokes, McKenna."

"Yes, sir. Sorry, sir."

"Snark," he said as he lifted her caftan enough to slip inside her, an experience that stole her breath as his lips met hers and breathing seemed unnecessary. A forever kiss, their bodies melding. Two puzzles, all their parts moving deliciously and perfectly in sync, the more so once he got Toffee moving a bit faster. "This wouldn't work if you weren't so long," she said against his lips.

"Thank you, Kenna."

"And the average bareback rider wouldn't be able to do this."

"Granted," he said. "I am above average."

"In more ways than one," she said, turning her mind to passion.

Their movement might hurt the horse, so they let Toffee's movements cause a ripple effect that escalated their union, their hands clasped, lips touching, his dragon lance working an effortless magick.

Wild pleasure Bastian found when loving one's heart mate bareback, until he realized that his inner dragon woke, so he sat a bit back, cupped Kenna's face, and watched pleasure wash over her.

"You're fighting your inner dragon," she said. "Watch me and let pleasure replace your struggle."

With their gazes locked, a soft word got the horse to trotting faster, the spade of Bastian's man lance, with a mind of its own, working that tender place on Kenna that made her rise and weep and beg and gasp. Then his thickness entered and stretched her, his movable scales exciting them both, shooting them nearly beyond a plane of endurance.

Kenna's pleasure, like her pain, belonged to him.

He whooped as he watched her come, while he came, too, and his inner beast lost the fight.

"Knowing you feel my pleasure enhances mine," she said breathlessly. "I can't believe we're making love on Toffee's back. She used to be such an innocent."

"So were you. So were we both." Bastian chuckled against Kenna's lips. "You finally admitted to 'making *love*,' my Kenna. Believe it."

Her eyes widened, and Toffee's sudden change of direction along the shore made Bastian surge inside her, so they unexpectedly rushed the stars, the ones in the sky—not the blue fluorescents frolicking about them—and they cried out together.

"Come again, Kenna, to the farthest plane, if only for a minute, where we can shine like suns and burn ourselves out. I'll wait. Come." Bringing her closer, deepening his penetration, he lowered her gown from her shoulders and suckled her, gratification bursting through him.

When she came, he did, too.

When she gasped, he hissed.

When she shouted, he shouted with her.

They climaxed together, calling each other's names, touched the island of stars and rode the scarlet sun.

He made Toffee go faster and faster, and the farther they rode, the more orgasmic his heart mate became. Multiple multiples, she experienced. Him, too.

"I am near to passing out," he said, finally, as he headed Toffee back toward the barn. "No man could be happier or more sated."

Kenna sighed and fell against him, and it was all he could do, after they returned to the barn, to lift her off the horse, groom Toffee, get the horse some oats, and walk Kenna inside.

In the house, he fell to the bed. "Men do not usually have multiple orgasms," he said against his pillow. "And now I know why."

McKenna giggled as Bastian began to make demented dragon noises, his snore like none she'd ever heard, and she took her first opportunity to examine his dragon lance at her leisure, with the soft light of dawn beaming through the window. She could see how much it looked like a dragon's tail, but she didn't care. It belonged to Bastian, the man who loved her body.

Who, apparently, and for no good reason, loved *her*.

Bastian's lance grew and woke the beast himself, the one on the outside. Another condom it was, but he took her slower now, with more purpose, looking godlike and imperfectly perfect.

He slept again soon after, his dragon noises a bit less demented.

McKenna sighed in contentment and snuggled deeper against his side, until she spotted a condom floating through the air, tumbling across her room, all pokes, grunts, and curses. "If you do not get me out of here, your tongue should grow warts and your bottom grow spines too painful to sit upon!"

"Bastian," McKenna said, shaking him. "Dewcup has been swallowed by a condom."

FIFTY-THREE

❧

Stark naked, Bastian chased a flying condom across the room, his sleeping lance and hefty dragon balls flying in the breeze as he leapt over her mother's hope chest, around the bed, over it, and back, while McKenna slunk deeper down into the bedding, pulling the blankets over her, so he wouldn't see her shoulders shaking or the grin on her face.

"Stop flapping your wings this minute!" he ordered the cursing faery, but if anything, Dewcup flapped harder.

"May you sprain your lance and need a splint," the faery shouted as the condom dipped and swayed, hit the door, a lamp, and knocked a picture off the wall.

Oh, man, where was a camcorder when you needed it? Would this get hits on YouTube or what?

A knock on the door startled them both, and it must have startled Dewcup, too, because the flying condom dropped to the bed.

As fast as Bastian put on his pants, McKenna slipped the

condom-trapped faery beneath the covers. She only hoped that whoever stood on the opposite side of the door couldn't hear Dewcup cursing them to life in a stink swamp.

"It's Lizzie," Steve said when Bastian opened the door. "She's having the babies."

"I'll call nine-one-one," McKenna said, reaching for the phone on her nightstand.

"Too late; she's on the floor in the living room delivering them herself. When I heard her in labor, thanks to your upper body workouts, Bastian, I was able to fall out of that bed and into this chair by myself. Get dressed," Steve said, as he rolled his chair away. "Hurry."

"We're coming," McKenna called. "Bastian, go with him. I'll be right there."

She called nine-one-one in case the babies needed help, got dressed, and went out to find Esther, the spirit who'd been a midwife.

When she got to Lizzie, Steve held one of the babies, his face ashen.

Bastian stood by Lizzie's head and his face matched Steve's, though his eyes were wide, his pupils dilated, as if he faced a loaded gun. "Having babies hurts, Kenna."

"So I've heard."

"But look," he added. "A new kidlet. A girl."

"And here comes another," Lizzie said.

McKenna caught the second baby, a boy, and wrapped him in the receiving blanket Lizzie had waiting. "You planned to do this yourself all along, didn't you, because you don't have health insurance?"

"Ya think?"

"I think this isn't the right time to give you hell."

"I appreciate that."

Esther gave instructions for cutting the second baby's cord, which Bastian followed to the letter. "McKenna," he said. "Lizzie really hurts."

McKenna wondered if he was suffering at the thought, as if . . . as if he might actually stick around long enough for them to have children. Speaking of which, "Where are Wyatt and Whitney?" she asked as she sat beside Lizzie on the floor so Lizzie could see her new son.

"Nothing wakes those kids," Steve said, wiping his new daughter's face with a towel. "Thank God."

Not that Lizzie was screaming. Right now McKenna found her eerily quiet and determined.

"Kenna," Bastian said, "give Lizzie a Midol for her belly pain."

Lizzie fell back and laughed. "Don't do that. I'm concentrating."

"Why are you concentrating?" McKenna asked. "You already have both babies."

"Wait," Lizzie said.

Disquiet filled McKenna as she got up and handed Steve his new son, returned to Lizzie, and sure enough, she delivered a second baby girl, which McKenna caught and wrapped. "You *do* have them fast."

"And easy. I'm a freaking baby factory. Do I hear sirens?" Lizzie pulled herself up on her elbows.

"I called them for the babies," McKenna said. "This way you'll all get checked out and since you look fine, I'm guessing you won't have to stay at the hospital for long."

Lizzie lay back and released her breath. "Thank you, for the sake of the babies. I planned to bring them to Dr. Carver tomorrow. He lets us pay on the installment plan. I would have let Steve call if it wasn't going as fast as it always does."

"I should beat you," Steve said. "For not telling me what you planned. How long have you known we were having triplets?"

"I found out after you got hurt. Our fifth was hiding behind her sister. I didn't want to add to your burden. You wouldn't have wanted a home delivery, especially with three. I knew that, but I did plenty of studying, and see . . ." She held up her cell phone. "In case I was in trouble. But babies fall out of me. You know that. We barely made it to the hospital the other times. You can be mad, but I'm pretty sure you won't beat me since I just gave you three beautiful babies."

"As long as you're all fine," Steve said. "Geez McGee, Lizzie, we have three! We don't have enough cribs!"

McKenna squeezed his shoulder. "They'll all fit in one for a while."

"Oh, right."

The paramedics took Lizzie and the babies to the hospital to get checked out. McKenna and Steve followed the ambulance in her truck, while Bastian stayed to take care of Wyatt and Whitney.

After an hour, McKenna left the babies for overnight monitoring in the nursery, while Lizzie and Steve stayed in a family room so Lizzie could nurse as needed. If all went well, they'd call her in the morning to bring them all home.

When McKenna got home, the house was still dark and she felt nervous as she called Bastian's name.

"In my room," he said.

Right away, she knew that he was leaving. The delivery had scared him into it, and she couldn't blame him.

"Look what I found," he said, no travel bag in sight.

Her cat, Jaunty, lay curled in the center of Bastian's bed, but not alone. "The snack gave birth to six niblets. This is happening all over the place tonight."

McKenna released a breath. "I told you, she's a cat, not a snack."

"That was a joke, McKenna. I know they're not niblets; they're kittens."

"Oh. Right." She touched his arm. "Bastian, are you okay?"

"I will be honest with you," he said.

Ah, she thought, here it comes.

"I do not like that our babies will hurt you."

"They'll hurt you, too." Listen to her talking as if it *could* happen.

"Pain is nothing to me," Bastian boasted.

McKenna swallowed her chuckle. "Did the children wake up?"

"I just looked in on them. They're sleeping like angels."

The next morning, the Framinghams, all five, were ready to come home. Lizzie's longtime doctor would check in daily. The babies all weighed in at around five and a half pounds, not bad for triplets.

McKenna and Bastian lent a hand whenever they could.

"Are newborn kidlets as breakable as they look?" he asked as they bathed them on their third day of life.

"Yes, and no," she said. "They look like Lizzie, don't they?"

"No, they look like Steve."

"Let's face it, they look like both their parents."

Both, McKenna thought, which was probably why it touched her so deeply when she placed the babies on the bed beside Lizzie, the way Steve looked at the four of them, and the way Lizzie looked back at him.

Bastian closed his hand around hers and squeezed.

Now, this was magick . . .

Unless she lost the fight for her home and put them all out on the street.

FIFTY-FOUR

Bastian sat in the rocker in the kitchen by the big hearth with two kittens in his lap. "Babies everywhere," he said.

McKenna nodded. "The human ones set Steve back a few weeks. Lizzie is weaker than we expected after three. How are you managing with the plumbing on your own?"

"You have a lot of bathrooms."

"I know. My grandmother was already thinking bed-and-breakfast when she had so many of them put in. That was before she got sick. Bastian, you've done a great job, moving all the furniture into the bedrooms by yourself. We used almost all the furniture I had. Those new mattresses set me back a bundle. Not that I didn't expect it. I'm just glad that we decided to be a romantic inn with no televisions in the bedrooms."

Jaunty dropped a third kitten in his lap.

"That cat thinks you're the niblets' daddy."

Bastian raised a brow as he petted the mewling things.

But all he could think about was how McKenna and Steve and Lizzie struggled because a blackheart like Elliott Huntley wanted the land this beautiful home sat on. "I need to go and investigate Huntley."

"Where? How?"

"Can I tell you when I get back?" Bastian got up and handed her the kittens, kissed her longer than he planned, pulled back, looked into her eyes, and kissed her again. "This is bad that I want to stay and never go."

"Is it?"

"No and yes. We cannot spend every minute in bed. Life is for more than sex. We have to do all those things you said you would do with a heart mate. Take care of the B and B, have children, run the farm, defeat Huntley, get our groove on—that means to dance, I think."

"You've been taking vocab lessons from Wyatt again, haven't you?" She kissed him. "I'd like to do all of it with you, Bastian Dragonelli, and more, including midnight bareback rides. Now, go run your errand, and don't get lost."

He probably would, Bastian thought as he tried to find his way back to the house where Steve fell off the roof. He made one wrong turn but eventually he found the place. Still, it looked empty. A big, beautiful, expensive house going to waste. He rang the doorbell, but no one answered. He wanted to say, *"Did you know that a man fell off your roof, got badly hurt, and lost his insurance and his home?"*

He wanted to but he didn't. Kenna told him not to, and he trusted her instincts. They were better honed for humans than his were.

He walked around to the back of the house, saw a sign for a burglar alarm company, and wrote it down, but when he was leaving, he also took down the name on the truck parked out front, which belonged to a property management company. A man with the name on the back of his shirt worked near the front door.

He got lost twice on his way to Salem proper, but he found Works Like Magick and surprised Vivica. "You found me without McKenna's help," she said.

"Huntley came to see her a few days ago. He is an evil man, Vivica. He is scared she will win. I am scared she will not. I got to thinking that maybe somebody who works at that house where Steve got hurt might have seen something."

"How about the person who lives there?"

"Someone with Alzheimer's who has a caretaker, Steve told me. They don't communicate except through the management company. No one ever sets foot outside. Here is the name and address of the property management company. They hired Steve, and accept no blame for his fall, and the name of the alarm company. Will you look into them?"

"You know I will. I'm not sure it'll do any good, though. How's McKenna?"

"Worried about losing her home. Hoping she can welcome those guests to the Dragon's Lair. Looking forward to doing a *Kitchen Witch* show this week. Enjoying Lizzie's babies."

"Enjoying you?" Vivica winked.

Bastian could not hide his pleasure. "She is rough on men, our Kenna, but I can take rough. I like that about her, that she will not break. Can you *see*, Vivica, how this will turn out for Kenna, her fight against Huntley, I mean?"

"I see nothing. The man's evil clouds everything. I know only that McKenna is strong and she has more power than she knows."

Bastian found himself pacing, his frustration boiling over. "I do not see why I am here if I cannot help."

"You might have helped by getting me this information. I'll rush it through."

He stopped to look up at Vivica. "You will come to McKenna's grand opening on October twenty-sixth?"

"I wouldn't miss it."

Neither of them said, "If the opening takes place."

Bastian hated that within the next few days, McKenna could lose her home, her hopes and dreams, and her heritage.

Not to mention the ripple effect on all the people they both loved.

FIFTY-FIVE

McKenna woke before dawn, disoriented at first, until she found herself in the warm cocoon of Bastian's arms. When he said her name in his sleep, she settled back into them.

October twenty-fifth. She could keep her home until midnight tonight, though she prayed she'd done enough to keep it forever. If she could afford to hire a lawyer, she'd get him to ask for a stay of execution, or whatever you called it.

Yes, she'd played it close, but she hadn't known, until after her mother's death, what kind of debt she inherited. That *must* be why Mom let her cancer take its course. Vivica had been right. Mom didn't want to deepen the family debt.

This opportunity to have the B and B and support herself, this was a gift from her mother.

McKenna wiped her tears. What was wrong with her? She never cried.

Hell, she'd hardly had time to mourn after her mother

passed before she was hiring Bastian and they were off to the races, in so many ways.

Last week, she'd signed a contract for the regular sale of fruit and produce to a local supermarket, and not a moment too soon. She could now add the advance to her mother's insurance money, Bastian's pay, her guests' deposit, and the income from the *Kitchen Witch* show. With all of it, she came close, damned close, to having what she needed to pay both the mortgage and taxes.

The reunion family wouldn't arrive until tomorrow, and she couldn't charge them for their entire stay until the end of it, *after* the foreclosure date. She hadn't heard back from the bank yet about whether they'd consider the week's income toward her mortgage and taxes. If the bank said yes, and she should know by noon, today, all she needed was an all-clear from the building inspector this afternoon.

If only for the moment, life stood on the precipice of looking up.

A roar of engines made her sit up, the chilling sound getting louder, closer, too close, aggressive, more threatening than the roar of a dragon. She sprinted toward the window. "That sonofabitch!"

"What?" Bastian came awake in that wild-animal way he had, ready to strike, but she couldn't laugh this time.

"Huntley is out there bulldozing his way toward the shed."

"No," Bastian shouted and nearly left the house naked.

McKenna balled up a pair of jeans and threw them at his head.

He pulled them on and ran back for one of his black T-shirts. "I could use some talons and maybe Cedrig's teeth right now," he snapped as he slipped his bare feet into his work boots and ran outside.

Before she finished dressing, McKenna looked out the window and saw Bastian waving down Huntley, driving the rumbling bulldozer himself. Bastian was acting as if he could stop a psycho developer.

No, not one developer. Two bulldozers and a backhoe pulled up behind Huntley. He'd brought reinforcements.

McKenna stepped outside and used her cell phone to call the police. They were on their way, but would her house still be standing when they got here?

Huntley shouldn't be able to claim the place until after midnight, at the soonest, and if she did default—which she damned well would *not*—she was supposed to have a time frame in which to move.

With all her disappointed ancestors watching, McKenna had never felt more like a loser.

Her cell phone rang. "McKenna," Vivica said, "Huntley owns the property management company that hired Steve to shingle the roof from which he fell. Steve could never have made the connection, because Huntley's ownership was buried in a maze of real and fake holding companies. It took two corporate lawyers all night to unravel the nightmare of paperwork.

"And another thing," Vivica said. "Neighbors saw a man on the roof with a hose the night before Steve's accident. The gunk on the shingle is a slippery, old, commercial floor wax that's no longer used because it's so dangerous. If not for Bastian, the weather would eventually have erased the evidence. The police are now looking for Huntley in connection."

"Send them here. He's trying to bulldoze my shed, maybe my house next."

"He must think he lost," Vivica said, "and that if he tears everything down, you'll give up and sell him the place."

"Viv, that would make him crazy."

"You just figured that out? I'm calling a friend at your bank to confirm. Keep your phone close."

McKenna made a beeline for Steve and Lizzie's. "Get everybody out. Go out my front door to your van and drive straight to Works Like Magick. Don't look back. Vivica will take care of you until it's safe for you to come home."

Worried about her property, but more about Bastian's safety, McKenna went back outside.

Bastian stood in the path of the bulldozer towering over him, too damned close, his predatory gaze on the man in the driver's seat.

"No," she shouted. "Bastian, move." A dragon wouldn't be afraid of a bulldozer, but a man *should* be.

At the same time Huntley sped up, Bastian disappeared. Beneath the dozer's wheels?

McKenna screamed like a madwoman as she rushed Huntley. He'd tried to kill Steve; he wouldn't care about killing Bastian.

Somebody needed to stop him.

FIFTY-SIX

Bastian strategically body-rolled into the dirt eater's giant plow tray, beneath Huntley's eye level, hoping the developer would *care* about mowing him down, but the machine didn't falter on its journey toward the shed.

Huntley raised the plow tray, but that could work in Bastian's favor, because he'd tower over the evil driver once he stood up in the tray and revealed himself. Since his arrival here on earth, he had not allowed himself to become so angry. Not since he fell from Kenna's roof had his inner dragon clamored so forcefully to be set free.

Bastian could feel his horns poking against his skin. Feel the itchy burn in his wing tracks, the lengthening of his claws. He couldn't let the transformation happen, yet *never* had he needed a dragon's strength more.

His inner beast's gnashing teeth almost meshed with his own, fire filled his nostrils, but Bastian kept himself in check to save his brothers, until he rode the earth eater's tray high enough to see Kenna fighting with Huntley in the dirt eater's cab, as if trying to drag the man from his seat, screaming his name.

Bastian realized then that she was trying to save *him*. Yes, he'd tried to give the impression that he'd fallen beneath the machine's wheels, but for Huntley's sake, not Kenna's. Bastian tried to get her attention. He shouted, he roared, but she could not hear him over the growl of machinery and her own wild panic.

Huntley knocked McKenna from the cab. Blood splattered everywhere. Her blood. She lost her footing and her body hit each jutting edge of the machine as she fell, until she landed, covered in blood and still as death in the dirt.

Agony overtook him, physical and emotional. Fury filled him. Bloodlust. Bastian knew a death blow when it sheared his heart in half. As he reeled from the knowledge, more than the pain, the dragon in him rose and took over his being, and he welcomed it. Reveled in it.

The need for vengeance overshadowed loss. Scales, spikes, and claws grew apace with his size and fury, and everything inside him sharpened, his strength, his skills, and his senses.

Bastian gnashed his teeth, and he breathed fire.

The tray of the earth eater broke under his new weight and jammed the wheels, stopping the machine in its tracks.

Beside it, McKenna did not move.

Bastian rose to his full dragon height, dwarfing the machine and its driver, raised his wings to an alarming span, and he roared.

Huntley screamed.

Killian had been biding her time, waiting for the worst moment to strike, and now she showed herself.

Lit by an arc of her own lightning, she smiled, and the funnel cloud shrouding her fell away. She sent a handful of lightning bolts his way, all five, but he lifted his hands against them, and turned them back toward the evil sorceress herself. What could be more powerful or more deadly? When the throwback struck, Killian vanished in a black mist, her howl chilling. This did not mean that she was gone forever. It meant only that he'd won the moment. Perhaps not even the battle. Definitely not his brothers' battles, in the event he hadn't already destroyed their opportunity to come to earth.

For Kenna, he'd turned back into a dragon, so enraged, he hardly acknowledged forfeiting his life and his quest.

For him, thinking him injured beneath the machine's wheels, his love had attacked her worst enemy.

Now McKenna, his heart, lay in bloody, broken pieces.

She had been dealt the final blow, and he was no longer a man.

With nothing to lose, Bastian bent his long neck and showed his teeth and his fire to Huntley. The greedmonger's fear fed Bastian's bloodlust as the man cowered in the far corner of the machine's cab, sweat dripping from his slimy skin.

At the sight of him charging, Huntley's men turned their earth eaters around and left the property. A retreat that came too late.

But it didn't matter anymore. Bastian's fire melted the bulldozer's controls and shattered the windshield.

With smoke still pouring from his nostrils, he snatched Huntley up between his teeth, dragged him from the cab, shook him until his bones rattled, and tossed him like so much trash.

Bastian then bent over McKenna, so still in the dirt. He lifted her limp hand, and held it to his face, almost glad that she could not see how he had failed her.

She opened her eyes and met his gaze. "The most beautiful dragon ever," she whispered, stroking his scales. "I'll love you, Bastian. Forever. Even in death. Fly away. Save yourself."

Her eyes closed as her hand went limp against him.

The mournful cry he sent into the universe shattered the silence and echoed over the valley. Birds took to the air. Animals ran. Bastian placed his dragon hands on McKenna's every bloody gash—so many—but she did not awaken. "Heal!" he shouted with another echoing roar, but nothing happened.

"Where is my healing magick?" he shouted to the universe.

He should have more magick as a dragon. Not less.

"Bastian." Andra's voice came on the wind. "You cannot heal the dead."

Life abandoned him as surely as it had left Kenna. His dragon heart clutched and shattered, the physical pain of losing her breaking him.

But his pain did not matter. The deep gash on Kenna's head would never close.

Bastian threw back his head and roared his grief, scorching the trees around him, and as their blackened leaves fell, nature wept with him.

He expanded his wings and tucked them around her, holding her for the last time, his shameless tears salting her wounds. "My fault. Mine. Forgive me, my Kenna," he begged, though she could not hear.

If he had not taunted Huntley, Kenna would not have tried to save him.

His anguish knew no bounds. He rested his face against his sweet, dead love, in that place where their babies should have grown, and he wept for them, too.

Cars with lights, he saw coming down the street through the trees. An ambulance. No, three.

Afraid to take his attention from McKenna, Bastian stood behind the barn to watch, hoping the paramedics would fix her and leave her, that he would see her get up and walk into the house.

But they took her away.

Kenna. Gone. Lost to him.

She had died, taking his heart, his life, with her.

The second ambulance took Huntley, but Bastian didn't care. He stayed behind the barn, watched Lizzie drive up to the house. Steve talked to the police. Vivica, driving in behind them, hugged Lizzie, and they wept against each other before taking the children and babies inside.

He had failed Andra and his brothers, but most especially, he had failed Kenna.

He had doomed everyone he loved to die.

Now he must wait for death to claim him, too.

FIFTY-SEVEN

McKenna woke calling Bastian's name in a hospital room with Vivica sitting beside her bed. "Where's Bastian?"

Vivica's eyes filled. "He seems to have disappeared. Huntley is in the psych ward telling people he was attacked by a dragon, but the workers who were with him are denying the report."

"But Bastian *is* a dragon."

Vivica squeezed her hand. "I know."

"A proud and beautiful dragon."

"I wish I'd seen him in all his beastly glory."

"He fought for me and tried to heal me." A beast with tears in his eyes. A paradox. A mystery from the beginning. "I hope he was able to fly somewhere safe." McKenna's heart clenched with a physical spasm. So intense, so filled with grief, tears would not come.

She shook her head and refused to give in to memories. As time went by, she would take them out for comfort. But not now. Not yet.

For now, she would mourn. Alone. Lonely. Without Bastian.

Dead. Both of them. Her, too.

"But you," Vivica said, falsely enthusiastic. "The doctors are calling you their miracle patient. You should have died, given the head trauma you suffered. You shouldn't have healed so fast. The paramedics said they could practically see you healing before their eyes."

Dragon magick, McKenna thought. He'd turned back into a dragon to save her. Why couldn't he save himself? "When can I go home? Oh, no. I didn't settle with the bank or get the house inspected. Huntley won, after all."

"He didn't. With the money you were able to give them, the bank accepted the down payment from your B and B guests and the anticipated income from this past week. Your long-term business plan helped, too, as did your website, especially the reservation inquiries, which Steve was smart to program in."

"Vivica, you talked to somebody at the bank ahead of time to make it happen, didn't you?"

"I simply pointed out some facts."

"Then what was Huntley doing at my place at dawn?"

"When he showed with the bulldozer, he knew you were square with the bank. That man wasn't used to losing, and your property might have been his biggest loss to date. He'd gone off the deep end, pure and simple."

The Dragon's Lair lived, McKenna thought. Only the dragon had died. "I have everything I've ever dreamed of," she whispered, "and the only thing I want is Bastian." She turned to look out the window. "How long have I been here?"

"Eight days."

Panic filled McKenna. "No! My guests!"

Vivica pushed her back against her pillows. "The Dragon's Lair is in good hands," Vivica said. "Lizzie and

Steve gave your building inspector the tour and accepted his stamp of approval. The following day, they welcomed your guests, cared for them, and after they left, Lizzie took their money to your bank. Oh, and they hosted your Halloween Grand Opening. Melody and her husband, Logan—the original producer of *The Kitchen Witch*— came. Logan now makes independent films, so he brought a video camera to give you some extra publicity. Melody's shown snippets like commercials a couple of times on her show."

"Lizzie's a good friend. Melody, too, maybe."

"The way Steve and Lizzie tell it, you're the great friend."

"Lizzie and I have always been like sisters."

"Did you know that Melody Seabright owns a nonprofit charitable foundation with several smaller foundations as holdings?"

"No, I didn't."

"One is called the Keep Me Foundation. It's for mothers who want to keep their babies but don't have the income. They supply cribs and such. The foundation gave Lizzie three cribs—well, three of everything for the triplets."

That nearly made her cry. "Lizzie and Steve needed a break."

"Lizzie said to tell you she'd be here if she wasn't a walking milk bottle, and that's a quote."

McKenna liked this distant cousin of hers. They'd become closer in the past few months. She'd always be grateful that Vivica sent Bastian to her. "I fell in love with him, you know."

"I know, sweetie."

"I never told Bastian the man, not in words."

"He knew. He was perceptive, our Bastian."

McKenna remembered wonderful times with him when all *she* could think about was the B and B. She'd never given him her whole self, her whole heart, not knowingly, not even when they were making love.

"I have something to tell you," Vivica said. "You can hear it from me or the doctors. It's up to you."

"You mean, Steve and I will be able to have wheelchair races?"

FIFTY-EIGHT

McKenna raised herself in the hospital bed and braced herself for the worst. "I'd rather have you tell me than the doctors," she said, clutching the covers.

Vivica took her hand. McKenna felt exposed. Vulnerable. Somebody takes your hand when there's bad news.

"You won't be confined to a wheelchair," Vivica said. "You're a miracle, remember? And so is your baby. Nobody can figure out how it survived the fall, but it did, and it's healthy and growing exactly as it should."

"It?"

"Too soon to know the baby's sex."

The night the condoms overflowed, McKenna thought, and though she smiled inwardly, her face felt wet. "I'm not so much worried about the sex as I am the species," she admitted.

Vivica chuckled. "On your nightstand, here, are the results from the checkup I had Bastian get when he first came to me. His child will be as human as he. 'Anything out of the ordinary'—and I don't know what—was 'a *physical* defect,' to quote the doctor who gives my clients their physicals."

Not a defect, McKenna thought. A gift. A baby maker, as it turned out. "How far along am I?"

"Nearly a month."

Bastian had left her his heart in their child. As much as she wanted Bastian himself, love overflowed in her for his baby.

"Your guests couldn't have been happier with the Dragon's Lair," Vivica said to break the silence. "They're booked for next fall, same week."

"How can I thank you for everything you did to help?"

"Get better and get home."

Without Bastian, it wouldn't seem like home anymore. What a bittersweet victory, going home to her successful bed-and-breakfast.

Had Bastian flown away and survived? Or had Killian taken him back to the island? Even if he'd lived—a long shot—he was lost to her.

The next morning, Vivica checked her out of the hospital.

"Viv," she said in the car. "I didn't see a hospital bill."

"Didn't you? Can't imagine why."

"I'll pay you back."

"No," Vivica said. "Consider it the investment in the B and B that my instincts said I shouldn't make so as not to hinder destiny. Not the slightest hint of intuition stopped me from paying that bill, so I knew it was the right thing to do. Besides, you're carrying on the family line. I'm all for that."

Her first day home, McKenna imagined Bastian in every room, but she had him, still, in the small being with his genes—not jeans—beneath her heart. She chuckled and wiped her eyes.

She looked for Dewcup and Jock, but they had disappeared as well. Still, her friends made sure she had no time to mourn or curl up on her bed to wallow in grief.

Lizzie was over the moon about her pregnancy. Her best friend's advice alone would keep her busy for the next eight months, not to mention baby practice with the triplets: Payton, Piper, and Patrice. Whitney and Wyatt's auntie kisses made for good distractions, too, and Steve's progress, which might come to a stop without Bastian, though she wouldn't mention it.

An investigation into Huntley's suspicious conglomerate revealed too many parcels of "coincidentally" acquired bargain property, so the police were digging deeper into his business practices and, thanks to Vivica, into Steve's insurance company for their refusal to pay after his fall.

On McKenna's second morning home, as she noted an e-mail reservation in her book at the registration desk in her wide front hall, a man knocked at her front door. He looked familiar, but she couldn't place him. He stood tall, his long, wild, sandy hair streaked with sunshine, his eyes a bright . . . violet? With that scar crossing his left eye, he looked a lot like the tawny gold dragon Bastian painted in one of her bedrooms. "Can I help you?" McKenna asked, the hair on her arms bristling.

"Vivica sent me."

Her heart skipped a beat. A connection. A reminder. Vague. Disturbing. "Thank you for coming, but I'm not ready to hire another handyman."

"I just got to Salem last night, and I don't need a job. Vivica hired me as her bodyguard. She has a bit of a stalker problem."

That journalist, McKenna remembered. This familiar man's story made sense. "So do you need a place to stay until you find an apartment?"

"No, thank you. My name is Jaydun Dragonelli, and I'm looking for my brother Bastian."

"Vivica didn't tell you?"

"Tell me what?"

No, wait. Confusion caught McKenna in its headlights until her mind cleared; hope shot through her and nearly buckled her knees. "Andra sent you from the island? That means—Bastian didn't fail?"

"Bastian made way for us and saved us at the same time. Are you his heart mate?"

"Bastian's not dead, then?"

Jaydun looked troubled. "I'm here, and Andra has her magick back."

"Lizzie!" McKenna shouted. "Excuse me, Jaydun. I have an emergency errand to run."

Bastian might not know he'd succeeded any more than she'd known. He could have flown, heaven knew where, or he could be somewhere in Salem.

McKenna made her way up the hall, not sore at all after her injuries. Bastian had healed her, though she thought she remembered him cursing his lack of healing power.

She looked out the window. Where could a huge dragon linger and not be seen? Unless he was a man again, weak, hungry.

A place to linger undetected. The caves? "Make yourself at home, Jaydun!" McKenna called.

Lizzie met her in the hall, a baby in each arm. "You rang?"

"Lizzie, sweetie, can you send Whitney and Wyatt into the parlor with a drink and snack for Bastian's brother? I'll be back."

"Bastian has a brother?"

"Lots of them." McKenna swiped every container of honey from a cupboard shelf into a canvas bag, and grabbed an empty bag to take with her.

"McKenna, where are you going?" Lizzie asked, looking worried. "You have a baby to think about."

"Precisely why I'm going. You always wanted me to throw caution to the wind and chase a rainbow. Wish me luck." McKenna let the porch door bounce behind her, and she'd no sooner gone outside than Jock appeared and snuffle-puffed purple smoke as he flew in circles slightly ahead of her.

Following the small blue dragon, McKenna packed the extra bag with lemongrass along the way. When she didn't see any sign of life at the near caves, she followed Jock to the farthest entrance, the one where she took Bastian the night they met Ciarra.

If transforming back into a man was a problem, which he expected it might be, and if he didn't fly away, she hoped he'd foraged at night. She should have looked for him sooner. After all, he'd been missing for nine days.

"Did you feed him, Jock?"

More purple smoke.

What did that mean? Bastian might not even be here. She'd *seen* him turn into a dragon, which he wasn't supposed to do. She'd seen Killian's satisfaction when Bastian turned. She knew then how much trouble Bastian was in.

Anticipation beat in her breast, made her hands shake and her step falter. She would hold on to hope . . . until she reached her destination, at which point, it could be ripped from her forever.

She would probably be safer and smarter to reject hope now, but she couldn't.

Practically speaking, Bastian could have gotten into trouble *after* Andra transformed Jaydun and sent him through the veil.

FIFTY-NINE

As McKenna rounded the corner of the cave mass, toward the waterfront entrance, she saw a dragon tail trailing from the cave. A ruddy red color, long and scaled, with an arrow-tipped spade, but enough scales had dried up and fallen off to cause alarm. The tail showed no sign of life.

Oh, God. Adrenaline rushed her, and nausea rose in her. With a hand to her babe, McKenna stroked the inert spade.

After a dead-space minute, it twitched.

Bastian could be alive. Barely. But for how long?

His huge body nearly filled the cavern. Only one way to reach him so he could *see* her. Climb over him. She started at the narrow end of his tail and worked her way up his back, continuously stopping to wipe her eyes so she could see what she was doing. The higher she climbed, the more that listless tail seemed to twitch.

Deep in the cave, she saw his wings tucked against his side. She stroked them, too, slid her hands along the velvet-like webs, and closed them around each wing claw. "Your scales tickle," she shouted, her words echoing in the caves, loud enough for him to hear her, she hoped.

To get his head into the room where they'd once spent the night, Bastian had managed to knock down part of the entrance that hid Ciarra's portion of the caves.

As McKenna reached Bastian's neck, his head came listlessly up, though raising it seemed difficult, and he couldn't seem to open his eyes. "Dreams," he whispered with barely a breath. "Sweet."

McKenna scootched down his neck—scales weren't made for sliding—and landed on his front paw, where she stood to stroke his jaw. As his jaw relaxed, his lips, if you could call them that, parted. She covered a handful of lemongrass with honey and shoved that in his mouth.

His entire being stiffened, then he sighed as if hope were a waste of effort.

"Chew, you stubborn Bastardon! You dragosapien tripod. Chew, damn it!"

His head came up a bit further, and he knocked her off his foot with the jut of his jaw.

She rolled onto her bottom while he pawed at his eyes as if to clear them. "Dreams," he said again. "Stronger every day. Makes no sense. Why can't I die?"

"Chew, Bastian. You nearly are dead. Who do you think you are, Dragula?" She sobbed with a rush of happy, and scared, and hopeful, and afraid to hope. "When you're better, we're going to talk about why you're lolling on your lazy ass while I have a B and B to run, and I don't mean a place where we sit in bed and eat bees for breakfast."

He swallowed, but his head lolled to the ground. He didn't have the strength to hold it up.

"What happened to the connection between us?" she shouted.

"It died with you." A tear landed on her hand. He was too far gone. How to get through to him?

"You're a dragon, you troglodyte. Get fired up. Go ahead. Work up some sweat. Huntley lived, you know. Okay, fire when ready—just let me get out of the way first."

When she got no reaction to her abuse, she opened his mouth and poured honey down his gullet. "There, does that help the burning sensation in your throat?"

Nothing.

"You came here to die, didn't you, you lazy beast? You will not die! You will *not*! I forbid it. Turn back into a man so I can beat you for abandoning me before I feed you and make you better." She pointed an imperious finger at him. "Turn, I say."

He coughed up a bit of smoke.

Panic rushed her. Made her dizzy. She opened two containers of honey and poured them into him. "You have to turn back into a man, because I don't know what to tell this baby about his daddy if you don't. I guess it'd go something like, 'Hey, little one, see the tail hanging out of that cave? That's your dad! Aren't we proud?'"

Bastian turned his head to the side and more rocks fell from the entrance.

McKenna hoped Ciarra wouldn't mind. Where *were* her ancestors? She hadn't seen a one since she got home.

Best concentrate on Bastian. "Eat," she said. "Think of it as eating for the three of us.

"Why don't you respond? Bastian, say something!"

He opened one eye while she stood pouring honey into him. She thought he saw her then, though he barely blinked, but he did begin to take an active part in swallowing.

After a few jars, he rolled, dragon belly up, to suck honey from the containers. "Now I know how Lizzie feels when she calls herself a walking milk bottle."

Bastian gave a snort, and a larger puff of smoke.

She had to get through to him so he'd at least *try* to transform. They could barely communicate this way. She wanted her man back. She wiped the smoke from her eyes. "Damned hormones."

His eyes looked a little, er, smoky, too, with tears like her own.

She had to jar him into making the transformation, or at least into making the effort. "Talk about taking the easy way out," she snapped. "Hey, is that your dragon lance stiffening up? What an itty bitty little thing. Nowhere near as impressive as your man lance. You're a sorry tripod in this condition. Hell, you barely qualify as a tripod. Let's see if I can make *this* lance dance."

But as she tried to climb over him to reach his lance, a tremor began in Bastian's chest, like a swell at first, then a full-bellied rumble, which knocked her off her knees and flat on top of him. "This is where you *want* me, isn't it?"

She rode his chest rumbles like waves at high tide, and the greater the rumbles, the lower she rode, and the more complete his transformation, until she blanketed Bastian, her own dear love, her man-beast, come back to her sporting a supersized trick dick in fine working order.

Funny how his lance could function without him, because he was terribly weak, probably because of the energy it took to transform.

McKenna kissed him all over his face and cried all over him, too.

His eyes still closed, his breathing shallow, she lay beside him, her arms around him, reveling in the beat of his heart, and praying for it to beat faster.

All at once, his chest expanded, the back muscles beneath her hand rippled, and they both breathed easier again.

"You live?" he whispered, as weak as he was, touching a wayward tear on her face.

She got herself together and fed him more sweetgrass and honey. "I know that you don't have as much Bastian to carry now that you're a man again, but I think I should get Toffee to carry you home."

"My Kenna," he said, cupping a cheek and eating her up with his gaze. "No wonder I couldn't die. I thought I was dreaming my continued connection with you."

A crash in the corner caught their attention.

"Humans!" Dewcup snapped, tossing small rocks from above the trough of spring water. "You have the attention spans of gnats."

Bastian ignored the faery and pulled McKenna kissing-close.

"May the dragons of life roast your hot dogs but never your buns," the flaky faery said before she flew into the hole she'd made in the formation.

Ping. Ping. Ping. One by one, coins flew from the opening. Gold coins. Ancient.

McKenna stood and took one to look at. "The McKenna family treasure?"

The bright discs flew faster from their centuries-old hidey-hole to mound on the floor. Dewcup flew out after them, hovered in the air, hands on her hips, as she grew bright, and in a burst of fireworks, a human-sized woman dressed in stars stood in her place.

Bastian pulled McKenna in front of him to cover himself. "Andra. You're Dewcup?"

"Blessed Be, my Bastian," the glittering woman said. "I couldn't let you face a new world alone, and I needed to see how my dragons would fare here. You did well. I worried when you turned back into a dragon, but that was the only way you could have saved McKenna. Dragon tears are powerful magick. That's how you healed her."

"But I wept only when I thought she had died."

"Killian's evil backfired. She masked her voice to sound

like me—she's a sorceress, after all. It was she who told you that McKenna was dead. She wanted you to lose hope, and you did, so much so that you wept, and your tears saved McKenna, causing you to vanquish Killian, on your own behalf, not on behalf of your brothers. They will have their own battles to fight with her."

"May I help them?" Bastian asked.

"No more than I was able to help you."

"But you didn't help me."

"I rest my case. Destiny is a funny thing. It needs to take its own time and follow its own circuitous route."

McKenna smiled. "Vivica said something similar to me not long ago."

"I'll tell you who did help you—Jock."

"Yes," Bastian said. "Jock is a fine guardian dragon."

"Did you know that it was Whyzind the elder's tears that saved you during your transformation on the island?"

"Whyzind, my old mentor?" Bastian asked. "I hadn't realized. I was rather preoccupied at the time."

"Aged and infirm but determined to serve you, Whyzind is here."

"I didn't think he could make the trip through the planes safely at his advanced age," Bastian said.

"By making him smaller, we conserved his life force, which gave him strength for the journey and a longer life. You know him as Jock, and he is determined to serve you till the end of his days, if you will have him."

"Does he babysit?" McKenna asked, winking at their guardian dragon, who puffed purple smoke.

"McKenna and I would be honored," Bastian said.

"McKenna." Andra looked her way. "You have set your ancestors free to move on in the circle of life. They leave you their thanks, their blessings, and their love. *You* are the champion that generations of your clan had been waiting for."

"That's not possible."

"Kenna, how can you say that anything is impossible, given the circumstances?" Bastian asked.

McKenna wiped her cheek with her hand. "It's good that they could move on, I guess." She'd never see or speak to them again, but how lucky was she to have the opportunity to see her parents again? McKenna swallowed her sadness and embraced the joy her family must have experienced at moving on.

"My work for you is done," Andra said. "I will move between here and the Island of Stars while I send your brother dragons back to earth as men, one moon at a time, each with his own quest." The Goddess of Hope bowed majestically and raised a hand. "May your warts and splints be few, your children many, and your nights filled with stars of your own making." She blessed them and vanished.

McKenna knelt beside Bastian and settled in the crook of his arm. She couldn't get enough of looking at him. "You're alive. I can't believe I didn't lose you." His unexpected return to her, here in Ciarra's cave, both of them from different planes and centuries, was a magick so incredible, she couldn't fathom it. Call it serendipity, or just plain destiny, but the universe and all its elements had aligned to bring them together, him, lost to one world but more alive than ever in hers.

McKenna found her true self in his arms, and she liked what she saw, thanks to him.

She stroked his every feature and scar, memorizing him all over again.

"You lived," he said, cupping her face. "I can't believe you lived. I've been waiting to die, because you died, and— Did you say something about a baby?"

"Mmm." Her smile grew. "We're going to have one. And it's your fault."

"I should hope so."

She took a swim in his violet eyes. "I love you."

"I have always loved you. Now I love you both. I will stand behind you always."

"Beside me, please, with my hand in yours?"

"What? No more grunt?"

"I love your alpha self, the man who turned into a proud dragon to protect me."

"Marry me," he whispered, kissing the palm of her hand.

She smiled. "How does a dragon marry?"

"In tails?"

Turn the page for a special look at
Annette Blair's next

A Works Like Magick novel

BEDEVILED ANGEL

Coming soon from Berkley Sensation!

Chance Godricson was supposed to live and Kenya Saint-Denis was supposed to die, but when rescue came, he gave her his place . . . and became her guardian angel. Now she's agoraphobic. But to be worthy of the life given her, she's become a surrogate—bearing children for those who would otherwise have none.

Chance Godricson, guardian angel, is overly attached to Kenya. When he discovers that her life is about to fall apart, he's ready to neglect the rest of his charges to care for her. The angel triumvirate of Everlasting is having none of it. Chance is knocked back to earth for Kenya's sake, during which time he's to make peace with his angelic role—or forfeit it—and suffer the consequences.

ONE

"How could you die at a time like this?"

Guardian Angel Fourth Class Chance Godricson rushed toward the new arrivals, his Technicolor dream robe flowing behind him. "Mountain climbing?" he shouted. "Really? With your responsibilities?"

The newly deceased couple stepped back as Chance's anger vibrated the rainbow sky dome of pre-everlasting.

Minion angels in pastel robes materialized and propelled him away from the distressed couple, a firm hand on each of his wrists.

Chance struggled against his wardens, until Isaiah, his mentor—an Albert Einstein double—appeared before him shaking his head, his bushy mustache making Chance want to scratch his own upper lip, though he resisted temptation as all angels *should*.

Isaiah, with his uncanny ability to discern the emotions of others, sighed and scratched his fuzzy upper lip. That done, he firmed his spine and his expression. "You have no purpose in this sector. Even if you belonged here, those souls are not yours to protect, much less to chide."

Chance fisted his hands. "But Kenya Saint-Denis *is* my responsibility, and she's carrying their child. In the remote location where they died, they won't be found for weeks, months, if ever. What happens to an unprepared surrogate when no couple arrives to take the child she's borne them? Kenya will be waiting, worrying."

Isaiah's unibrow undulated like a fuzzy white caterpillar on the run. "You've already been warned. You spend too much time guarding that girl when others in your charge are also in need of your guardianship."

Chance's thick feather wings snapped open and bristled of their own accord before he could draw them in. "Kenya's needs are more in number and more urgent than the rest of my charges put together."

"Granted, the girl has fears . . . with good reason. Her fears have caused problems, however. Holy halo, her solutions have caused problems, but there is a limit to your role as her guardian. Her free will is her own. Not yours, and not to be toyed with. You cannot protect her from life, Chance." Isaiah made a motion that dismissed his pastel-robed guards.

The minions disappeared while Chance rubbed his wrists, from habit, not pain—pain did not exist here. When he looked up, Isaiah, too, had vanished.

Chance found himself standing beside a precipice from which earth sat bared to his view, a brink, razor sharp in its implications, the earth's pull and beauty both mesmerizing and frightening. From here, more than from anyplace else in heaven, the earthen plane loomed: visible, vulnerable, and open.

Dangerously open.

TWO

Chance looked up to find Tavish, one of his trainees—a pupil who might someday outshine his teacher—standing before him.

"Et tu, Tavish?" Chance asked as he watched Kenya in her living room, nothing but a huge flat TV for company, her belly big with child, flowers on her head, and scarves of every shade flowing around her while she ungracefully danced with the stars—alone—from the safety of her home.

Agoraphobia: An abnormal fear of being in public places.

Learning that her babe's parents had died would not help her overcome her self-imposed isolation.

"Are you here to warn me away from her, too?" Chance asked his friend.

Tavish, a younger soul with an older body and a reasonably recent arrival, rocked on his heels. "Gabriel and Raphael are worried about you."

"And here I thought Isaiah sent you."

"No, Isaiah has washed his hands of you."

"Glad tidings. So what message do you bring from the high holy duo, precisely?"

With the toe of his sparkling high-top Flyers, Tavish scratched a triangle in the pearlescent angel dust beneath their feet before he made eye contact. "Gabriel and Raphael believe that you reside too much in your heart, not here, but on the earthen plane . . . with Kenya."

"That's not much of an accusation," Chance said. "Kenya's more angelic than I am."

"I will, unfortunately, grant you that, since you are more worldly than most, including the girl."

Chance straightened, relief washing over him. At least someone understood. "So you see my problem?"

"I see it better than you, I believe. You are besotted. By a mortal."

"No . . . No," Chance said. "No, I'm empathetic, like any guardian angel worth his wings."

Tavish smoothed his beard. "That's the problem. To your neglected charges, you're *not* worth your wings."

Chance kept the subject of their discourse—his unruly wings—from escaping and snapping in indignation. "That's a harsh opinion."

"It's not an opinion, but a judgment."

"A judgment?" Chance threw back his shoulders as understanding dawned. "Only the triumvirate can pass judgment."

Tavish held his tongue, though one Scot's red brow rose on its own accord.

Chance bristled and took his attention from Kenya to focus on Tavish. "You mean that Raphael and Gabriel called Michael—a bold move—and convened a Tribunal because of *my* behavior?"

Chance's distress dissolved in a blink, caught as he was,

heart and soul, by observing and encouraging Kenya to sing to the unborn child. The babe she loved but would give away for the generous joy of making two people happy, three if you counted the babe in addition to its parents—who, it turned out, were too irresponsible to stay alive and raise it.

"How long will Michael and the others observe me?" Chance asked.

Tavish sighed. "Neither your mind nor your heart is here. You belong to earth and to *her* even now."

Chance dragged his gaze from Kenya and caught up with his friend's words. "I do not."

Tavish shook his head. "What is that song she sings?"

"*Toora, loora, loora.* She's half Irish and half Kenyan, but adopted by Irish parents, so she can toss the *blarney* with the best of them. I like that about her."

"You like a lot about her," Tavish said. "Remember this: I am a better friend than you think."

"Fond of yourself are y—"

Before Chance knew what Tavish was about, the Scot went shoulder to shoulder with him and shoved him off the precipice.

The tear and burn of the feather torn from his wings accompanied Chance on his free fall, his scream lost in the whoosh of air filling his lungs.

Keep reading for a special look at the next
novel of the Lupi by Eileen Wilks

BLOOD MAGIC

Coming February 2010
from Berkley Sensation!

On a blistering noon at the tag-end of July, Balboa Park in San Diego offered plenty of green to sun weary eyes. The paths in the Palm Canyon section were some of the park's prettiest byways, though shade was scant now. With the sun directly overhead, it was reduced to furtive puddles at the feet of the palms' arcing trunks.

A tall man walked one of those paths alone, dressed head-to-toe in black.

His hair was dark, his skin lightly tanned. His eyes were hidden by expensive sunglasses. From a distance he looked like a clump of shadow visiting its more dappled cousins along the bone-colored path.

Rule Turner touched his sunglasses lightly. They didn't need adjusting. He just liked the tactile reminder. They'd been a gift, a surprise present from Lily when the two of them returned from North Carolina with his son yesterday. She'd even found a smaller, identical pair for Toby, which the boy wore constantly. So Rule touched the shades and thought of Toby, and of Lily, and why he was here.

Two men rounded a curve in the path, heading toward Rule. Neither wore sunglasses. The older one looked like a blacksmith or some primordial earth deity—bearded and burly and as if he might burst out of his slacks and shirt at any moment. His beard and hair were rusty brown shot with gray; his eyes were the color of roasted nuts. Tanned skin creased around craggy features in a way that suggested smiles came easily and often.

He wasn't smiling now.

The other man looked younger and more dangerous . . . which was true in a sense. Benedict could kill faster and more surely than anyone Rule knew. He shared his companion's muscular build, but fitted over an additional five inches of height. His features reflected his mother's heritage, the cheekbones flat and high, the mouth wide, and his black hair was long enough to club back in a short tail.

No smile lines around those dark eyes. He moved with the economy of an athlete or martial artist, which he was; he wore athletic shoes with jeans and an oversize, untucked khaki shirt.

The shirt did nothing for his build or the bronze of his skin, but Benedict wouldn't have thought of that. Clothes, like most things, were tactical tools to him. The shirt was appropriate for the setting and hid whatever weapons he'd deemed appropriate. Knives, certainly. Probably a handgun.

Neither of them looked like Rule. Nor did they much resemble each other. A stranger wouldn't have guessed the three of them were a father and his two living sons.

The older man stopped some fifteen feet away. Benedict dropped back a few feet, guarding his rear. Rule continued walking until he was only three feet away, then stopped, too. Waiting.

"Do you not kneel?" Rule's father demanded.

"I'm waiting to see who greets me."

Now there was a smile. A small one, but it reached the nut-brown eyes. "Your Rho."

Immediately Rule dropped to one knee, bending his head to bare his nape. He felt his father's fingers brush his nape, and in Rule's gut the portion of mantle that belonged to his birth clan—to Nokolai —leaped in response.

The other mantle—the complete one—remained quiet. Leidolf didn't answer to Nokolai.

"Rise."

Rule did. And still he waited. Isen Turner might be wolf in his other form, but his son thought of him as more like a fox—canny, tricky, highly maneuverable. Isen could trip Machiavelli on his assumptions, so Rule did his best not to possess any.

For once, Isen was blunt. "Why did you assume the Leidolf mantle?"

Rule had already told him how it happened, though over the phone. For some months he'd carried the heir's portion of the Leidolf clan's mantle, due to trickery of the man who had been Leidolf's Rho. Then Lily had been possessed by the wraith of one who, in life, had been Leidolf. Rule had needed the authority of the full mantle to command the wraith and save Lily. He'd taken it, killing the former Rho—and becoming leader of his clan's enemies.

But if anyone understood the difference between a chronology of events and a revelation of motive, it was Isen Turner. Rule kept his answer brief. "To save Lily."

"Was that the only reason?"

"No."

Isen hmphed. "Taught you too well, haven't I? Very well. You don't speak of your other reasons. Is that because they are Leidolf business?"

"In part. Mostly, however, I am bound by a promise I gave."

Isen's bushy eyebrows climbed in surprise that might have been real. "A promise! Obviously I can't ask what you promised, but who . . . that *is* my affair, as your Rho. Who did you promise?"

Rule had considered what to say on this score already. He'd hew to the words of his promise, but give his father some meat to chew on. Cullen wouldn't mind. "I can't in honor give you the name, but he's Nokolai, and you already possess the information he gave me, if not the conclusions he drew from that information."

"Do I, now?" The bushy eyebrows drew down, but in thought, not anger.

One of the tactics Rule had learned from his father was when to shift the subject. "Benedict is angry with me."

Isen brushed that aside. "That's a matter between brothers, not clan business. How can you be both Rho to Leidolf and Lu Nuncio to Nokolai?"

With great difficulty. "If we speak of status, I'd suggest some default settings. When I'm at Nokolai Clanhome, I'm your Lu Nuncio. When I'm away from it, I'm Leidolf Rho."

"You assume you will remain my Lu Nuncio?"

For the first time Rule smiled—small and wry, perhaps, but a genuine smile. "I assume only that your decision will not be based on anger or affection, but on what you think best for Nokolai. You asked how I could be both. That's what I answered."

"True, true—though that's a tiny dab of an answer, compared to the size of the problem. Do you see any advantage to Nokolai in having my heir be Rho to another clan?"

"Certainly. Leidolf won't be trying to kill you anymore."

Isen chuckled. "A refreshing change, yes, and one I'll appreciate. But I think that with you as Rho, Leidolf will stop its assassination attempts whether you remain my heir or not. What else?"

Rule stepped out on shaky ground then, but he stepped surely. Hesitation, doubt—both were reasonable, but revealing them was seldom useful. "No lupus has held two mantles in over three thousand years. Our oldest enemy has been stirring. Times are changing. I believe this is our Lady's will. That it's part of her plan to defeat the one we do not name."

This time Isen's surprise was unmistakably real. Both eyebrows shot up—then descended in a scowl. "You think you're privy to the Lady's plans now?"

"I'm guessing, of course. If the Lady has spoken to any of the Rhejes, they haven't told us. But it's a guess based on my gut, on . . ." Rule hesitated, then did his best to put words to what didn't fit into words. "The mantles I carry are pleased by the situation. They . . . help. They make it easy for me to separate my roles."

"Hmm." For a long moment Isen didn't say anything. Then he asked, "And can you carry both full mantles? If I dropped dead right now, could you assume Nokolai's complete mantle?"

"If I thought I couldn't, I'd ask you to remove the Nokolai portion from me immediately. I will not risk the clan."

"A good answer, but a simple 'yes' would have been even better."

"A simple 'yes' would mean I was confusing fact with opinion."

"Your opinion."

"Yes. It's based on unique experience, however. Assuming the full Leidolf mantle was . . ." He paused to fit words around what he meant as best as possible. "Simple. Not

easy, no, but much simpler than when I was first forced
to carry portions of two mantles. There's . . . room now.
They're both already here. I've no reason to think assuming the full Nokolai mantle would be beyond me."

Isen nodded slowly. "Very well. I trust your judgment.
I'll make no definite decision yet, but for the time being you
will remain my Lu Nuncio. We will use the protocol you
suggested, but the parameters must be different. On this
side of the country, you are my Lu Nuncio. On Leidolf's
side, you are their Rho."

"No."

This time only one eyebrow shot up. "No?"

"If you and I meet on the street and I submit to you, the
other clans won't see your Lu Nuncio submitting. They'll
see Leidolf's Rho submitting. I can't agree to that."

"Who am I speaking to now—my Lu Nuncio, or
Leidolf's Rho?"

"Both. The other clans are uneasy about what they see
as Nokolai's growing power. We don't want to feed that."

A grin broke out on Isen's face, folding up the creases
in the way they were meant to go. "You're good," he said
happily. "You're damned good. I've done well with you.
Yes, I agree, with some stipulations to be worked out—but
that discussion will take place between the Leidolf Rho
and the Nokolai Rho." His eyes twinkled. "You can put
me in touch with him later. Right now I want to embrace
my son."

Isen was a world-class hugger. However much he held
himself apart when he was being Rho to Rule's Lu Nuncio,
when he dropped that role and was a father, he brimmed
with love, support, and hugs.

When they broke apart Rule was grinning as widely as
his father. He braced his feet—and sure enough, here came
the clap on the back, hearty enough to stagger the unprepared. "Lily's good, right?' Isen said. "And Toby. I can't

wait to see that boy. You'll bring him to Clanhome soon. Today."

Isen could have come to Toby, but Rule didn't suggest it. Today's meeting was very much the exception. His father seldom left Clanhome—though that might change, with Leidolf no longer a threat. "I will. He's eager to see you and his Uncle Benedict." Rule glanced at the silent man still standing guard behind their father. "Speaking of whom—"

Isen squeezed Rule's arm. "Leave him be. He's brooding. Always been a hell of a one for a good brood, my Benedict. Leave him be for now."

Rule looked at his brother's unrevealing face. "I didn't expect him to object so strongly to my becoming Leidolf Rho."

"No, no. He considers that good strategy. It's getting yourself engaged he has problems with. Now, when do I get to see my grandson? He'll stay at Clanhome for the rest of the summer," Isen announced. "Once school starts, well, we'll see how that works out. But it's summer still."

That was all he said about Rule's upcoming marriage. They walked and talked for another half hour as father and son, arranging for Toby to spend time at Clanhome, if not quite as much as Isen wanted. And Rule's father didn't again refer to Rule's intention to break one of the strongest taboos of his people. When Rule tried to raise the subject, Isen dodged it neatly.

It would have been nice, Rule thought as he headed for his car, if he could trust that silence meant support, or at least a lack of opposition. But this was Isen Turner. By definition, he was up to something.

ABOUT THE AUTHOR

Annette Blair admits to having fallen *accidentally* into the enchanting world of her characters in visiting the Witch City of Salem, but these days, witches, dragons, and angels are only a small part of the magickal, supernatural ancients inhabiting her high-spirited imagination. She's solving mysteries in one series, and making way for time travelers and werecritters in another, and not to mention the return of the old friends you've been asking to see in their own stories. She loves sharing her zany, whimsical worlds and hopes you enjoy them as much.

Please visit her website at www.annetteblair.com.